The Infamous Ellen James

By

N.A. Alcorn

D1562769

Copyright
Published by: N.A. Alcorn
N.A. Alcorn
The Infamous Ellen James
Copyright 2013, N.A. Alcorn

ALL RIGHTS RESERVED. This book contains material protected under International and Federal Copyright Laws and Treaties. Any unauthorized reprint or use of this material is prohibited. No part of this book may be reproduced or transmitted in any form or by any means, electronic or mechanical, including photocopying, recording, or by any information storage and retrieval system without express written permission from the author / publisher. The characters and events portrayed in this book are fictitious. Any similarity to real persons, or dead is coincidental and not intended by the author.

License Notice
This book is licensed for your personal enjoyment only. This book may not be resold or given away to other people. If you wish to share this book with another person, please purchase an additional copy for each person you share it with. Thank you for respecting the hard work of this author.

Disclaimer
This is a work of adult fiction. The author does not endorse or condone any of the behavior enclosed within. The subject matter is not appropriate for minors. Please note this novel contains profanity and explicit sexual situations.

Cover design: Copyright Arijana Karčić, Cover It! Designs
Editor: Mickey Reed- www.mickeyreedediting.com
Formatting: White Hot Ebook Formatting

For, Georgia. The most beautiful, kindest, sweetest dog in the entire world. I miss your big brown eyes and soft ears. I miss you lying at my feet as I type on my laptop.
Rest in peace, sweet girl.

***

Prologue

"Every once in a while, someone will catch your eye. Someone you can't seem to get out of your head—a once-in-a-lifetime kind of girl. A girl who makes you feel like a complete pussy for even entertaining the idea of love at first sight, and sometimes it takes you off guard so much that you might even have to reach down and make sure your balls are still intact."

Between the delay in my flight from Seattle and the cougar at the hotel bar who kept insisting I go back to her room last night, I'm running really late for this morning's presentation. And to answer your question, no, I did not hook up with that cougar. Although the idea of her lips wrapped around my cock were extremely intriguing, I decided against it despite my dick's continual insistence. Normally I'm all for a little hotel sex, but it was getting late and I didn't want to miss this conference that Seattle Medical Center was so generously paying me to attend. Plus, I'm getting a little tired of the impersonal, lack-of-emotion hookups I've been indulging in over the past ten years. I'm still a guy though, and the morning wood I'm sporting at the moment is making it difficult to *not* jerk off before heading down to the first presentation.

The summer morning sun is filtering through my hotel window as I hurriedly get dressed. I fix my tie, adjust my now semi-hard cock in my pants, and throw my suit jacket on as I head out the door of my hotel room.

I jump on the elevator and head quickly towards the conference room on the lobby level. The conference room door is already shut, and I can make out a woman's voice speaking. I check my Rolex and see it's only a few minutes past nine. I'm not too late, but obviously they've started without me. I open the door and notice that an *extremely* attractive woman, who manages to be adorable yet fuckably hot at the same time, is standing in the front of the spacious room, starting her presentation.

The room is painted in neutral tones, typical of any business conference area. Hotel chains most likely hire interior designers to keep rooms like these *conducive to professional settings.* Go ahead and insert a sarcastic tone with that last statement. You see, I know I'm kind of an asshole when it comes to things like this. I honestly don't give a shit about appearances and making the perfect impression. I'm a fucking trauma surgeon. I'd much rather have my hands elbow-deep in a gunshot victim's chest than sit around and play "I'm a prestigious doctor, make over five hundred grand a year, and drive a Mercedes" bullshit.

Because that's what it is—complete *bullshit.* Most surgeons walk around with this better-than-you persona and that kind of crap makes me pissed off. I became a trauma surgeon because I wanted to spend my days—and a shitload of nights—in the OR attempting to save lives. I live for those moments. The adrenaline rushes. The high-stress pressure of being the one to make all of the decisions. The decisions that could potentially mean life or death for my patients.

The ridiculously attractive presenter makes eye contact with me, and I know that my attempt at sneaking in unnoticed isn't going to happen. She's in the middle of her introduction, and I continue to watch her as I make my way towards the only empty seat near the front of the room. My eyes roam her body from head to toe. I manage to mouth, "Sorry," as I sit down and shoot a wink and a smile in her direction.

She smiles back and I feel my cock twitch against my zipper. *Fuck, this chick is hot.* Too hot. I'm not quite sure how I'm going to stay engaged in this presentation. Don't get me wrong—I'll be engaged all right. Just not on the actual material. This chick's body is practically singing to my cock.

"And for those of you who have joined us a little late, my name is Ellen James. I'm a nurse for the ED at Regency Memorial in Charlotte." She shoots a slightly pointed look my way. I laugh to myself at her ability to be sarcastic despite the noticeable nervous energy she is giving off.

I can imagine presenting in front of a group of well-known physicians and hospital board officials is nerve-racking. Most of this crowd is men, and I know from experience that they can be extremely intimidating. And being a man, I'm sure I'm not the only one focused on the tight, black knee-length skirt and fuck-me heels Ellen James is wearing while strutting around this room.

Ellen James. This woman has my full attention. She is talking about Regency Hospital's staffing protocols and procedures, but I'm honestly just focused on her full, pink lips that are accentuated by the perfect amount of gloss. She is a natural beauty. Classically beautiful. Long, wavy auburn hair and minimal makeup, and this girl is no doubt drop-dead gorgeous. Downright stunning. Her natural beauty in combination with her fuck-me heels makes her look like a cross between the girl next door and a porn star. Okay, maybe I'm saying porn star because of all the filthy things I'm imagining doing to her right now, but can you honestly blame a guy? I consider myself a nice guy. I treat women with respect, but that still isn't going to stop me from thinking about sex the majority of my day. And damn, does this chick have me thinking about sex.

She has my mind daydreaming about fucking her forty ways into Sunday all over this god damn conference table. Her ability to be sensual and sexy without even realizing she's doing it has my dick nearly bursting through my black dress slacks. Now I'm really started to rethink my decision to not rub one out this morning. I'm definitely taken aback by the instant attraction and undeniable intrigue I feel towards a woman I've never even spoken with. Ellen James is making me feel like some shmuck on a Lifetime movie. Well, maybe it's more like a cross between a shmuck on a Lifetime movie and a teenage boy desperate to get laid on prom night.

And the only thing that's going through my mind right now is that I have to find a way to meet her...talk to her...wrap her legs around my waist...

She's making that offer to temporarily take over Dr. Grey's practice more tempting by the second. Dr. Grey is a well-known trauma surgeon located in Charlotte who primarily scrubs into surgeries at Regency Memorial. Now can you see why that offer is starting to look so enticing. What a coincidence, huh? A fucking perfect coincidence if you ask me. Honestly, the offer Dr. Grey extended will more than likely only help my career. Regency is Charlotte's main hospital for trauma surgeries, and this will only add to the experience I've already got under my belt from working at University Hospital in Seattle.

Yes, the job offer is looking better by the second, and it has almost everything to do with the girl in the black fuck-me heels and white button-up blouse. A blouse that reveals just enough cleavage to allow the assumption that Ellen has fucking perfect tits. I'd say she's a full C, maybe even a D cup. I discreetly adjust myself in my seat and attempt to reel in my wayward thoughts about Ellen's perfect tits in my hands—and my mouth. This girl makes me feel like I'm eighteen years old, hornier than a motherfucker, and ready to stick my teenage dick into anything wet and willing. I honestly can't remember the last time a girl had me this turned out without actually talking to her—or touching her.

God, would I love to touch her.

Fuck, Trent, get your balls in line.

I'm sitting here daydreaming about fucking some woman I've never even spoken to, a woman I've seen all of fifteen minutes. I'm Trent Hamilton, prestigious trauma surgeon, for fuck's sake. There are hospitals all over the country begging to get me into their OR. See, that's what a normal prick of a surgeon would think to himself on a daily basis, but I'm not like most surgeons. I tend to have more of an "I don't give a fuck" attitude. Honestly, I think it suits me well—*really* well. Materialistic bullshit and prestigious awards don't impress me. I prefer to go in, do my job, and then go about my day. I'm not the type of guy who flaunts his money or title in order to receive some sort of acceptance or approval. *Fuck. That.* I'd rather drive around in my Ford F-150 truck than be caught dead in some pretentious car like a Jag or Benz.

Ellen continues her presentation, smoothly running through each slide while discussing her main points informatively and with precision. The more she talks, the more I find myself wanting to get to know her. The more she struts around the conference room, the more I find myself wanting to fuck her.

What? I'm not a prick—I'm just honest. Any hot-blooded, straight man in this room who isn't thinking about what it would feel like to be between Ellen James's thighs should check to make sure their balls are still there. Seriously, this girl has my dick screaming for attention, and I'm not sure I can pass it off as just the pleats in my pants.

I continue to watch Ellen and try like hell to focus my attention on her actual presentation instead of her long, shapely legs or perfectly round ass. An ass that is practically begging for me to grasp in both of my very willing hands.

She turns to the next slide as she continues to highlight some of Regency's preferred methods of staffing protocols, and that's when my mouth drops open. The next slide is a picture of a very scantily clad Ellen James sporting a huge strap-on. *Shit, that rubber cock must be at least eleven or twelve inches.*

She's oblivious of the current picture that is up on the screen, and I find myself unable to pull my eyes away. She is dressed in sexy little boy shorts and a provocative lace top. A top that leaves little to the imagination. A top that confirms my suspicions of her having perfect tits. *Dear god, she really does have perfect tits.* I can almost see a hint of her perfect, rosy nipples poking through. So much for even attempting to hide my arousal...

I would put money on the fact that Ellen did not plan for this picture to be displayed during her presentation. I'm curious to know who is behind this unfortunate-for-Ellen-but-very-fortunate-for-me change in presentation agenda. When Ellen finally realizes why the entire conference room has ridiculous smirks on their faces, she is completely mortified. This moment of mortification only lasts a few seconds before she quickly changes the slide and addresses her audience with a sarcastic quip about wanting to make sure she had their full attention.

You definitely had mine.

Even in embarrassing situations, she manages to pull through with grace. *Really sexy, grace.* I'm in awe of this woman. Undeniably intrigued. I think she has me under some kind of spell. It's either that or someone has drugged the complimentary coffee that sits in front of me. I discreetly lift my Styrofoam cup and glance inside to make sure I don't see any evidence of an odd powder or residue floating around.

Nope, nothing.

I can't write this unquestionable attraction off.

I only have myself and my ever-willing cock to blame.

I know this makes me sound like a complete jackass, but I can't remember a time where a woman managed to get my attention without even really trying on her part. She's just up there being herself, presenting to a group of people, and I'm nothing but in awe of her.

She manages to smoothly finish her presentation without further assistance from her slides. I'd take a wild guess and say Ellen did this to avoid any other unexpected pictures to become front and center in a room full of surgeons and hospital officials. Mostly male surgeons and hospital officials at that.

I spend the rest of the time formulating a plan on how to get Ellen alone to chat after her presentation. Unfortunately for me, once she gives her closing speech, she rushes out of the conference room like her ass is on fire with the excuse of not wanting to miss her flight.

In this very moment, I have decided that Regency Memorial will be seeing the face of a new trauma surgeon very soon. That's right—Trent Hamilton, will be willingly taking that temporary offer to oversee Dr. Grey's practice.

I just hope Ellen James is ready...

Chapter One

"Not every moment in life is worth the purchase of a Hallmark card..."

Exhausted and starving, I sit down in the breakroom to enjoy a little R&R away from the trenches. I've got to stop agreeing to double shifts. For some reason, Regency has seen an all-time record this July in ER patients, and my manager might as well have me on speed dial. If I even see Nurse Ratchet headed my way to beg me to pick up another shift, I am running in the opposite direction. I don't care if the crazy bitch offers me triple time!

Nurse Ratchet is the less than friendly nickname that has been bestowed upon my wonderful manager, Shirley. She is a beast of a woman who has been a nurse longer than I have even been alive. She lives and breathes her job, and being stylish isn't one of her priorities. Her Groucho Marx eyebrows and gray roots are a testament to that.

I don't even want to imagine what the carpet looks like...

I am newly single, twenty-eight years old, and working over sixty hours in the ER most weeks. Yeah, my life is fucking fantastic right now. I reside in Charlotte, North Carolina, and have been working at Regency Medical for over seven years. Nursing is my job, and I'm thankful it pays my bills, bar tabs, and addiction to smut novels.

My name is Ellen James. Elle for short. I'm ornery and sarcastic, and my favorite word has four letters, starts with an F, and ends with U, C, and K. I'm loud, obnoxious, and inappropriately honest. I have a girl crush on my yoga instructor and take pride in the fact that I can double plow. I promise it's a yoga position!

With that being said, I'm also an advocate of equal opportunity and do not discriminate against any type of plowing. I feel completely certifiable most days, and my therapist's recommendation is Prozac. I'm actually partial to a bottle of tequila and a rough ride to Pound Town. Can you feel my sexual frustration?

Three months ago, I came home early from a nursing conference to find my fiancé in bed with another woman. Not just any other woman though—my friend and coworker, Veronica Morris. Shit hit the fan, and let's just say we won't be sharing Pinterest recipes or braiding each other's hair anytime soon. And to top it all off, I still work with the two-timing asshole and his hooker slut.

I'm not bitter.

Okay, I'm a little bitter, but can you honestly blame me?

I mean, my soon-to-be husband dicked one of my coworkers in *our* bed. Our god damn bed! Who does that? An asshole, cock-sucking, lying scumbag, that's who. If I could cut his balls off and make him wear them as a necklace, I'd do it.

Just thinking about the night I walked in on them banging it out makes me feel stabby. I've fantasized about running over my ex, John, with my car, more times than I'd like to admit. Nothing can bring out your inner-psycho-bitch like seeing your spouse's cock inside another woman. The only thing that could have made that situation better is if it would have broadcasted on that show *Cheaters.* I would have found a decent amount of sick-and-twisted enjoyment out of seeing that moment televised for the world to see. John butt-ass naked and begging for my forgiveness while sporting a raging erection with his whore's pussy juice dripping off of it, attempting to hide his face from the cameras…

A god damn Hallmark moment right there.

And again, just thinking about that night is making me feel *extremely* stabby.

Dr. John Ryan. ER Physician. The man I found to be sexy, charming, and utterly irresistible. He was once the most important man in my life. I'd started dating him when I was twenty-two years old, and things just escalated from there. We fell in love, moved in together, got engaged, and planned to live happily ever after in a beautiful home with a white picket fence.

Fortunately, our relationship ended before purchasing our dream home, because three months ago I probably would have lit that motherfucker on fire.

Chapter Two

"Sometimes surprises surprise the fuck out of you, and sometimes those surprises come in the form of a big red flag—a two-timing cocksucker with a hard-on, thrusting into a dirty pirate hooker."

Three months ago...

I decided to surprise him. I knew he would be home in bed by the time my flight got in. As I got out of the cab, the cool night air caused shivers up my spine. Charlotte was uncharacteristically cold for April that night, and I noticed our bedroom light was on in the apartment. I remember thinking it was odd that John was still awake.

It's 2 a.m. Maybe he's on call tonight?

I paid the driver and dragged my suitcase through the front door.

I could hear faint moaning.

What? Is John watching porn?

I actually giggled at the thought of this. I had no idea what or who was coming—pun intended—I walked down the hall and opened our bedroom door to find my fiancé balls-deep in Veronica.

I wanted to vomit.

I could feel the bile rising in my throat, and honestly, it was a shame that I couldn't attempt an exorcist-style projectile puking session all over those two. I just stood there in shock while I watched

John roughly thrust into another woman over and over and over again. *My John.* The man I thought was my best friend. The man I was planning to spend the rest of my life with.

I remember loudly dropping my bag to the hardwood floor, causing John to still, and Veronica looked up. "Oh my god, Ellen!" Veronica said with an expression of horror on her sweaty sex face. I found her expression ironic, because she was still spread-eagle on my bed, with her hairy muff lips flapping in the wind. Okay, maybe she wasn't *that* hairy, but she still had more pubes than any woman should sport unless she's planning on re-enacting a '70s style porno.

John quickly stood up and turned to look at me. "Ellie... Baby... Ellie... Oh shit! Oh fuck! Let me explain..." He was standing there, dripping in sweat, with a god damned hard-on, telling me to let him explain.

I looked John in the eyes with a cold, hard stare, took a deep breath, and then slowly picked up my bag and turned for the door. John grabbed my arm while looking at me with absolute terror etched on his face. "Ellie... Babe... Wait... Please don't leave me! Oh my god, sweetie, I'm so sorry!"

I roughly pulled my arm from his grasp. "Don't fucking call me Ellie. You lost those fucking rights when you fucked this bitch in our bed!"

I could feel the tears starting to fill my eyes and slowly drip down my cheeks.

I was devastated.

I felt like someone had ripped my heart out of my chest and left me open to bleed out every last ounce of dignity I had left. I can vaguely remember John attempting to talk to me, but it was too late. My mind had already gone into shock. The last thing I remember about that night is taking off my engagement ring, placing it on the dresser, and walking out of our apartment for the very last time.

That was three months ago.

Three long months since John Ryan broke my heart into a million tiny pieces.

It was a night that completely turned my world upside down. A night that took a little part of my happiness and flushed it down a diarrhea-filled toilet. A night that, when I look back, the only words that come to my mind are *fucking dickheads*.

John and Veronica are the biggest dickheads I have ever laid eyes on. Those two selfishly put their horny needs first and didn't worry about the consequences. They gave in to their slutty, cock-sucking, whore-filled desires and ruined a long-term relationship that was soon to turn into a marriage.

A soon-to-be marriage that had all of the wedding details planned to a T. Dress was bought, venues were booked, flowers were ordered, and invitations were ready to be sent in the mail. What a complete and total shit-storm those two put me through. The headache of explanations to friends and family, the endless phone calls, the attempts to cancel everything that had been put into motion for the wedding...

I would have been better off getting ass fucked with a twelve incher, minus the lube. There would have been a heck of a lot more enjoyment, that's for sure.

Chapter Three

"Breakups are hard. They can turn your life upside down and send you on endless journey to pick up the pieces and find yourself again."

After John trampled my heart, my best friend Amy was my rock. Our relationship is different than most. I know a lot of people don't really understand our sarcastic, raunchy sense of humor, but Amy has been nothing but a true friend to me. She is my best friend and has been a huge support system since day one. She's my shoulder to cry on, my drinking partner to let loose with, and everything else in between. Despite all of our witty banter and constant pranks on each other, I love her dearly. Amy has seen me through one of the lowest points in my life and managed to help me come out of that situation with my head still held high. Walking in on John having sex with another woman quite literally destroyed me. He betrayed me in the worst possible way, and for that, I will never forgive him.

John spent the first month after our breakup vying for my forgiveness. There were endless phone calls, text messages, unwelcome visits to my apartment, emails, and daily flower arrangements.

You name it and John attempted it.

The man was a force to be reckoned with, and somehow, I think he really believed we would get back together. In his warped, screwed-up head, I think John thought that I would eventually just forgive and forget his ultimate betrayal to our relationship.

At first, he even refused to cancel the wedding we had planned together. Eventually, after several weeks of no breakthrough, I think it finally sunk in that I was never going to get back together with him. The wedding plans were officially canceled, and I can only imagine the exorbitant amount of money John lost on deposits.

I hope it was an unbelievably, ridiculous amount.

The first thirty days were the absolute worst. I moved in with

Amy. Well actually I was *forced* to move in with Amy. She refused to take no for an answer. Amy is nothing if not persistent and extremely stubborn. She does not understand when someone is trying to tell her no. Her stubbornness was a life-saver; moving in with her was one of the best decisions that had ever been made for me.

Our conversation regarding me becoming Amy's new roommate consisted of the following:

"You're fucking moving in with me."

"No I'm not. I'm not letting you do that."

"Stop being such a dumbass. You're moving in with me or else I will tell Dr. Simon you want to bang his brains out."

"You're playing dirty. God! Why are you so damn bossy?"

"I'm going to your old apartment tomorrow and packing your shit. I'll probably tell that dick-munch ex of yours to go fuck himself while I'm there. I love you, roomie."

"Ugh. I love you too."

Amy moved my stuff from John's apartment the very next day. I can only imagine the nasty things she'd managed to spew at him when she was packing up my stuff. I spent countless hours watching mind-numbing reality shows while stuffing my face with Rocky Road ice cream. I refused to leave the apartment, and if it weren't for Amy being such a prying, nosy bitch, I would have shut everyone out of my life. I am fortunate that she stood by my side and helped me pick up the pieces of my battered, pathetic heart.

During the first week, I went into a severe depression.

I couldn't eat, sleep, or even find the motivation to shower. After five days of lying around in my own filth, Amy shoved my stinky ass into a bath and even took the time to wash my hair. Let's face it. If it weren't for her, I'd probably still be lying around in my panties and an old Patriots t-shirt, shoving ice cream down my throat.

As time passed, I began to have moments where I felt like myself again. Although these moments were few and far between, I was happy to know the old Ellen was still in there somewhere.

The second two months were the most interesting to date. I attempted to drown my sorrows in alcohol and find drunken solace in a string of one-night stands.

Nothing says "I'm trying to get over my ex" like going on a tequila bender and waking up with some random, faceless guy passed out in your bed. When guys talk about "beer goggles," I always kind of thought they were full of shit, but now I can say I understand this term one hundred and ten percent. I have had my share of leaving with a hot fucking ten and waking up next to a sweaty, smelly, and far-too-hairy five.

Don't get me wrong. There were a few really attractive men, but there were also some disturbingly pathetic drunken hookups. I guess I just thought that by refusing to date and taking any man I wanted to bed I was somehow getting back at John for what he did.

Deep down I know that most of these random one-night stands were motivated by my newfound trust issues and never-ending yet nonconventional quest to move on. There is one hookup that Amy loves to remind me of, because frankly, it's pretty ridiculous. Not many girls can say she took a deaf guy home, had sloppy sex with him, passed out, and then forgot the next day that said guy is actually hearing impaired.

Yes, you heard me correctly.

I drunkenly screwed a deaf guy, and the next morning, I forgot the guy was in my bed and, more importantly, that he was hearing impaired.

Chapter Four

"Sign language is useful. You never know when you'll find yourself being thrusted by a guy with a hearing impairment and you want to tell him to plunge that dick harder."

I felt the sunlight filter through my bedroom window and winced from the already prominent hangover headache that was pounding inside of my brain. My head felt as if someone was banging my skull into cement, and the unfortunate tequila aftertaste was making bile rise slowly up my throat. My mouth tasted like someone had shit inside of it, and I could only imagine the breath I was sporting. I jumped out of bed and raced to the bathroom, knowing full well that I was going to be praying to the porcelain gods for a while. Tequila and I had a serious love-hate relationship. I loved to drink her all night long, and then the next day, I hated that bitch something fierce. With my head in the toilet, I proceeded to heave everything out of my stomach until I was sweaty, shivering, and had tears streaming down my cheeks. *Worst feeling ever.*

"Elle, you okay in there?" I heard Amy say outside the bathroom door.

I groaned out a pathetic yes and continued to go for round two with the toilet bowl. I was having one of those awful hangovers where you truly believed you were going to vomit your entire stomach up and still have no relief in sight.

Dry heave… Vomit… Dry heave… Vomit.

I might have unintentionally cracked three ribs and given myself an appendectomy.

This was the moment where I'd promise myself I would never drink again, despite the fact that I'd be ready to hit the bottle once I was fully healed.

Yes, I was having one of *those* hangovers.

"I feel so bad for you right now. I'm just thankful that I don't feel as shitty as you. Holler if you need anything." I heard Amy step away from the bathroom door and head down the hallway.

After I'd proceeded to vomit like a bulimic girl who'd just binged herself through a pack of Oreos and several McDonald's Quarter Pounders, I hopped into the shower to wash off last night's alcohol and remnants of today's puking marathon.

The warm water felt soothing on my now achy muscles, and I took my time washing my hair. I could only imagine the shenanigans I'd gotten myself into last night. If I was this hung over and couldn't recall how I'd gotten home, things probably had been out of control. I jumped out of the shower, brushed my teeth, dried my hair a little, and put on my favorite comfy robe before heading back into my bedroom.

"Ahhhhhh! What the fuck!" I screamed as I realized there was a sleeping man in my bed.

I was shocked my shrill yell hadn't startled him awake. I wouldn't have been surprised if I'd woken up the entire apartment complex. Amy came running in with a look of terror on her face and then abruptly stopped when she realized what my dramatics were about. We were both standing at the foot of my bed, staring at the still sleeping guy, with puzzled looks on our faces.

Amy looked over at me with a goofy grin before putting her hand over her mouth in attempt to hide her laughter. I elbowed her in the stomach in hopes that I could shut her up and then proceeded to grab her by the wrist and quickly drag her out of my bedroom. We headed into the kitchen and did what any girl would do in this situation—tried to recount last night's events.

"How in the hell did you not see this guy when you woke up?" Amy was grinning, her perfectly white teeth practically shining back at me.

"Well, let's see. I woke up with a pounding fucking headache and then had to make a mad dash to the bathroom, where I proceeded to vomit for like an hour. I'm pretty sure you should have called a priest. I could have used an exorcism in there!"

Amy started to laugh a little and shook her head at the nonsensicality of this scenario.

"Okay. Let me get this straight. You didn't happen to notice that *a man*, who looks to be about six foot and a muscular two hundred pounds, was lying in your bed? Seriously, Ellen? Are you that clueless?"

"First of all, who the hell are you? Do you secretly write height and weight statistics for the NFL? Secondly, I was too focused on how god damn awful I felt! My head was pounding and I could barely open my eyes! I was probably still kind of drunk when I woke up!" I said a little too loudly.

Amy motioned for me to quiet down, and we both glanced down the hall in hopes that Mystery Guy hadn't woken up and overheard our conversation. The entire apartment was uncannily quiet, and we assumed that my unexpected guest was still sound asleep in my bed.

I abruptly sat down at the kitchen table and put my head in my hands, huffing out a deep breath of frustration. My mortification was at record-breaking levels.

How in the hell do I find myself in these situations?

"I've got to get my act together. This one-night stand shit is starting to get out of control," I said in the whiniest voice possible with my head still buried in my hands.

"Elle, it's fine. We've all been there before. Okay, let's look on the positive side. At least he's attractive and not covered in back hair like that one guy from—"

I quickly interrupted Amy and gave her a serious look. "Enough! Now is not the time for a rehashing of my past hookups. I just need you to help me get this guy out of here so I can still maintain a tiny bit of my already scant amount of dignity."

She glanced at the clock and sat down next to me at the kitchen table. "All right, well in my opinion this guy has already overstayed his welcome. It's almost ten, and in proper one-night stand etiquette, his ass should have been out the door over an hour ago."

"Proper one-night stand etiquette? Do you realize how absurd you sound right now?"

"Ellen, there are some unwritten but very well-known one-night stand rules, and having your ass out the door before ten in the morning is definitely one of them!" Amy threw her arms in the air, indicating she was irritated with Mystery Guy for not following the so-called one-night stand book of etiquette.

I rolled my eyes skyward. "Whatever. I'm not discussing this with you right now. Let's just get this idiot out of here. We need to be really loud so we wake him up."

Amy stood up from the kitchen table and loudly grabbed a frying pan from the cabinet. "Good idea. I'll make us something to eat and make sure I'm extra noisy so we interrupt ass-clown's beauty rest. Go turn on some music."

I plugged my iPod into the stereo and blasted Incubus while Amy proceeded to bang shit around in the kitchen.

Forty-five minutes later...

Amy and I had now successfully cooked breakfast, eaten said breakfast, cleaned up the kitchen, and listened to the entire Morning View album by Incubus on surround sound. Yet, there was still no sign from Mr. Sleeping Beauty. I decided to take matters into my own hands and leave my dignity in the kitchen. I headed into my bedroom and forcefully shut my door, the slamming vibration nearly sending shockwaves throughout the entire apartment. I looked towards my bed, hopeful that Mystery Guy would start to stir.

No flinch.

No startle.

Not a single budge.

What the hell?

If I couldn't have visibly seen this guy breathing, I'd have been worried that he was dead. I cleared my throat loudly. "Excuse me... Uhhh...are you awake?"

Still no response.

Now I was starting to get a little pissed at Mr. Sleeping Dead. Again, I cleared my throat as loudly as humanly possible. "Hey. You. Guy. Could you wake the fuck up?"

And still, no response. This guy might as well have been in a coma.

Who sleeps this deeply and doesn't hear a single thing all morning?

I looked towards the night stand to make sure there wasn't a small hearing aid missing its owner. . And just thinking that thought brought up drunken flashbacks from the previous night into my head...

I'm looking down at this incredibly attractive man as I continue to ride his cock. He's looking up at me in a seductive, euphoric way. Who cares that he's deaf right? I mean, this guy is unbelievable sexy. Blond hair, chocolate brown eyes, and a set of washboard abs that would make any girl's panties wet.

I've taken care of people with hearing impairments. I know sign language...a little.

I managed to get him back to my apartment and undressed, so that's all that really matters at this point. He flips me on my back and starts thrusting deeper inside of me.

Damn, this guy knows how to use his dick.

He's average-sized, but he has nice girth and I know he's got the tools to bring me to orgasm.

"Oh yesssss! Harder! Harder!" I yell and can't ignore the fact that my drunken slur has it sounding more like "Uh Yessss! Hardhurts!

Hardhurts!"

Oh well. He can't hear me anyway.

He abruptly stops the thrusting and just stares down at me with a look of concern.

What the fuck? Why isn't this guy continuing to screw my brains out?

"No! No! No! Keep going! Go! Now! Move your dick! Keeping moving your dick!" I say with urgency.

He's still not moving and is just looking at me. Oh no. He was good at lip-reading at the bar, but I bet he's having a hard time understanding my Tequila English.

What's the sign for harder? Think, Ellen! Think! Sign for harder? Pelvic thrusting motion? That would probably work...

I blinked back the drunken flashback and flushed cherry red with embarrassment.

Holy mother of pearl! This guy is actually hearing impaired!

I'd brought a deaf guy home, and I'd been trying to wake him up all morning by making noise. Noise he couldn't hear because he was motherfucking deaf! I slapped my forehead with my right hand, dragged it over my eyes, and then slowly shook my head.

How in the hell had I managed this one? I drunkenly brought a deaf guy home from the bar, blacked out, and woke up without remembering any details. Oh wait, I had some details. The mortifyingly embarrassing ones! I was pretty sure I'd attempted to sign "harder" to him by motioning a pelvic thrust with my hips and arms.

Ground, please swallow me up! Lightning, strike me dead right here in my bedroom!

After several moments of self-deprecation, I decided to end this embarrassing moment by tapping his back with my foot. Mystery Guy rolled over on his back and sleepily looked over at me. I forced a tight smile on my face and gave a slight wave.

Oh great. Now I'm waving hello at this guy.

I was waving hello at the guy I was standing three feet away from, and less than twelve hours ago, he'd been muff-diving like a god damn professional. Now that I was starting to recall bits and pieces of last night, I could definitely remember that this guy had some serious oral skills. If the Olympics had muff-diving as an event, he would definitely be on the medal stand with the Star-Spangled Banner loudly playing while the American flag hung proudly behind him.

That guy had eaten my pussy like a fat guy on death row smothering himself in a box of Twinkies.

Mystery Guy smirked back at me before grabbing his cell phone from my night stand and checking the time. I could tell by his facial expression that he was shocked it was almost noon.

Yeah, fucker, haven't you read the one-night stand book of etiquette?

He abruptly stood up and began to collect his clothes while simultaneously giving me a full-on naked view of his very nice ass.

And that's the story of how I brought home a deaf guy and had drunken one-night-stand sex with him. You're welcome for the comedic entertainment.

In that moment, I promised myself I would never drink tequila *or* have one-night stand sex again until I manage to get over this terrible hangover and seek therapy.

God damn drunken one-night stands...

I've got to get my act together and stop doing this.

Chapter Five

"'Pull on my pubes' and 'handcuff my balls' are never useful instructions from a physician attempting to run a code."

Right now, my life feels like it's probably at an all-time low. Take my current situation for example: I'm sitting in the ER breakroom, attempting to eat shitty hospital cafeteria food, while having flashbacks of my ex-fiancé banging it out with loose lips Vagina—I mean Veronica. Ha!

And now I'm even laughing at my own jokes, but seriously... That's a little funny, right?

Shirley rushes into the breakroom looking visibly frantic. "Where have you been?! We've got a code in bed three and I need you there!"

So much for sitting down for a few minutes...

"Obviously I was under the very wrong impression that hospital employees get lunch breaks around here."

"I don't need the attitude today, Elle," Nurse Ratchet replied with a raise of her unibrow.

Deep breaths, Elle. Deep breaths.

I get out of my chair, throw my crappy food away, and head for the god damn code that's interrupting the only five minute break I've had since clocking in ten hours ago.

"Excuse me, nurse. Someone needs to pay for my cab ride back to my house. I called an *amalance* to get here, because I don't got a car." This demand is coming from a guy who is updating his *Facebook* status on his brand-new iPhone.

I briskly walk around that idiot without even acknowledging him. I do this for several reasons. One, I obviously need to get to this code, and two, I probably would have said some things that would have been deemed highly inappropriate by Human Resources.

I know I'm a little jaded, but you trying working in an ER for over seven years and then tell me if your view of the world has changed. I continue to quickly rush to bed three while silently repeating my mantra in my head.

I love my job. I love my job. I love my job.

I get into the room and can already tell this is going to be a complete clusterfuck, because the new ER physician is attempting to run this code. Dr. Bill Simon is a thirty-five-year-old physician who is a few inches shy of five foot five and as skinny as Olive Oil, and he also happens to have Tourette's.

Now, don't start judging me. I really don't have anything against people with Tourette's Syndrome, but it can become quite hard to ignore when an ER doctor's Tourette's is more pronounced under stressful situations. That's right—*stressful situations* make this man's Tourette's go haywire. And yes, he actually chose Emergency Medicine as his specialty.

Some things just can't be explained.

So here I am, watching shit hit the fan while good ol' Doctor Bill attempts to run a code despite his ill-timed outbursts. Oh, did I forget to mention that Bill's Tourette's cause him to yell out sexually explicit comments?

Sometimes it really is the little things in life.

"So what do we have here?" I ask Amy.

"He's a forty-five-year-old truck driver who was brought in by squad after being found nonresponsive at a truck stop. No known medical or surgical history. Next of kin has yet to be contacted," Amy responds as she continues chest compressions. The girl couldn't look ugly even if she tried. She's standing there pounding on some guy's chest and still managing to look like she's just walked off a fucking runaway. If she wasn't my best friend, she'd be one of those girls I'd love to hate for always looking so damn gorgeous. Her big brown eyes framed with thick, black lashes, her long brunette hair, and her adorably curvy body that can even be seen in loose scrubs. Yeah, she's kind of a bitch that way.

"What's… PICKLE PISS! What's our rhythm?" Dr. Bill yells out.

"He's still in V-fib, Dr. Simon," I tell him as I take over chest compressions to give Amy a break.

"Okay, okay. Go ahead and intubate. Let's continue CPR and prepare to…SWEET MOMMA'S PUSSY…BIG-LIPPED VAGINAS…prepare to defibrillate…PULL ON MY PUBES!" Dr. Bill sputters a little too loudly while making it quite obvious he is pretty worked up and extremely nervous.

I don't know how long I can hold back laughter if he keeps demanding someone pulls on his pubes. I look over at Amy, raise my eyebrow, and slightly shake my head while I continue chest compressions on this poor truck driver. She looks back at me, indicating that she agrees that this code is going to be a shit show.

I am just thankful this man didn't have any family with him. There is nothing about a doctor yelling about "big-lipped vaginas" that will make you feel like your loved one is in good hands. Unless, of course, your loved one has a problem with their big-lipped vagina; then you know you came to the right place and might think, "Boy, this doctor is passionate about his practice."

Unfortunately, that isn't the case here.

Amy starts to draw up epinephrine, already anticipating what actually needs to be done. Amy and I have been running our own codes for so long now that it's old hat, but Dr. Simon needs some practice. So here we are, attempting to defibrillate a man out of V-fib (irregular, life-threatening heart rhythm) while becoming more uncomfortable by the minute because Dr. Simon is shouting about "momma's pussy."

Don't let your thoughts wander with that scenario or else you will end up some place extremely disturbing. Don't do it! Save yourself! Think about happy things, like Ryan Gosling's abs…

"Let's attempt to defibrillate him out of…TITS…out of BIG TITTIES…out of V-fib. All clear. Hands off the patient," Dr. Simon hollers as he attempts to shock this patient into some type of life-sustaining rhythm.

"'Defibrillate him out of big titties'? Didn't know they added that to one of the ACLS Algorithms," a husky voice whispers into my ear.

ACLS Algorithms are basically standard protocols that we follow when faced with code situations. I smirk and laugh quietly to myself before I look up to see where that voice came from. I see the most striking blue eyes staring back at me. Eyes that nearly take my breath away and make me forget my name.

This man is extremely muscular, well over six foot, and looking like absolute sin in a pair of simple navy scrubs. His blue eyes are even more pronounced under his thick, black lashes and messy, jet-black hair. His badge reads Dr. Trent Hamilton.

God, even his name is sexy.

I look over at Amy and see that she notices this hot piece of eye candy standing near me. She's looking at me with a huge grin on her face. I give her the 'holy shit, this guy is hot!' look and she discreetly nods her head. Then, in true Amy fashion, she proceeds to stroke her epinephrine syringe while she bites on her bottom lip.

I swear I can't take her anywhere.

My eyes widen a little in a desperate endeavor to get Amy to stop showing off her hand-job techniques in the middle of a code. She just continues to fondle her syringe to satisfaction, and this leaves my best friend with two options: either she knocks it off *or* I'll give her a swift cunt punch after work. I'm being completely serious here, too. Just ask Amy about the infamous Slackers vs. Mallrats argument. After numerous shots of tequila and being thrown out of Murphy's Pub, she found out that getting punched in the vagina really does hurt like a motherfucker.

After giving Amy several 'I'm going to donkey-punch your taint' looks, she decides it's in her best interest to stop the stroking. I notice that Dr. Beautiful continues to stand back and watch Dr. Simon run an extremely attention-grabbing code.

I have a suspicion that he came to observe the notorious Dr. Simon for his own amusement, because word tends to spread like wildfire around this hospital. Luckily, we are able to defibrillate the truck driver out of V-fib and get him stable enough to be transferred to the ICU vented and in critical condition.

Drugs that include cocaine, meth, and barbiturates were found in the trucker's system. The man most likely had a massive heart attack and honestly is damn lucky to be alive at this point. I'm just thankful we were able to get through that code with only hearing a few more inappropriate comments from Dr. Simon. "Whip me," "handcuff my balls," and "vibrating anal beads" were a few of my favorites. My guess is that he's probably a Fifty Shades of Grey fan.

Chapter Six

"The first step in fixing a problem starts with admitting you have a problem. My name is Ellen and my traitor nipples have an addiction to sexy physicians."

As I'm sitting at the nurses' station, updating some patient charts, I look up to see Dr. Hamilton leaning over my computer screen, smiling. "Uh, can I help you with something?" I say, sounding a little irritated.

He shakes his head slightly while still grinning at me and then mumbles quietly to himself. The only thing I managed to hear was "doesn't remember." My eyebrows turn in as I contemplate the notion that this hot doctor might be a little crazy.

After an awkward silence, he introduces himself. "Hi, I'm Trent Hamilton, the new trauma surgeon that's temporarily taking over Dr. Grey's practice. You must be the infamous Ellen James?"

Infamous? What the hell? Is that like a code word for 'I hear you're a good fuck'?

He puts his hand out towards me and I hesitantly place my hand in his; the warmth of his palm makes my nipples tighten immediately.

Jesus, Elle, you're at work! Calm your tits!

I'm in complete shock over my body's reaction to a simple handshake. I quickly compose myself and remove my hand from his scorching, muscular grip.

"Infamous, huh? Well I'm not sure why, but hopefully it's for good reason. It's a pleasure, Dr. Hamilton."

"Yes, Ellen, the pleasure is all mine, and please, call me Trent," he replies with a smirk.

Damn, sexy, smirking, too-hot-for-my-own-good doctor. And of course he's a surgeon! After John, I already promised myself…NO MORE DOCTORS! This guy is going to make that promise very hard to keep.

I'm already mentally taking pictures of him for my spank bank.

Don't judge me. Everyone has a spank bank. Your go-to mental pictures that you keep stored away for when it's time to finger-bang yourself.

Diddle your skittle. Flick your bean. Fluff your muff. Double-click your mouse…

Anyone who denies the need for a spank bank is an uptight prude who could use a good double plow. See what I did there with the yoga sexual innuendo?

"Okay, *Trent,*" I retort with a tight smile. A tight smile because my nipples and snatch have betrayed me and seem to find Trent Hamilton worthy of hot, dirty sex.

"So, is it just Ellen, or do you go by anything else?"

"Yes, it's Ellen, but I also go by Ellie—I mean Elle. I also go by Elle."

What? Why did I say Ellie first? Freudian slip?

The only man who has ever called me Ellie is John.

"Well, I look forward to working with you. Would you mind showing me around the department?" He asks expectantly while continuing to hold my gaze with his beautiful blue eyes. I reluctantly pull away from his stare and glance over at Tony. I'm trying to find a way out of this scenario, because I really don't trust my sexually frustrated body near this man.

"I've actually got a few patients to see, but I'm sure Tony would love to. Right, Tony?" I say to Tony, who is sitting at the computer next me.

"Sorry, Elle, I'm a little busy here," Tony responds without even looking up from his computer screen.

I can tell he's furiously attempting to catch up on charting. Obviously, he waited until the end of his shift to chart for all of his patients, because he's a procrastinating asshole with horrible timing and no sense of how his procrastination MAY AFFECT MY LIFE! Ugh!

Damn you, Tony, and your shitty, shitty time management skills!

"All right, well I guess I can take a few minutes to show you around, Dr. Hamilton." I get out of my chair and motion for him to follow me. "Let's head back towards our supplies and work our way out."

"Sounds like a plan," Dr. Hamilton—or should I say Dr. Beautiful—answers with a voice that does things to me I am not even ready to admit. My muff, on the other hand… Well, she is practically wetting herself right now.

We walk into the supply room, and this man has me so on edge that I jump a little as the door closes shut behind us.

"So this is the supply room. Pretty much everything you could possibly need is back here. I doubt you'll be spending much time here though. That's what nurses are for, right, *Doctor*?" I ask sarcastically.

I turn away from him and attempt to point out some specific supplies, but warm breath on the back of my neck makes me forget my train of thought.

What is with this man?

He's already got me fantasizing about all kinds of kinky sex positions with him: Double plow, triple plow… Hell, any kind of plow as long as *he* is plowing *me!*

I slowly turn around, and my breath catches when I find myself face to face with Trent Hamilton. Without giving me any time to think or protest, he roughly pulls my hips flush to his then proceeds to place his lips on mine. I weakly attempt to pull away, but his hand is in my hair, holding me in place.

His tongue slowly licks my bottom lip and begs entrance into my mouth. I can't help the moan that escapes me, and then he's in my mouth, exploring me, kissing me with more passion than I've ever felt in my entire twenty-eight years.

My body melts into his and I'm completely lost in this kiss—this amazing, sexy, passionate kiss. I'm kissing a man I just today maybe spoke a total of ten minutes to and will be working with on a daily basis. *Clearly I've lost my ever-loving mind!* But my mind has left for lunch. The only one running the show at this point is my vagina, and boy oh boy, is she loving her some Trent Hamilton right now.

His hand slowly slides up under my scrub top and grazes my thin cotton bra. My nipple hardens as the pad of his thumb rubs against it. His tongue stroking inside my mouth and hand firmly grabbing my breast have me so turned on that I think I might spontaneously combust. I have no self-control left and I find myself putting my hands all over his hard, muscular body.

I grind my body into his, and that's when I feel his erection pressing into my belly. He has me so aroused that I start to feel that familiar, delicious clench from deep within, and I know my panties are drenched.

"Fuck, you taste amazing," he whispers into my mouth.

Oh, sweet Jesus…

My moans become embarrassingly loud. My body has taken over and doesn't seem to be bothered by the fact that I'm currently grinding on a physician, in the supply room, at my place of employment. Scratch that— *our* place of employment. That's when I hear voices outside the door, quickly push away from him, and attempt to act like I've got my shit together.

The door opens abruptly and in walks my ex-fiancé John with that procrastinating asshole Tony. They are loudly discussing supplies for a dressing change on a patient as they step through the door. Both suddenly stop talking when they see us standing there looking a little out of breath and slightly disheveled.

"Uh, h-hey Tony, Dr. Ryan. I was just, uh, showing Dr. Hamilton around. Have y'all met?"

Y'all? Where in the hell did that come from?

I hate that my nerves always manage to bring out my Louisville twang. I know John can sense this. He is practically penetrating my skull with his intense stare.

"Yep, we've met." John's tone is clipped, and he doesn't so much as glance towards Dr. Hamilton's direction. I can't quite read the expression on John's face, but I think he almost looks pissed.

"Yeah, Elle, I met Dr. Hamilton a few minutes ago. Remember?" Tony conveys to me with a curious look on his face.

"Must've slipped my mind. Well, let us get out of your way." I attempt to quickly escape this extremely uncomfortable situation.

"Have a good one, guys." Trent gives a smug grin.

I try to get some distance from Dr. Hamilton but he manages to catch up with me as I hastily walk away from the supply room. As I head back towards the nurses' station, I glance over at him and can't help but notice that he's the epitome of every woman's fantasy. He had my body so riled up in that supply room that I'm not sure if I would have ever stopped.

Was I really going to fuck him in the supply room?

Oh my god! I was going to fuck him in the supply room! I'm pathetic! A pathetic, dirty little slut! I can feel my blood starting to boil at the thought of being so reckless and out of control.

"I'm pretty sure that kissing a staff member in the supply room could be considered sexual harassment," I whisper sternly to him before we make it back to the nurses' station.

"I'm pretty sure it's not sexual harassment when said staff member actually kisses back and grinds her scandalous little body right into my hard cock." He gives me a treacherously sexy smirk.

Nothing comes out of my mouth.

I have no words right now.

None. Zip. Zilch. Nada.

I have no idea what to say, because he's technically right. I was grinding all over him. I was basically climbing up his body like a god damn spider monkey! Before I can even respond, he grabs my wrist and pulls my body close to his. We are so close that I can feel his warm breath on my lips. I get lost in his penetrating blue eyes.

"Elle, I will be thinking about that kiss *all fucking day*," he slowly

Chapter Seven

"Never mess with a baby sporting a Fu Manchu."

I'm standing in this kitchen that looks oddly familiar. Everywhere I look there are little, dark-haired babies in chef hats.

Am I having a psychotic break?

Oh god, my therapist was right! I DO need Prozac!

The babies are running around this kitchen and seem to be chaotically cooking some type of chicken dish. *Chicken cacciatore maybe?* I then realize that the kitchen uncannily resembles the Jersey Shore house. Oh! Maybe it's Sunday dinner and these are all of Snooki's kids!

I thought she only had one baby, though. What's that baby's name? Lonnie… Leon… Luigi… I know its L-something. So how did she end up with this many babies?! Holy shit, that Gianni must have some powerful spunk!

"Snooook? Vin? JWOWW?" I scream over the crowd of cooking midgets.

I look down and notice that the baby to my left is scowling at me under his tiny Fu Manchu while furiously chopping a green pepper. Wow, he sure looks like an angry little man. Where is this child's mother? I bet she'd shit herself if she found her creepy Fu Manchu-wearing baby using a butcher's knife.

"Hey, little buddy. Why don't you go ahead and hand me the knife?" I calmly ask the scowling baby with a disturbing amount of facial hair.

Uh, oh. Baby Fu Manchu looks pissed. Really, really pissed.

He stops chopping his pepper and proceeds to yell some sort of baby-talk code word, and then all hell breaks loose. All of the babies stop what they're doing and seem to be yelling profanities at me. Now they're running towards me! Oh my god! These babies are coming after me! I'm going to die by the hands of Snooki's kids!

Damn you, Gianni and your nuclear spooge!

"AHHHHHHHHHH!" I'm screaming at the top of my lungs as I attempt to run away from the midget mob. "AHHHHHH! SNOOKI, YOUR FUCKING KIDS ARE GOING TO KILL ME! AHHHHHHH!"

Then I can barely hear someone saying, "Elle! Elle! Wake up!"

Snooki's little bastards start to slowly fade away and I open my eyes to the familiar surroundings of my bedroom in my and Amy's apartment. The July summer sun is shining through my curtains, and my eyes squint in reaction.

I was dreaming. Oh thank god.

I've always thought dying in a fire was the absolute worst way to go, but now I'm thinking that being burned at the stake by Snooki's Fu Manchu-wearing little bastards is definitely the *worst* way to die.

I notice that Amy is sitting on the edge of my bed, looking at me curiously.

"What was that all about, Elle? You were thrashing around and screaming about Snooki having bastards that were conceived from super spunk. I told you we shouldn't have had tequila last night. You *always* have the weirdest dreams when you drink tequila. And I told you that Jersey Shore marathon was a bad idea last week."

"Don't get snippy with me. I love tequila, and that mind-numbing bitch loves me. Tequila and I are the best of friends, and you will *never* suggest that I quit her!" I wail as I attempt to slowly sit up and lean against my headboard.

"Chill out, dickhead. No need to re-enact Brokeback Mountain on my account."

I roll my eyes at my sarcastic asshole of a friend and look down to realize I'm currently sporting a white t-shirt that has "Shirley Swallows" sloppily written in black sharpie and nothing else.

What happened last night?

"First of all, I owe you an apology because I honestly didn't realize how serious you and tequila were about each other. Secondly, as much as you love that crazy bitch, tequila makes you dream the creepiest shit. Last time you drank tequila, we had an hour-long discussion on why you had a dream that you gave Honey Boo Boo shaken baby syndrome," Amy says while attempting to find a pair of my pants on the floor.

"Hey there, Ms. Judgy. I was seriously freaked out from that dream about Honey Boo Boo! That little pageant queen was so pissed that I'd taken her Red Bull and Pixy Sticks away that she threatened my life! I honestly had no other choice but to shake the ever-living shit out of her. I still don't understand how a grown child hopped up on energy drinks could get shaken baby syndrome."

I slide on the pair of black yoga pants Amy threw on my bed and attempt to stand up without falling face-first into the hardwood floor.

"Calm down, crazy. There is no explanation for that, because it was a *dream*. A tequila dream at that. Anyways, I think Honey Boo Boo might already have shaken baby syndrome," Amy says with a smirk before she walks out of my bedroom.

"Tequila does not make me dream crazy shit!" I scream at the top of my lungs towards the hallway, which unfortunately causes a throbbing pain inside my skull.

"Denial is the first step towards realizing you have a problem!" Amy yells back.

She is quite the sarcastic bitch.

Chapter Eight

"Technology makes it impossible to escape moments of drunken insanity."

I walk out into the kitchen to find Amy making coffee. Two mugs are already set out on the counter with my favorite French vanilla creamer.

What a sweetheart.

"If I liked vagina, you would definitely be my number one lesbian lover," I tell Amy as I grab ibuprofen from our communal medicine basket. We might as well have a bowl of them on our coffee table like damn M&Ms.

"Aw, Elle, you always know just the right things to say to a girl." Amy smiles at me.

"So are we going to talk about what the hell happened last night?" I glance down at my Shirley Swallows t-shirt.

Amy lets out a loud laugh and shakes her head at me. "Oh, Elle, I'm not even sure how to start this conversation with you."

"Is it really that bad?"

"Depends on what you consider bad. If you attempting to get the bar to make a Harlem Shake video is something you would consider bad, then yes. Prepare yourself to hear the worst." She pours coffee into both mugs.

"Whaaat? A Harlem Shake video? Oh, fuck me. Please tell me there is no documentation of this."

Amy picks her phone up off the counter and hands it to me. "Actually there is video proof."

"Video proof!?" I quickly take the phone out of her hand and scroll to her videos.

I don't even have to ask which one it is, because I see a video icon that is a picture of me with my Shirley Swallows shirt. I'm assuming this shirt is in reference to our nursing manager Shirley. I am praying she is not directly involved with last night's shenanigans.

I take my coffee mug off the kitchen counter, toss back the ibuprofen, and sit down at the table. Amy sits down next to me, and I can tell she is fighting back a smile. I don't even have to look over; I can feel her enjoyment. I sigh in anticipation before pressing play.

The video starts with Amy turning the camera towards her; she smiles, her brown eyes sparkling as she drunkenly says, "You can thank me later for this."

Add 100 cunt points. Supreme cunt status achieved by the dickhead sitting next to me.

The camera turns towards the corner of the bar. I notice that someone with a motorcycle helmet is standing completely still while everyone else in the bar is going about their business, conversing, and drinking. Then I notice that said person is wearing a Shirley Swallows t-shirt.

Oh, no.

The intro to the Harlem Shake begins to play loudly in the bar, and that is when I begin to awkwardly thrust my pelvis to the beat of the music. Don't worry, the motorcycle helmet is still on my fucking head.

I'm going to *kill* Amy for this.

The song continues, and I am still in the corner of the bar, gyrating and pelvic thrusting like a god damn idiot. The camera swings back towards Amy, and she says, "Wait for it." Then you hear the lyric "Do the Harlem Shake" blaring from the jukebox as the camera turns back towards me in the corner.

Oh, god.

Fuck my life and my ability to continually make terrible decisions when I'm shitfaced.

The motorcycle helmet has now been replaced by my t-shirt.

Yes, my t-shirt is now tied on top of my head and I am thrashing my body around in nothing but my cut-off jean shorts and black lace bra. Someone plan Amy's funeral because this girl is not going to live another day.

But it gets even better...

The Harlem Shake is still blaring in the background, and I abruptly stop thrash dancing because I am finally realizing that everyone in the bar has stopped what they are doing to watch my crazy ass act a fool.

No one is joining in on this little Harlem Shake revival.

We have reached the part in the video where I get very angry and begin to scream at everyone in the bar. I am now standing on top of the bar and roaring profanities I didn't even know existed while still wearing nothing but my bra, cut-off jean shorts, and t-shirt still wrapped around my head.

Could this get any worse?

Yes, actually it *can* get worse. And it *does*.

The video continues with me shouting while I can barely hear Amy's giggle in the background. The bartender grabs me by the knees and throws me over his shoulder. I am thrashing around and yelling for him to put me down, but this doesn't even faze him.

He proceeds to haul my stupid ass out of the bar. The video ends with the bar cheering and clapping when the bartender comes back in sans the idiot drunk girl who just managed to make a complete fool of herself.

I set the phone down on the kitchen table and slowly lift my eyes to look at Amy. She is doing her famous silent laugh as tears are streaming down her cheeks.

"Amy! What the hell?!"

She isn't holding back the laughter now. Amy is laughing so hard that she is snorting. Her chest is vibrating with laughter as she slaps her knee and wails in hysterics. My anger level is rising to new heights at the moment, and I decide its best to leave the kitchen before I start re-enacting Fight Club. I am so unbelievably pissed that I just stand up, throw my mug in the sink, and stomp my way back towards my bedroom.

"Elle, come back! I'm sorry, but that is some seriously funny shit!" Amy chokes out through continued bursts of laughter.

"I take it back, Amy! If I liked vagina, there is NO way you would be my number one lesbian lover! You wouldn't even be in my top three! You'd be behind the fat girl in Pitch Perfect!" I scream at her before slamming my bedroom door.

Dear Hangover,
I'm your bitch.
Sincerely,
Ellen

Chapter Nine

"Karma can be a snarky little bitch."

I am finally fully recovered from my hangover after the infamous Harlem Shake night. Although I love that bitch dearly, tequila rocked my ass, and I found myself severely hungover all day yesterday. Even ibuprofen and greasy fast food couldn't save me from the nasty headache and all-day nausea.

I know, poor me, right? But seriously, my whole body is still aching today!

I'm presuming the muscle soreness may be a direct result of all the dancing I apparently took part in. I'm using the term dancing very loosely here. The moves I was displaying on Amy's video were nothing short of pathetic, looking more like I was having an actual seizure rather than the sex kitten I was probably picturing in my drunken head.

So here I am, facing another exciting day in the emergency room. I have officially made it halfway through my shift, and I'm getting close to being able to sit my tired ass down for a few minutes. I told Nurse Ratchet I would see this last patient before going on break.

I pull back the curtain in bed one and find this frail, little elderly woman quietly sitting on my gurney. She's an eighty-year-old petite little thing who's about five feet tall and couldn't weigh an ounce over one hundred pounds soaking wet.

"Hi, Mrs. Franks. What brings you in to see me today?" I ask as I pull the curtain back for privacy.

"Oh, honey, I've been having this awful pain down in my undercarriage and I feel like everything is going to fall out." She nervously fidgets and adjusts the stark white sheet around her legs.

Did this woman really just say undercarriage*?*

"Okay. So how long have you been experiencing this pain and discomfort in your *undercarriage*?" I attempt to ask with a straight face

"Hmmmm. Well, dear, I would say it's been at least a month now," Mrs. Franks replies quietly.

"A *month*, Mrs. Franks? What made you wait so long before seeing a physician?"

"Well, I have always just been able to push my undercarriage right back inside until today, so that's why I came in here to see you." She somehow manages to tell me this without a hint of emotion on her face.

Push her undercarriage right back inside?

God help me if this is going where I think it's going...

"Mrs. Franks, have you had any surgeries on your lady parts? Like maybe a hysterectomy?"

"Oh no, dear. I have all my lady parts, undercarriage included!" she says a little too excitedly.

Yeah, this really is going where I think it's going.

I do a quick assessment and vitals check on Mrs. Franks. Everything is stable and within normal limits. I politely tell her that the physician will be in to examine her shortly before closing the curtain behind me. I have a suspicion that this woman's uterus is quite literally falling out of her vagina. I'm pretty sure any time a little old lady is telling you she pushes her "undercarriage" back inside on a daily basis, we're most likely dealing with something falling out of her hoo-hah.

I hand John the chart for this patient to ensure that he's the one who gets to witness her "undercarriage dilemma." He's taken aback by the fact that I'm actually acknowledging his presence, and it's just too bad he hasn't quite grasped my motives yet.

"Here ya go, Dr. Ryan. Mrs. Franks is waiting patiently for you in bed one," I say to John with a sickeningly sweet smile plastered on my face.

"Thanks. Would you mind assisting me with her?" He asks while glancing through her history and physical.

"Sure, no problem." I'm waiting for his reaction when he finally realizes what this little old woman is here for.

"Uh, Elle. *Undercarriage*? I'm pretty sure that's not a medical term."

"Well, that's what the sweet old lady kept telling me, so that's what I wrote down."

God, I'm such a bitch, but honestly, I can't help myself when it comes to him.

I follow John into bed one to *assist* with Mrs. Franks's examination. I'm acting like a good, resourceful nurse by obtaining a speculum, but I know that once this little old woman drops her pants, her uterus is most likely going to be sitting on the bed.

I can hardly hold back the laughter.

I tend to have an issue with laughing at inappropriate times, such as church, funerals, extremely awkward moments, or like this magical moment we're about to experience right now. I'm finding myself slightly overwhelmed by the hilarity of this entire situation. Unfortunately, John is completely aware of my issue with holding back laughter, and I notice that he's practically scowling at me.

I quickly turn around and act like I'm busying myself with one of the cabinets while John asks Mrs. Franks to remove her pants and underwear.

Damn my tendency to laugh at the most outlandish scenarios possible!

I'm practically shaking with quiet laughter at this point, and occasional snorts are escaping my nose while tears stream down my face. The fact that I know that John knows I'm laughing at him is making this situation even more comical.

I speedily attempt to pull myself together and turn around to help him when he sternly asks me to hand him a pack of sterile gloves. No way should I expect a physician to grab his own gloves. That would be absolutely crazy, right? I mean, that's a *nurse's* job.

Are you sensing my sarcasm? It's mighty heavy right now…

I discreetly wipe the tears from my cheeks before I grab a pair of size eight gloves from the cabinet. After I hand John the gloves, Mrs. Franks gives me a look of concern and asks if everything is all right.

"Of course, Mrs. Franks. I think I managed to get some dust in my eyes," I tell her while still trying to hold back the overwhelming urge to burst out laughing. I assist Mrs. Franks with placing her legs in stirrups while John continues to explain the type of examine he will be administering.

Sure enough, once I place her little chicken legs in stirrups, her "undercarriage" is hanging all the way out. That's right—Mrs. Franks's uterus is actually hanging out of her vagina.

John slowly glances my way and I quickly turn my head before I am faced with his pissed off glare. The quiet laughter threatens to take over again and I have to suddenly excuse myself before I cause an embarrassing scene right there in bed one.

Let's be honest. This entire situation is like a comedy sketch. I'm in a patient room witnessing my ex-fiancé's face all up in eighty-year-old saggy va-jay-jay, which also happens to have a giant uterus attempting to make the great escape.

Oh thank you, karma, you snarky little bitch.

Chapter Ten

"Sometimes you feel like alcohol is the fuel to greatness. Then you wake up the next day and realize you're just one YouTube video away from becoming the next VH1 reality star with a giant clock hanging around your neck, desperately trying to get Flavor Flav to shoot his special sauce on your face."

Amy and I decide to make it a girls only night and stuff our faces with large amounts of chocolate and red wine. We choose to watch the movie *Bridesmaids* because Kristen Wiig is a riot and the plane scene is our absolute favorite.

We have a nice selection of Reese's Cups, M&M's, cookie dough, and whipped cream.

The dinner of champions, my friends.

We agreed to just drink one bottle of our favorite Merlot.

We stick to that plan hardcore…for about forty-five minutes until we realize that we're out of alcohol. You'd think a bottle of wine would last longer than forty-five minutes. I head into the kitchen and pull out two more bottles of Merlot from my secret stash, pop the corks, and hand one to Amy before resuming my designated spot on the couch.

"What. The. Fuck? Where did you find these?" Amy is giving me an evil stare.

"Uhhhhh…my secret stash," I state with a laugh before taking a large swig from my bottle.

"I can't believe you've been hiding alcohol from me! I thought we were friends! What else is there? What else are you hiding? Candy? Ice cream? Condoms?"

I nearly spit out my wine when she mentions condoms. Luckily, I manage to contain my laughter and avoid staining our living room carpet red. There is one thing I refuse to do, and that is waste alcohol. I never *ever* waste alcohol.

"Of course I have a secret stash. Are you blind? If you knew about my secret stash, then you wouldn't have that bottle in your hands right now, because you would have already drunk it," I answer with a serious look on my face.

Shit gets real when we're talking secret alcohol stashes. I'm a grown-ass woman, and if I want to hide my alcohol like I'm on the show Hoarders, that's my own personal right.

Amy looks pensive as she thinks about my last statement. After a good thirty seconds of silence, which is rare in this apartment, she finally gives me a response. "Okay. You win. You're one hundred percent right that I would have already drunk this alcohol if I'd known about your secret stash."

I let out a large sigh of relief at her willingness to wave the white flag. I honestly didn't have the strength to be involved in WineGate 2013 tonight.

"How many Reese's Cups do you think I can eat in fifteen minutes?" I attempt to change the subject and choose one of our all-time favorite topics of discussion.

"You bring this up at least once a month, but you never actually prove yourself. Bring it, James. Show me what ya got!" Amy cheers loudly before running into the kitchen.

She comes back with a stopwatch, an extra bag of Reese's Cups, a notepad, and a pen.

"What's the pen and paper for?" I sit down in front of the coffee table, mentally preparing myself to crush a bag of Reese's Cups' like a woman who just got her period and is gorging herself after two weeks on a low-carb diet.

"To keep tally of how many Reese's Cups you can eat. Duh." Her tone is completely serious, and I glance up to see if she's actually joking.

She's not. She's one hundred percent serious right now.

"Are you fucking with me right now? You know you could just count the wrappers or even just count out loud as I eat them. I mean, it's only fifteen minutes."

"Oh. Well, maybe I was kidding with you."

"Let's just go with that assumption." I'm laughing a little at her expense, but I can't help myself. Occasionally, Amy has these rare moments that are absolutely hilarious and have me temporarily questioning what goes on inside that head of hers.

Fifteen minutes later...

I'm lying flat on my back, trying to avoid throwing up chocolate covered peanut butter. My mouth is watering like a faucet and my esophagus feels like it's boiling in undigested candy. I'm so nauseous that I can't even sit up straight, and I'm sure the large amount of wine I've consumed isn't helping my cause.

When I was eight minutes into my Reese's Cup challenge, Amy and I ran out of wine. We both decided that I obviously could not go on with the challenge unless I had more wine to help wash the candy down. *Logical, right?* Amy managed to find another bottle of some cheap red wine in the kitchen pantry. Now, I'm two bottles-of-wine deep, and I just consumed eighteen Reese's Cups in fifteen minutes. *Fuck.*

"What do you think about that new surgeon who's watching over Dr. Grey's practice?" I continue to stare up at the ceiling of our apartment, counting the tiles and tiny cracks that are dispersed throughout. I'm trying desperately to get my mind off the fact that I might hurl all over our living room carpet.

"I think he's pretty hot and seems to make 'fuck me' eyes at you," Amy answers before beginning her routine of drunken hiccups.

"'Fuck me' eyes? You're crazy, you know that?"

"Yes, I know I'm crazy. That's why you love me so much. And yes, 'fuck me' eyes. Dr. Hamilton wants to thrust you something fierce."

Well, his dick sure seemed interested when he kissed me senseless in the supply room the other day...

"I feel like I've met him before. I get this feeling of déjà vu whenever I'm around him."

Amy giggles a couple of times and then glances over at me from the couch. "You need to start working on your 'Thrust me, Dr. Hamilton' campaign.'"

I just look over at Amy and start laughing.

There is no way I'm going to let her know about the supply room incident. If I let her know that Dr. Hamilton and I kissed, she would seriously lose her shit. And Amy with two bottles of wine in her system and losing her shit is not a good scenario for me. I can already picture her tracking down his number and inviting him over to our apartment tonight with, "Hey, Dr. Fuck-Me-Eyes, you should come over and bang my Elle into next Tuesday."

Yeah, that definitely wouldn't make things awkward for everyone at work tomorrow.

"What, Elle? I'm serious. With a body like that, I bet that man would screw you senseless. Can I at least be in the room when you two bang it out for the first time?"

"Sure thing, dickhead. If Dr. Hamilton and I get our freak on, I'll make sure you have a front-row seat. Actually, I'll just bring him back to your room and let him bang me while you're sleeping right next to me."

"Yessssss! That's what I'm talking about! And I most definitely will not be sleeping while he's pounding your snatch," Amy says before she starts singing a song that consists of one only verse...

I get to see Elle and Dr. Fuck-Me-Eyes thrust.

Yeah, definitely not a good idea to tell her about the kiss in the supply room.

I stay on the floor for a good thirty minutes and manage to recover from my sugar-alcohol overdose. I'm still shitfaced, but that feeling is always welcome in this apartment. Amy and I continue to laugh hysterically as we watch Bridesmaids. We're both drunk to the nines, and this can be a dangerous scenario when we are left alone together.

The Merlot has stained both of our teeth red and we take at least fifty selfies with our phones while giggling uncontrollably. We take a few minutes to drunk dial a few of our closest friends and then decide to take a gander at funny YouTube videos. Amy scrolls to a Harlem Shake video and we both start laughing, remembering my performance the other night at Murphy's.

"Hey, friennnnd, we should post my Harlem Shake video on YouTube!" I slur to Amy as I pet her hair.

"Whaaat? No way! Are you sure you want that on YouTube?" Amy is already scrolling to the saved videos on her phone.

"Hell yes! My video is awwwwwwesome and YouTubers will love me!" I throw my hands in the air and fall back onto the carpet.

"Everyone will love you, Ellie Belly! I'm gonna load it up right now!" Amy announces as she drunkenly starts to upload a video to YouTube.

***

The next day at work is grueling, and working through a wine headache is always a little bit of a struggle. Amy and I take turns seeing patients in the emergency room. We keep up a constant supply of coffee and Tylenol, and this seems to get us through the day.

As I head towards the nurses' station, I notice Tony and Amy sitting around one of the computers, laughing riotously as they look at his phone. I quietly sneak up behind them and attempt to figure out what they're watching. I can tell YouTube is pulled up, but Tony's giant head is blocking my view of the video.

"Hey!" I shriek in attempt to scare both of them.

They both jump and then turn around quickly at the sound of my voice. They have this deer-in-headlights look as they try to discreetly hide Tony's phone screen from my view.

"What are you guys doing?" My voice is laced with irritation, and

I'm sure the wrinkle lines in my forehead are showing with my scowl.

"Uh, nothing, Elle. We're just browsing the web, looking at stupid stuff." Amy looks nervous and Tony is frantically trying to click out of YouTube on his phone. I swiftly move around Tony and snatch his phone from his hands.

"Shit! Elle! Give that back!" Tony shouts at me while furiously attempting to retrieve his phone.

"Tony, stop grabbing for your phone or I swear I will tell Nurse Ratchet to float you to Med-Surg tomorrow." Tony slowly puts his hands to his sides, and that's when I notice the title of the video they are watching—Harlem Shake Epic Fail.

Oh, fuck me.

I push Tony out of the chair and slowly sit down before clicking play. I'm then faced with the video that Amy recorded of me at Murphy's.

Oh my god! Why is this on YouTube?!

I glance down in the right-hand corner of the screen and see that there have been over five hundred thousand hits.

"Five hundred thousand hits! Amy, you are so dead!" I scream as I watch a video of myself awkwardly thrusting my pelvis in the background at Murphy's Pub.

"You made me upload it last night! Tony just happened to find it while scrolling through YouTube on his break!" she shouts back at me while still trying to contain her laughter.

I made her put this ridiculous video on YouTube?

And then…it hits me.

I remember drunkenly petting her hair and telling her to upload the video to YouTube, saying, "Youtubers will love me!"

Son. Of. A. Bitch.

"Motherfucking fuck. Fucking shit!" I stomp my foot on the ground like an insolent toddler.

I sluggishly start scrolling through the comments and see Shirley Swallows Goes Viral posted over and over and over again. My best friend and I have managed to make me an overnight YouTube sensation.

I will forever been known as the girl in the Shirley Swallows t-shirt who awkwardly pelvic thrusts.

Well, that's just fan-fucking-tastic.

Chapter Eleven

"When life gives you 550-horsepower and a little cocksucker challenging you to a street race, you burn rubber and show him that women can drive muscle cars just as well as men."

By the end of my shift, I decide that I'm not actually going to kill Amy for posting the infamous Harlem Shake Epic Fail YouTube video. Although, I'm still entertaining the idea of cunt punching her tonight while she is sleeping.

I sit down next to Tony, who's feverishly charting his patient assessments on one of the computers in the nurses' station. I have no doubt that these are assessments that most likely should have been charted hours ago. This is typical Tony. I love the guy to death. He's a fantastic nurse, but his time management skills blow some serious ass.

"How's Rachel doing?" I ask him as I type out a note on the last patient I discharged.

"She's great." Tony's face lights up with a huge smile. "I think I'm going to propose to her."

"Seriously? Oh my god, that is awesome! I'm so happy for you!" I jump up out of my chair and wrap my arms around his broad chest, hugging him tightly.

Tony laughs and gives my arms a gentle squeeze. "Thanks, Elle. I really appreciate that."

Despite his lack of time management skills, Tony is truly an amazing man. He started dating a sweet girl named Rachel over a year ago, and they've been inseparable ever since. I have no doubt in my mind she will say yes, and Tony will get his much deserved happily ever after.

I finish up with my last patient and let out a huge sigh in relief. I'm exhausted, it's after nine p.m., and I'm in desperate need for a drink at Murphy's. I see Amy sitting at the nurses' station and decide to extend a tequila branch her way. Yes, *tequila* branch instead of *olive* branch. Amy and I are notorious for our alcohol consumption, and this is one part of our friendship we both proudly embrace.

"Hey, I'm going to head out. Meet me at Murphy's after you finish up?"

Amy looks up from her large stack of patient charts. "Is this you offering a tequila branch my way?"

I feign frustration and give an exaggerated sigh. "Yeah, I guess I forgive you for being such an asshole and allowing that video to go viral on YouTube."

"All right, sweet cheeks. I'll see you there once I'm done charting."

I glance up at the large white clock that sits above the nurse's station. "It's nine o'clock right now. How about you try to get out of here before ten, slacker?"

Amy scratches her cheek with her middle finger before saying, "Hey, why don't you get off my ass and go change your stank-ass scrubs?" She grins widely at me. "I'll see you around ten."

I laugh a little at her inappropriate gesture. "Like you should talk. I'm pretty sure you still have remnants of bed four's GI bleed on your pants."

She smiles at me and then looks down at her pants. "Just for that comment, I'm wearing these to the bar so you can smell me all night long."

"Okay, nasty. I'll see you around ten." I blow Amy a kiss and walk towards the locker room.

"Love your tits!" Amy yells a little too loudly for a professional hospital setting. I just shake my head, knowing full well that if I turn around, the inappropriate banter will start spewing from her mouth, so I do what any sane person would do…I keep walking.

I head to the ladies' locker room to change out of my scrubs and into something more appropriate for drinks after work. I throw on my faded skinny jeans, black knee-high riding boots, and my favorite vintage Pink Floyd tank. I love this tank because it is so comfortable and shows just enough cleavage to give a little sex appeal. I brush my long auburn locks up into a pony tail and put on just enough makeup to hide the fact that I've worked sixteen hours in the emergency room.

As I head for the parking lot, I notice Trent Hamilton leaning against the wall just outside of the ladies' locker room. His jet-black hair is tousled, and his piercing blue eyes are covered with thick black lashes. His attire gives no hints to the fact that he is one of the most respected trauma surgeons in the country. A black leather jacket, a white V-neck tee, faded jeans, and black boots make him look more like he just got off of a Harley rather than just having finished a long shift in the operating room.

Mmmmmm. Hot guy eye-candy. Is there anything better?

After visually eye-fucking him for a good thirty seconds, Trent finally looks up at me as he slides his Blackberry in the back pocket of his jeans. *I bet his ass looks fantastic in those jeans.*

He flashes a big, warm smile when we lock eyes. "Well, hello there. We meet again."

"Yes, we meet *again*, Dr. Hamilton." I can't help the sarcasm that drips from my voice.

"Remember, it's Trent, and I'm glad we meet *again*." He mimics my sarcastic tone. "Where are you heading now?"

"Well, *Trent*, I'm just going to a bar called Murphy's. My friend Amy is meeting me there after she finishes up. What are you still doing here?"

"Waiting for you to get dressed so we can grab a drink at a bar called Murphy's." Trent's mouth blazes a sexy smirk.

His response gives me a slight thrill of excitement. This man definitely intrigues me. Well, he intrigues my vagina, that's for sure. The bitch is practically screaming from my panties for me to throw myself at Trent and start dry humping his leg like some sort of horny, rabid dog. Ever since he kissed me in the supply room, I honestly can't stop thinking about his lips on mine, his body against mine, his cock pressed against my belly. I pull myself away from my incessant dirty thoughts and attempt to act like I'm not affected by his very presence.

I laugh a little at his very forward response. "Do I get a say in this little plan of yours? I mean, you basically assaulted me in the supply room the other day. I'm concerned for my lips' safety around you."

"No, sweetheart, you only get to choose who's driving over there. And for your little assault comment, you wanted that kiss just as much as I did. But your sexy mouth is probably never going to be safe around me." Trent's blue eyes lock with mine, and his demeanor oozes sex.

I can't believe I'm even allowing this banter to occur. Red flags are flashing in my brain. I told myself that I would *not* fall for another man for a very long time, especially another physician, and yet here I am, engaging in a game of flirtatious banter with a sexy trauma surgeon whose body I just ogled for a good minute.

My hands itch to touch him.

My body seems to crave him in a way I never knew was possible.

My eyes keep attempting to wander southward on his body, just to get a glance at the bulge in his jeans. He makes me feel like a horny eighteen-year-old girl. A girl whose mind just keeps thinking about what a good, hard dicking from Trent Hamilton would actually feel like. If my vagina were running the show, my panties would be nonexistent and I would be rubbing myself all over his tight, muscular physique. *Thank god my brain is still working.* At least it's managing to work right now. Later, after I've had a few drinks, I can't make any promises.

I pull my keys out of my purse, give them a little jingle in front of his face, and say "Well, *sweetheart*, let's head out."

He coughs out a barking laugh and motions for me to walk ahead. "Ladies first."

We step out of the hospital and the warm summer breezes brushes against my face, leaving me feeling warm and gooey on the inside. I love summertime in Charlotte. I will admit that the weather can be blazing hot at times, but the easy access to nearby beaches makes it worth my while.

As we approach my car, I hit the unlock button and the headlights and interior of my red Shelby Mustang automatically light up.

"What the hell is this?" Trent has a shocked yet amused expression on his face.

"Trent, meet my baby, Shelby. She's quite the looker and has 550 horses to boot," I say with a little grin. I get in the front seat and push the key in the ignition so I can hear my Shelby's engine purr.

Trent slides into the black leather passenger seat and just looks at me with a pleasant smirk while shaking his head. "You are just full of surprises, Ellie."

"So I'm taking it that you like my Shelby girl?" I ask as I slowly pull out of the hospital parking lot. I can't ignore the fact that he just called me Ellie, but I honestly like it too much to correct him.

"I more than like this car. I fucking *love* this car. I hope one day I can take this car for a test drive."

"If you're a good boy, I might let you take her for a spin someday." I glance over at Trent before turning left onto Main Street and head towards the bar.

I can't even believe the words that are just flowing out of my mouth. I never let anyone drive my baby. Amy begs me on a daily basis to take this car for a drive and I always say no without hesitation. Trent seems to have a secret key to my brain or something. He seems to unleash a side of myself I didn't even know was there. I've known this guy for a hot second, and in this short span of time, I've already dry humped him in a supply room and given him hope that he can drive my Mustang.

If he is managing to unleash a hidden part of my mind, what will he do with my vagina?

"A sexy girl like you is driving around a badass Mustang. This should be illegal."

I make eye contact with Trent in the passenger seat and let out a girlish giggle. This man just oozes sex. I decide now is the best time to hook up my iPod and turn on the stereo in hopes that music will distract me from pulling over and showing Trent just what his unadulterated sex appeal does to my now very horny snatch.

You will not dry hump the surgeon again. You will not dry hump the surgeon again.

I keep repeating this silent mantra in my head.

Since it's almost ten o'clock on a Sunday evening, most of downtown Charlotte's streets are empty. I pull up to a stoplight and notice a young kid, probably eighteen or nineteen, revving his older Camaro's engine and looking over at my tinted windows.

He gestures for me to roll down the passenger window. This kid is kind of adorable, with his shaggy blond hair and dimpled grin. Trent just looks over at me with an entertained expression. I bet he can already figure out that *this* is a common occurrence when you're driving around in this car. Young guys love to race, and I'm not going to lie, I indulge their competitiveness frequently.

Once the window is down, the kid looks into the car and seems a little shocked. I'm guessing it's because a woman is actually driving. This is also a common occurrence, one that I get a huge kick out of. Trent just sits back comfortably with his arm resting on the outside of the door, his fingers tapping to the beat of the The Rolling Stones playing on my iPod, and of course, he's still managing to look sexy as hell.

"Can you handle this car, little lady?" The kid bellows over to me before nodding his head towards the road.

Little lady? Is he for real?

"I'm not sure. How bad do you want to find out?"

"When the light turns green, I'll race you to the next light. It's about a mile from here. Think you can handle it?" he asks as he's revving his engine. His confidence is endearing, and I can't wait to give him a reality check.

The song switches over to Led Zepplin's Whole Lotta Love, the bass pumping through my speakers, vibrating deep in my chest.

Fucking perfect.

"Yeah I think I can handle it." I rev Shelby up a bit.

Green light.

I put Shelby in first gear, press the gas pedal to floor, and quickly release the heavy clutch.

After spinning the tires and leaving a little smoke, I switch to second gear so I can leave this little cocksucker in the dust. Shelby's horsepower pushes Trent and me back in our seats.

Damn, I love that feeling.

The initial rush of adrenaline that fills my veins, coursing throughout my body, practically pulses through my chest. That in combination with the feel of the engine vibrating my ass could quite literally bring me to orgasm. That feeling is the exact reason I bought this car, the exact reason why I love this car. I hear people joke about marrying inanimate objects, but I honestly think I would consider marrying my Shelby.

By the time I switch to fifth gear, we are coasting at around 110 mph and the kid in the Camaro isn't even close to us. I gradually slow down and come to a complete stop at the next light. The young kid in the Camaro finally pulls up next to us, and he is just shaking his head with a slightly embarrassed look on his face. "I guess you can handle that car, huh?"

"Yeah, I guess so," I respond with a confident laugh. The light turns green and I give the kid in the Camaro a slight wave before turning left and pulling away. I look over to the passenger side and see that Trent is looking at me with intensity in his eyes.

"What? Why are you looking at me like that?" I can't hide the shy tone in my voice.

The look on his face is making me feel slightly self-conscious. I'm wondering if I've pissed him off. Doing something like that would have made John angry with me. He hated riding bitch in my Mustang, and if he was riding bitch while I was street racing some young guy, hell would have probably frozen over. And honestly, John never really let me drive him around. His ego is far too big for that. He came up with every excuse in the book to avoid sitting in the passenger seat.

"Ellie girl, you really are a little spitfire. I don't think I've ever seen a girl handle a muscle car like you just did. That was hot, Elle. Really hot."

I can't hide the smile that has taken over my face. "I like it when you call me a spitfire and give me compliments about my hotness." I give Trent a suggestive expression as I pull into a parking spot at Murphy's and turn off the engine. "How about we go get that drink?"

"I think that's a damn fine idea, little spitfire," Trent says before opening the passenger door and getting out of the car.

I take the time to watch his fine ass exit my vehicle, and my assumptions were correct—his tight ass looks fantastic in those jeans. If I could sink my teeth into those muscular cheeks, I would.

I'm starting to think that this night isn't going to be so bad...

Chapter Twelve

"If you find yourself willingly enjoying getting sexed by a man with a fetish for dressing up in a bear costume and fucking in the woods because you dig him that much, then I'd say you have just found your soul mate."

Trent and I stroll into Murphy's and manage to find two seats at the bar. The crowd seems to be bigger than normal for a Sunday, but I'm sure this has everything to do with all of the college kids that are enjoying their summer break.

Johnny, my favorite bartender, heads our way with a big, dimpled smile across his face. I've known Johnny since I started coming to this bar a few years ago with Amy. He is a bear of a man. He stands at well over six foot and has to weigh at least two hundred and eighty pounds. His bald head and numerous tattoos make him appear extremely intimidating, but the man has a heart of gold and is a complete sweetheart.

"My favorite girl! What can I get you to drink, Elle?" Johnny is leaning against the bar, chocolate eyes grinning at me.

"Just give me a Corona. Johnny, this is Trent. Trent, this is my favorite bartender, Johnny."

Trent shakes his hand. "Nice to meet you, man. So how long have you known this little firecracker?"

Johnny lets out a loud laugh. "I've known Elle for years now and have all kinds of stories."

"Hey now! Let's not get into those stories. I'd like to have a night where I'm not reminded of how easily I can embarrass myself." I poke Johnny's shoulder. Johnny dramatically feigns injury while Trent smiles at my remark.

The very last thing I need is for Johnny to start dishing out my crazy drunken stories. I'm obviously notorious for shenanigans, and Murphy's bar has seen a lot of them. Trent orders a beer and hands Johnny his credit card, instructing him to put all of the drinks on his tab—mine included. I try to refuse, but the man is stubborn and insists that he cover my drinks since I drove him here.

We make small talk about random things, and I'm finding that conversation with Trent comes easily. There are never any awkward silences or uncomfortable chitchat. Things just seem to flow between us, and I find myself loving this fact while simultaneously hating it. I'm scared shitless to get attached to someone, to risk my heart and fall in love again. My heart was battered just a few short months ago, and I just can't fathom experiencing that for a second time. I'm nearly one hundred percent certain that if another man breaks my heart I will start working on my muff-diving skills.

Trent and I are enjoying each other's company immensely. He is witty and adorable, and somehow he manages to maintain this sexy-as-hell demeanor that has my insides clenching with each husky laugh. He keeps brushing my hair out of my eyes and tucking it behind my ear. I find myself thinking about how much I enjoy feeling his touch.

His skin on my skin.

This man makes chill bumps appear all over my body. The more drinks I get in me, the more my vagina is starting to call the shots. This night is either going to end really badly or *really well*. I don't want Trent as a one-night stand though. I find myself wanting more than that.

How can I already want more than that when I've known the guy for all of a few days?

These are the incessant thoughts that are racing through my brain. I'm having a hard time wrapping my brain around the fact that I'm digging Trent Hamilton—*a lot*—and I barely know the guy. He's turning me into a flaky, emotional, involuntary vagina-clenching, constant nipple-hardening mess.

Amy taps my shoulder and sits on the bar stool next to mine. "Well, I'm here and it only took an extra hour to finish charting."

"I was wondering when you were going to get here!" I grab her shoulders and give her a quick hug.

"Uh huh. Suuuuuure ya were." She gives me a pointed look before nodding her head in Trent's direction.

I discreetly roll my eyes. "Stop being so damn ornery."

"Well hello there, Dr. Hamilton. Fancy seeing you here. I hope you're keeping my best girl entertained." Amy puts her arm around my shoulder and smiles sweetly in Trent's direction.

Trent's blue eyes are completely mesmerizing, and I find myself zoning out of their conversation as he engages Amy in a discussion about our drive over here. This man, this too-hot-for-my-own-good man, has me grinning from ear to ear like an idiot. I can tell he's aware that I'm gawking at him, but I just can't seem to pull my eyes away. I'm blaming the alcohol.

Yes, blame the alcohol. That seems like a damn good plan.

Amy, Trent, and I continue to enjoy a few beers and several laughs. He seems to find our stories and sarcastic banter back and forth amusing. Trent is the complete opposite of my ex-fiancé John and I find myself loving…I mean…really liking him.

The alcohol. Keep blaming the alcohol.

John was a complete douchebag when it came to Amy and me spending time together. Eye rolling and annoyed sighs were common occurrences whenever we graced him with our sometimes rowdy presence. I'm sure there are times when Amy and I can be quite overwhelming, but John never seemed to enjoy us together. *Ever.*

Sometimes I wonder how I was ever able to get past how much of an asshole he could be at times. I think it was the quiet moments, the moments we spent together in the privacy of our old apartment. The moments when he wasn't such a dick and actually showed glimmers of being kind, caring, and most of all, loving. Those moments were what kept me invested in our relationship and able to move past the times where he would rather appear uptight and cold than risk people seeing him carefree and letting loose.

And speak of the devil.

"What the fuck is he doing here?" Amy interjects a little too loudly. She's glaring toward the front of the bar as John strolls in with a few of his buddies.

"It's okay, Am. Just ignore him," I say as I peek over my shoulder. Of course John is going to start coming to this bar. He never showed any interest in grabbing a drink with Amy and me after work when *we were actually a couple.* I wonder what caused him to lower his standards and slum it at Murphy's tonight. And for the first time in a long time, I find myself not even really caring about John. Trent is looking at both Amy and me inquisitively, and I decide I need to lighten the mood a little.

"We're here to enjoy ourselves so let's do just that. Shots?!" I look eagerly at them.

Amy smiles at me "Anything for you, sweet cheeks. You in for some shots, Trent? "

"Let's do it, ladies. Hey, Johnny! Bring three shots of Patron, salt, and a few lime wedges."

Trent is obviously game with our plans of getting a little shitfaced tonight, and I love the fact that he chose tequila as his shot of choice. Tonight, we will most likely be cabbing it home. After we down our first tequila shot of the night, I can slowly feel myself relaxing into oblivion.

"I'm gonna go play some tunes on the jukebox. Any suggestions?"

I get up from my barstool and pull a few singles from my purse.

Amy shakes her head. "You all right?"

"Yeah, I'm good. I just want to hear something else besides Lynard Skynard and Kid Rock."

Amy laughs loud enough for the entire bar to hear. "Yes! Please save us from awful rock music selections! And no country or my ears will start to bleed!"

Trent smiles at me and motions with his finger for me to step closer to him. On shaky legs, I walk towards him and stand between his jean-clad thighs. His breath is warm on my skin and his smile feels like home.

The alcohol. Keep blaming the alcohol, Elle…

"I forgot to tell you something, Elle."

I'm looking back at him, softly questioning him with my eyes.

"I forgot to tell you how beautiful you look tonight." He takes my face in his hands and kisses my forehead softly before slowly brushing my hair away from my face, tucking it behind my ear. This little intimate encounter, brushing my hair away from my face, has become his signature move, and I find myself loving every second of it. I give him a warm smile and whisper, "Thank you," into his ear before turning around and walking away.

Standing in front of the jukebox, I'm doing my best to ignore the fact that John is literally six feet away from me. I can feel him staring at me. He is practically eye-fucking my skull, and honestly, I feel nothing but annoyance and aggravation. I'm sure he just witnessed the fact that I'm here with Trent and I hope it's driving him insane.

"Hey, Ellie."

John comes to stand next to me in all his glory. He's still as handsome as ever, and I internally wish he would have a sudden outbreak of teenage acne. John has always been good-looking. And although this sounds extremely vain, his attractiveness was one of the things that caught my eye, what spurred my interest for him. To put it bluntly, John is…*hot*. Dirty blond hair, green eyes, and muscles for days. Yeah, he's a teenage girl's wet dream.

John clears his throat and brings me out of my annoying thoughts regarding his indisputable sexiness. "Ellie?"

"Please don't call me that," I sigh in displeasure as I continue to scroll through the music selections.

"What? Call you Ellie?" he asks with a furrowed brow.

"Yeah. Please don't call me Ellie. I'm not your Ellie anymore." I'm still avoiding his stare. He doesn't deserve my attention. He doesn't deserve anything from me.

"You will always be my Ellie." His voice is soft and warm, and my mind is thinking that he is such a complete shithead for even endeavoring to have a conversation with me.

"John, this needs to stop. You need to move on. It's been over three months and I'm most definitely moving on. I'm living my life and you are no longer a part of that life."

The alcohol is making me brave, and maybe, just maybe, Trent has managed to put a little ray of hope in my life. Right now, I feel like I can just tell John to fuck off. I actually believe every single word that is coming out of my mouth, and it feels *amazing*. This is the best I've felt in a very long time. Someone should bottle up this emotion and put it in a pill, because it could probably solve world peace or at least aid women into having multiple orgasms.

I finish choosing a few songs and start to walk away.

John grabs my elbow. "Elle, wait. Babe, I'm so sorry. So fucking sorry. Please talk to me. Let me explain."

Seriously? Will he ever give up?

I quickly pull my arm away from his grasp as I roll my eyes skyward at his lame attempt to talk to me. "Let you explain? Really, John? Please enlighten me with exactly how you are going to explain fucking another woman in our bed? Did you trip and fall over something and your cock just so happened to be hard, she just so happened to be naked on *our bed,* and you just so happened to fall directly into her gaping hole of a vagina? Don't play me for an idiot, because I'm not stupid. That thing between you and Veronica, it was going on for a while before that night. That may have been the first time you actually stuck your dick inside of her, but it wasn't your first encounter. You were emotionally cheating on me with her way before that. I'm just sorry it took me so long to figure it out. I'm sorry I was naïve enough to trust you for as long as I did."

"I have never regretted something so much in my life." His eyes are serious, even sorrowful, as he looks down at me.

I put my hand up to cut him off before I have to hear anymore. "Please, John, I'm begging you to stop this. I'm done. *We're* done. I'm moving on and I suggest you do the same."

"Elle, I'm not going give up on this. I'll show you how sorry I am and prove you can trust me again."

A heavy sigh escapes my lips. "John, I'm only going to say this one more time and then I'm not wasting my breath on another conversation with you. It's over. We. Are. Over." I turn away from the jukebox and brush past John to head back to the bar.

I see Trent and Amy laughing about a story Johnny is busy telling them, and feelings of relief wash over me. I'm relieved that I don't have to hear my idiot ex ramble on about wanting me back and begging for my forgiveness. I'm more than over the entire situation, and that in itself is a miracle, considering the emotional state I was in just three months ago.

Is three months too soon to move on from a relationship? A relationship that was headed for marriage, that had an entire wedding and future planned out to every last detail. I'm not sure what the right answer is, but I think somehow Trent has helped me take the final step towards recovery. I find myself wanting more from him. This entire assortment of emotions he spurs from deep inside of me are overwhelming, and I'm well aware that most people would see them as slightly crazy, but I can't help how I feel. I can't help the fact that I am really into Trent Hamilton. I want to get to know him, and let's be real with ourselves; I most definitely want to get him naked.

Well hello there, vagina! Nice to see know you're still there.

I sit back down at the bar and listen to Johnny tell his latest bar story of a guy's jealous girlfriend lighting his truck on fire in the parking lot. I can definitely relate to this story and the fact that crazy bitches need to light shit on fire. I was more than ready to set John's cheating pecker ablaze when I caught him mid-thrust in another woman's cock pocket. I may be partially evil, but the satisfaction I would have received to witness John's dick and balls going up in flames would have been like five Christmases, twelve birthdays, and ten Fourth of Julys all rolled up into one delightful holiday.

The more John pisses me off, the harder it is for me to even remember the good times we shared. After his lame attempt to pour his heart out by the fucking jukebox, my brain only seems to be able to remember the bad times, the really shitty times, and the times that make me wonder how I ever accepted his proposal of marriage. Maybe his dick's need to fuck whores with sloppy juice-boxes actually saved me from making the biggest mistake of my life. I should probably write his dick a letter and thank him for saving me from a life of misery and regret.

It's a shame Hallmark doesn't have cards for occasions like these.
What would you say to a penis?
Do penises even like thank-you cards?
These are the kind of thoughts that run through my mind. I start thinking about what I would actually write if I wrote a penis a letter…

Dear John's Dick,
You, my horny friend, have saved my ass from a terrible life with
your dickbrain owner.
I only feel gratitude towards you and your ability to find every
whorish snatch in a one-hundred-mile radius. You and my vagina
had some great times. Lucky for me, your
average-sized length and slightly-too-small girth were able to
bring me to climax...on occasion. I enjoyed your enthusiasm,
especially for my tits and my mouth's ability to make you blow your
load. In an odd way, you will always be remembered as the penis
who saved my life.
Thanks for the subpar thrusting!
Ellen

Someone clearing their throat causes me to glance up from my daydream about sending John's penis a thank-you card. Amy and Trent are both looking at me with curious yet amused expressions. I look down and realize that I wasn't just day dreaming. I have written the entire letter on a paper napkin.

I just wrote a fucking thank-you note to my ex's penis on a bar napkin.

A small laugh escapes me as I attempt to nervously crumple up the napkin before either of them sees it. Amy is like a god damn cat hopped on speed-laced kitty litter and quickly manages to get the pseudo penis letter out of my grasp. She begins to read the napkin and I can see her eyes getting more excited with each word. By the end of the note, Amy practically falls off of her barstool in hysterics. Her laugh is so contagious that I just start giggling right along with her. Both of us are leaning on the bar, tears streaming down our cheeks as we gasp for air. Trent is looking at us like we are complete lunatics, but I can see a little spark in his eye. That little spark tells me more about him than he will ever know. He looks genuinely happy seeing Amy and me laugh, and I feel my vagina warm up to him a little more.

Yes, my vagina is obviously a sucker for guys who are sexy and hot and well, sexy. I just might be crushing hard on Trent Hamilton. And no, it's not the alcohol or my vagina talking this time.

"So do I get in on this little inside joke?" Trent flashes an adorable grin.

"I'm not sure if you want in on this. It has something to do with my ex-fiancé." I'm sure my facial expression shows my discomfort with the idea of telling him about my past relationship with John.

"You mean your ex-fiancé John Ryan?"

"Shut the fuck up! How do you know about Dr. McDouche-A-Lot?" Amy has generously given John this nickname, which is really kind of perfect.

"Dr. McDouche-A-Lot? Holy shit, that's hilarious!" Trent's husky laugh echoes throughout the bar.

Sheesh, that husky voice makes my nipples harden instantly; it's like his voice has a direct line to my tits, making them act like little puppies begging for his attention. And now it's safe to say that I'm more than just a little buzzed. Whenever I find myself comparing my tits to puppies, I think we can all say the alcohol is copiously coursing through my bloodstream.

I decide that now is as good a time as ever to let Trent know about my past with John. I give him the short and sweet version of the story, skipping over the horrible details of witnessing John with his pants around his ankles, sliding his dick in and out of coworker's meat curtains. Trent just listens and takes it all in, not judging or scrutinizing my past. He only shows understanding towards my shitty relationship and how terrible the past three months have been. I find myself opening up and explain my motivation for writing that ridiculous thank-you note. In my mind, John and I are most definitely in the past. I know we shared happy times together, but as I look back and ponder on our relationship, albeit drunkenly, I realize things weren't exactly fairytale perfect.

John and I had our issues, and I think deep down I figured getting married would help us work through those. Obviously, that was an extremely warped way of thinking. A completely terrible idea of a solution to a problem that may or may not have been resolved had John not cheated on me. I'll never know if John and I could have lasted in the end, but I have a deep, sinking feeling in my gut that's telling me that I was saved from making a huge mistake.

I get the balls to let Trent read the penis thank-you note and it's quite obvious he only finds it entertaining. As Trent continues to shake his head and laugh at my absurdness, Amy gives me a look that says, "Don't let this one go."

I think she might be right. *Trent Hamilton seems like a keeper.*

"Another shot, ladies?" Trent grins at us and slides two shot glasses of tequila our way.

"Hell yes!" Amy and I both yell out simultaneously.

"If we're doing tequila, we have do it right!" I whoop towards them. Trent looks at me questioningly and Amy just smiles big.

"Uh oh, Trent. You're in trouble, because my college Elle is back." Amy chuckles to herself and then downs her tequila shot, finishing it off with a lime wedge.

"All right, Dr. Hamilton. You're going take this shot with me, *Elle style*." I attempt to give him a seductive smile, but I'm sure the alcohol is making me look like an idiot.

Oh well. He seems to be enjoying my little display of confidence. I shake the salt on my hand, place the shot glass on the bar, and put the lime in my mouth. Trent's eyes go wide for a second before he eventually gives me a wicked smirk. He is not so secretly digging this setup. I lift my hand to Trent's mouth, and without breaking eye contact, he slowly licks the salt off. The feel of his tongue on my skin makes me imagine all types of very dirty and extremely pleasurable scenarios, all of which end with my legs in the air and Trent giving my vagina some delicious face time.

Trent downs the shot in one fluid motion while keeping our eyes locked. He leans in and softly presses his lips against mine to retrieve the lime that's securely held between my teeth. I swear he keeps his lips pressed to mine for a good thirty seconds before pulling away with a grin that shows off his pearly whites and prized lime wedge. I look over to see Amy fanning herself with her hand.

"If you guys get your fuck on tonight, can I at least watch?"

"Amy! Filter please!" I swear she is going to be the death of me. Lucky for me, Trent seems to find her ability to never hold anything back delightful.

I'm watching Trent as he engages Amy in conversation about a specific patient he had to perform surgery on the other day. Jet-black hair and piercing blue eyes, two-day-old scruff that only he could make look good. God, this man is devastatingly sexy. He is so ruggedly handsome and he exudes so much testosterone that I feel like my panties are going to fall right off. My snatch is now in serious lust with him and my brain is definitely in full agreement. Normally I would be extremely overwhelmed by my feelings for him…

How can I want someone that I just met a few days ago so badly?

And why is he so good-looking?

If I could order the perfect man, Trent Hamilton would be that man. Women write books about guys like Trent Hamilton. I masturbate on a daily basis to fantasies with guys like Trent Hamilton. And now, since I actually know a real-life version of this dream man, I will be masturbating with him in my mind from now on. Every time I rub one out, I'm dedicating that orgasm to Trent motherfucking Hamilton.

Hell, I think I'll just name my vibrator Trent Hamilton.

At this point in the game, I'd settle for a session of hardcore dry humping with him. Just thinking about the way he kissed me in that supply room is making my muff clench. Every time I look at him, I seem to get this feeling of déjà vu. I can't ignore the feeling that I know him from somewhere else besides Regency…

Have I met him before?

"Have you figured it out yet?" Wow. Just hearing his voice is making my little juice-box drip. Deep, masculine, and slightly husky, it's like the god damn trifecta of sexy male hotness. Trent pulls me out of my fantasy, and I notice that he's intently watching me pull the label off of my beer bottle, a weird habit that surfaces whenever I'm deep in thought. *I'm obviously a very deep thinker.* Naming my vibrator after a hot surgeon I just met a few days ago is a testament to that.

"Figured it out yet?" The shots of tequila are probably making the fact that I keep undressing him with my eyes very apparent, and I wonder how long I've been sitting here daydreaming about double-clicking my mouse to Trent Hamilton. I notice that Amy isn't even sitting with us anymore. She managed to find a small group of friends to chat with at the other end of the bar.

"Figured out that we've met before the day I came to Regency and scandalized you in the supply room?" He winks at me before taking a swig of his beer.

"So I'm not going crazy when I get a sense of déjà vu every time I see you?"

"No, you are most definitely not crazy. But you definitely have the most mesmerizing green eyes I've ever seen. They are driving *me* crazy." His gaze is determined and exuding enough heat that I could probably go ahead and take my clothes off right now…

"Are you trying to hit on me, Dr. Hamilton?" I look at him coyly.

"Maybe. Is it working?"

"Maybe." I'm lost in his eyes. Deep, blue, and completely overwhelming. Trent's eyes are like nothing I've ever seen before. I would crawl across this dirty bar floor on my hands and knees just to get a chance to gaze into his baby blues. I would agree to let Amy watch us have sex if it meant those eyes would be staring down at me the entire time, watching me come hard around his cock. I would do a lot of things for those eyes, and not a single one of them would be deemed okay to discuss in the company of other people. Those eyes make me visualize a thousand different sexual positions. If I ever found a porno that had a man with Trent's eyes, I'd end up with carpal tunnel from incessant masturbation.

"All right, little spitfire, it's your turn to take a shot." Trent places salt on his index finger, the shot glass on the bar, and the lime in his mouth, smiling big and wagging his eyebrows suggestively.

I laughed loudly. "You are ridiculous."

He just nods yes and continues to grin at me.

I lean down and slowly lick the salt from his index finger then suck his finger into my mouth for a minute, long enough to let him know what my tongue is capable of. He gives an almost pained look and I swear I hear a small groan escape from his lips. I slowly take his finger out of my mouth before leaning down towards the bar. I wrap my lips around the shot glass and, without using my hands, tilt my head back and let the tequila flow down the back of my throat.

Trent's gaze gets a little darker as I place the shot glass back on the bar and go for the lime. I lightly lick his bottom lip with my tongue and then take the lime out of his mouth and proceed to suck the juice out.

"Mmmmmmm," I purr before placing the lime into my empty shot glass.

I think I prefer my tequila Trent style.

Trent just stares back at me, eyes wide. He finally seems to come to his senses when he shakes his head slightly and smirks as he runs his fingers through his hair. "All right, Elle. It's my turn again."

"Only if you promise to tell me how we've met before." I point a finger at him, letting him know I mean business with this request. I *need* to know why I get this feeling of déjà vu every time I'm near him.

"Deal." He shoots a wink my way as he stacks our empty shot glasses and slides them towards the edge of the bar.

I order another round from Johnny. My horny vagina and puppy tits—yeah, I said it—decide to take charge of this one and make things interesting. I place the salt on my hand, shot glass between my tits, and lime wedge in my mouth. Trent meets my gaze for a second before his eyes focus in on my chest.

"You're going to be the death of me."

"Are you talking to me or my tits?" I'm mentally applauding myself for wearing my favorite Pink Floyd tank that shows off the perfect amount of cleavage.

"Does it really matter?" He unwillingly pulls his eyes back to mine.

I just grin back at him and shrug my shoulders slightly. He slowly licks the salt off of my hand and, without breaking eye contact, leans forward to take the shot glass from my cleavage. Just feeling his hot breath near my chest makes my nipples harden instantly. With perfect finesse and several intentional face-to-breast brushes, Trent removes the shot glass with his lips and tilts it back. He surprises me a little by actually taking the time to place the shot glass back where he got it from.

Oh my...
Nipples hard? Check.
Panties wet? Check.

I'm going to need my newly named Trent Hamilton vibrator tonight.

Trent slowly comes up to my lips and starts to suck on the lime while it's still in my mouth. This is the hottest, most painful foreplay I've ever experienced. My foggy brain decides that the lime is in my way of tasting this fine specimen of a man. I quickly slide the lime from my mouth, grasp the back of his neck, and then kiss him softly on his lips. A small moan escapes my mouth as that soft kiss turns fierce. His tongue slides passed my lips and I accept him with nothing but horny enthusiasm. Trent possessively pillages my mouth with passionate, rough kisses.

Nipples still hard? Check.

Panties still wet? Check.

Panties really wet? Double check.

Can I just have the actual Trent Hamilton tonight?

I have never been so turned on in my life. This ruggedly handsome man might literally kiss me into a sexual stupor. I begin to come to my senses and remember that we are in the middle of a bar, not in the privacy of my bedroom. I begrudgingly end the kiss, pulling away slightly breathless.

Thrust me. Thrust me. Thrust me. My vagina is practically screaming for attention. She's in full-on "let's get laid mode" and I'm one hundred percent on board with this brilliant plan.

"Wow." Trent's eyes are lustful, and it's very apparent that he is as turned on by that kiss as I am.

"Yeah." He's basically stunned me into some sort of horny silence. I watch Trent take a swig of his beer and find myself being jealous of that fucking beer bottle.

Lucky bottle.

As my brain finally starts to work again, I remember his promise from before our public display of horny shot-taking commenced. I hope this story doesn't end with an embarrassing twist or pathetic display of drunkenness. This is me we are talking about here; I managed to become a YouTube sensation overnight with my obscene demonstration of pelvic thrusting to the Harlem Shake.

"All right, fess up, Casanova. There is obviously some sort of story that I'm not aware of and *you* are going to tell me every detail." I lightly poke him in the chest.

Trent sets his beer bottle on the bar and grins back at me with amusement. "I have one word for you. Nashville."

"Nashville? As in Nashville, Tennessee? I don't see how that…"

I abruptly stop talking as my brain begins to catch up with the conversation. The last time I was in Nashville, I was presenting to a group of surgeons about the most recent changes to Regency's staffing protocols and nurse-to-patient ratios. My manager Shirley had convinced me to do this presentation in hopes that it would positively promote Regency's new state-of-the-art facilities, and that little presentation didn't end so great. Calling it a disaster is actually putting it nicely. This is just another perfect example of how I somehow manage to find myself in the most absurd situations. Trent is watching me intently as I slowly come to the realization that he witnessed my presentation.

Holy shit!

Trent Hamilton saw my moment of complete mortification. He was a spectator to one of my most embarrassing moments. *Ever.*

Oh my god! Someone put me out of my misery!

I put my hands over my face and drop my head to the bar. "Oh my god. Oh my god. OH. MY. GOD! You were there? You saw my presentation?" I ask into my hands as I shake my head in pure disbelief.

I can faintly hear Trent laugh a little and then feel his large hand rub my back. "Ellie, don't be embarrassed."

I quickly lift my head up off of the bar and give him an annoyed look. "Don't be embarrassed? Are you screwing with me right now? You witnessed one of the most embarrassing moments of my life! That moment was more embarrassing than the stupid *YouTube* video Amy posted of me!"

"YouTube video? Wait, what YouTube video?" Trent's voice is filled with curiosity.

"No way, buddy! You are not seeing that YouTube video! One ridiculous display of my uncanny ability to make an idiot of myself is enough for you. And stop trying to change the subject!" I turn away from his deep blue eyes in a lame attempt to hide the mortification that is plastered all over my face.

Trent grasps my chin and pulls my gaze back to his.

"When I first laid eyes on you in that conference room wearing your fuck-me heels and tight black skirt, my cock was hard instantly. I had to adjust myself before I busted my fucking zipper. And then you were so god damn adorable during that presentation, Ellie, that I couldn't take my eyes off of you. I know you were embarrassed, but, sweetheart, I haven't stopped thinking about you since I saw you in Nashville."

"You calling me adorable is not helping to ease my mortification."

I don't want Trent to think I'm adorable. I want him to think I'm sexy and irresistible; I want him to feel like he can't keep his hands off of me. Adorable is something you call your kid sister, not a girl you plan on taking home and fucking until she can't even remember her name.

Trent closes his eyes for a second, and when he opens them, his expression is serious, almost seductive. "Did you hear when I said my cock was hard instantly at the sight of you? Let me spell it out for you, because you obviously do not understand what I'm telling you. When I was watching you during that presentation, my mind was not thinking about patient ratios and hospital bullshit. My mind had you naked in forty different positions while I was fucking you senseless on that conference table."

Well, fuck me sideways.

"Oh."

Speechless.

This man has left me entirely speechless and aching for him to do everything he just said. There's a moment of silence between us as we continue to gaze at each other. I feel my breath hitch a little at the increasing intensity in his deep blue eyes.

"Ellie, I need to kiss you. *Right. Now.*" He cups my face with his hands and brings my lips mere inches from his.

"Okay," I manage to breathlessly say before he pulls me in for a heart-stopping, mind-blowing, panty-dropping kiss.

After Trent practically kisses me into submission, we continue to talk about the infamous presentation. I explain to him what exactly happened and he finds every detail comical. If I would have been with John when that fiasco occurred, he would have been pissed at me—and *really* pissed at Amy. I'm kind of baffled by that fact that Trent just finds the story funny. I feel like this guy is just too good to be true. There has to be something wrong with him. Maybe he has webbed feet or a third nipple or some weird sex fetish where he likes to dress up in a bear suit and fuck women in the woods. I just can't imagine that there is actually a guy out there who is sexy, funny, and caring and who manages to embrace my frequent displays of awkwardness.

The rest of the night with Trent is perfect. He continues to make me laugh as we enjoy each other's conversation. He is a complete gentleman at the end of the night, instructing Johnny to call two cabs. To my vagina's disappointment, Trent doesn't attempt to go home with me. He softly kisses me goodnight and makes me promise to let him take me out on an actual date. I program my number into his Blackberry and silently pray that he actually calls.

Amy and I chat the entire way home. She asks me a thousand questions about Trent and makes me tell her every single detail about what it felt like to have his face between my tits. She apparently witnessed our pervy display of tequila shot-taking. After Amy grabs my boobs several times to see if my nipples are still hard, we finally make it back to our apartment. I quickly get ready for bed and practically face-plant into my mattress. The long day at work in combination with the amount of alcohol I consumed at Murphy's has me nearly comatose from exhaustion. As I begin to close my eyes, I hear my phone vibrate on my nightstand. I glance at the screen and see a text message from an unknown number.

Unknown: Three things, little spitfire. 1. Save my number. 2. Remember to wear those fuck-me heels on our date. 3. Goodnight, Ellie girl. -Trent

He manages to leave me speechless.
Again.
I fall asleep with thoughts of Trent Hamilton dancing around in my mind. He's in a bear suit, screwing me in the woods, and I'm just yelling for him to growl louder. Webbed feet, third nipple, and weird sex fetishes be damned. Even if Trent happens to have some flaws, there's no doubt in my mind that I really like this guy.

Chapter Thirteen

"It's all fun and games until you're caught with a twelve-inch rubber cock strapped around your waist."

I wake up the next day in a fan-fucking-tastic mood all thanks to Trent—or Dr. Beautiful as Amy has so generously nicknamed him. Well, she actually wants to call him Dr. Thrust Me, but we managed to agree upon something that didn't have the word thrust in it. Amy and I are chatting over coffee about last night. She might as well start a fan club for Trent Hamilton, because I'm pretty sure Amy is his number one fan. She just keeps gushing over how hot he is and how I need to let him take me to Pound Town.

I take a sip of my coffee and give Amy an annoyed stare. "Let's not turn this into something more than it really is. Trent and I barely know each other, and I think it would be in my best interest if we take things slow. John put me through absolute hell, and I really need to protect my heart right now."

Amy sets her cherry red "Eat Me For Breakfast" coffee mug on the kitchen table and smirks at me. "So letting him take a tequila shot from between your tits is taking it slow?"

"I was kind of drunk and I think my muff was calling the shots by that point in the night." I flush a little with embarrassment as I remember the events of the night.

Did I really let him take a shot from between my tits?

Yes, yes you did, and you enjoyed every second of it.

"Stop acting embarrassed. I was really happy to see you and your vagina living in the moment and not worrying about the consequences." Amy stands up to wash her coffee mug in the sink.

"So that explains why you're always encouraging me to consume obscene amounts of alcohol." I tap my fingers on the table and look at her inquisitively.

She laughs loudly. "Exactly!"

"So you remember how I told you I kept getting a feeling of déjà vu around Trent?"

"Yes." Amy turns off the faucet and leans against the counter, crossing her arms and giving me her full attention.

"Well, I was right. I've met him before, prior to his arrival to Regency." I slowly take a sip of my coffee.

Amy begins edgily tapping her foot against the hardwood kitchen floor. "Out with it!"

I leisurely set my coffee mug back on the table and clear my throat. Amy is the most impatient person I have ever met, and I find absolute joy in prolonging things just to get her worked up.

"He saw my presentation. In Nashville."

Amy's jaw drops and her eyes go wide with shock.

"What?! He was there?!" She is practically screaming, and I wouldn't be surprised if she just woke up the entire apartment complex.

"Calm down, crazy," I whisper-yell to her. "Yes. Trent Hamilton was present for one of the most embarrassing moments of my life." I give her a pointed stare.

"Fucking shit! I'm such a cunt!" Amy visibly feels terrible for her very large part in the Nashville presentation.

"Yeah, you kind of are." I chuckle a little to lighten up the mood.

Amy only gives me a tight smile in return.

"Don't worry about it, labia face. In your defense, when you emailed those slides back to me, you put in all caps, *Read through these one more time*."

"I know, Ellie, but I should have known you were too nervous to figure out I was secretly messing with you." She looks so remorseful right now. She's giving me her full-blown puppy-dog look, and I swear if I were a lesbian, I would just kiss her face off.

"Stop looking at me like you're going to thrust your tongue in my mouth." Amy grabs my empty coffee mug off of the table and rinses it out in the sink.

"Sorry, but you just look so pathetic with the puppy-dog eyes." Somehow this girl has a way of always knowing what I'm thinking. She is probably one of the only people in my life who *really* knows me. Amy knows me better than my own sister, Elizabeth. Although she can be a total pain in my ass some days, I honestly don't know what I would do without this crazy girl in my life.

Flashback to Nashville one and half months ago...

After begrudgingly agreeing to be the sole presenter for Regency

Memorial Hospital, I found myself sitting alone in my hotel room the night before my big presentation. I was scheduled to present in front of several very well-known trauma surgeons along with numerous board representatives from hospitals around the nation. Hell, the god damn CEO of the Cleveland Clinic was supposed to be at this conference. Thank god I wasn't the only presenter, but still, I was nervous as hell. I found myself wired and unable to sleep, which was only worsening my anxiety towards this very nerve-racking experience. I'm not sure why my nursing manager Shirley decided that she wanted me to represent Regency. Sometimes I question her ability to rationally make decisions. I had done several presentations and educational lectures for the staff at my own hospital, but I had never been faced with anything of this magnitude. To say I was freaking out was definitely putting it mildly.

My flight from Charlotte to Nashville was a fucking nightmare. The scheduled one-hour flight took three times longer due to mechanical difficulties, and this cunt of a flight attendant rudely cut me off after four glasses of wine. Who does that? A cunt, that's who; a god damn cunt named Gina whose bleached blond stripper hair will most likely fall out from incessant amounts of peroxide and hairspray. Don't worry; I left her a kind note on my beverage napkin...

Dear Va-Gina,
Learn some fucking manners before you rudely cut someone off from alcohol on a fucking flight that was delayed for over two hours. Four glasses of wine is barely enough to give me a buzz. Lick my asshole,
Passenger 32B

P.S. I fucked your pilot, Bill, last weekend in New York. He's ah-mazing.

No, I hadn't really screwed a pilot named Bill last weekend in New York, but I could guarantee that Va-Gina was sleeping with him. I had a good friend in college who'd become a flight attendant, and she used to tell me all the dirty details and juicy gossip. Apparently flight attendants and pilots sleep around—a lot. I was hoping my little white lie about Pilot Bill would get her all kinds of pissed.

Obviously, this conference had me on edge.

I never really had a problem speaking in front of large groups of people, but this presentation was huge for Regency Memorial Hospital. We were hoping to bring a positive spotlight to our new state-of-the-art facilities along with cultivating additional donations towards our ongoing cause in perfecting patient care in the emergency department setting.

I managed to eat half a cheeseburger and a few fries I'd ordered from room service. My nerves were really getting the best of me, and I was starting to panic about the slide presentation I'd prepared. I decided to email Amy my slides and beg her to look through them one final time. I sent her a quick text telling her to check her email, and she responded quickly with some smartass remark saying she'd get right on it.

Since the hospital was paying for everything, I decided to dive head first into the liquor bar that was so generously on hand. I ordered a horrible romantic comedy on pay-per-view, practically emptied the vending machine of candy, and continued to drink myself into a stupor. I managed to pass out sometime after midnight.

I woke up to the alarm I'd thankfully remembered to set last night and realized I'd been unknowingly pushing snooze for over an hour. I now had less than thirty minutes to shower, get dressed, and be ready to present downstairs in the conference room.

Shit!

I rushed through my shower so quickly that I nearly fell face first on the white tile floor. I hurriedly got dressed in my black pencil skirt, white button-up blouse, and favorite pair of black heels. These heels dressed up any outfit and seemed to add a little bit of sexy to my very professional attire. I decided to leave my auburn locks down and slightly wavy. My makeup was kept to a minimum because I honestly had no time for details. Mascara, blush, and lip gloss were the best I could do. All I could say is thank god I wasn't hungover. I grabbed my purse, laptop, notes, and cell phone before quickly walking out of my hotel room toward the elevators.

I managed to make it to the conference room with just enough time to set my laptop up to the projection screen and get myself settled in. I nervously ran my sweaty palms down the length of skirt and silently hoped I wasn't visibly showing pit stains. I was literally sweating like a whore in church. Why was it so fucking hot in there? Was Nashville supposed to be this hot in May? I checked the thermostat on the wall behind the projection screen and dropped that baby down as far as it could go. The last thing I needed was an audience of mostly men focusing in on my sweaty pit stains. I swiftly checked my email and saw that Amy had sent back the slides, stating she'd made a few minor changes and that I should review them before presenting.

Well, fuck.

I didn't have time to review each and every slide. I was sure whatever she'd decided to change was fine and I probably wouldn't even notice. Amy is a huge stickler for grammar and spelling, and I had a feeling that was what the minor changes entailed.

    I was sitting in one of the cushy black office chairs while everyone filed in, taking their seats around the overwhelmingly huge conference table that was in the center of the room. Everything was set up and ready to go, and I was just anxious to get this whole ordeal over with.

    I was so nervous that I could barely remember anyone's name upon introduction. My mind was just kind of on autopilot. Luckily, I'd managed to snag business cards of almost everyone, which I would kindly hand to my manager Shirley when I got back to Charlotte. A few minutes after nine a.m. I decided to start my presentation, feeling I'd given everyone more than enough time to arrive.

    As I cleared my throat and began to introduce myself, I noticed a ridiculously attractive, dark-haired gentleman stroll in and take a seat. My mind was foggy from nerves, but it wasn't too foggy that I couldn't notice the sexy piece of ass that had just strolled in. After mouthing "sorry" in my direction, he gave me a wink and a smile. I just smiled back and continued on with my introduction.

    About fifteen minutes into the presentation, I felt like things were going smoothly. The physicians and hospital board officials seemed excited about Regency's new state-of-the-art facilities and recent changes to the emergency department staffing protocols. Their positive reactions towards my presentation gave me a small boost of confidence. I found myself engaging my audience more as I sauntered around the room and continued discussing the positive aspects of my hospital's staffing protocols, policies, and procedures. Yeah, I knew it was extremely boring crap. I knew from the slides that I was nearing the end of my presentation, and the butterflies in my stomach were slowly dissipating as I got closer to the finish line.

    I was facing my audience as I turned to the next slide and noticed several small smirks cross their faces as they glanced up to the projection screen. I just brushed it off and continued on discussing projected cost savings in relation to our newest policies and changes. As I looked up at the screen before turning to the next slide, I finally became aware of why several physicians and hospital board officials were no longer making eye contact with me and mostly just gawking at the current slide with amused grins on their faces. The slide that was up on the projection screen, which seemed like it was the size of a giant billboard, was a picture of me from a Halloween party last year.

    Unfortunately, the theme of the party had been sex toys. I'd been dressed in boy shorts, a lace camisole top, high heels, and a strap-on with a twelve-inch rubber cock attached to it. Right now, I was screaming, "Screw You, Amy!" in my head. I was pretty sure I was frozen in complete mortification for a good thirty seconds because I was in absolute shock.

Hell, shock didn't even begin to describe the emotion that had turned me into a statue. I was literally frozen in place. An entire room of prestigious trauma surgeons and hospital board officials were currently staring at a picture of me scantily clad with a giant dildo strapped to my waist.

Could you die from embarrassment?

I hastily changed the slides and turned back to face my audience, who were currently in various states of emotions.

Shock.

Amusement.

Awkwardly gawking at me.

Holding back laughter.

"Just wanted to make sure you were all awake." I cleared my throat and then gave a small, nervous laugh.

"Well, sweetheart, you definitely have my attention," an older, heavyset gentleman said from the back of the room. This thankfully broke the awkward silence; I could hear several loud chuckles fill the room.

I somehow managed to continue on with my presentation and gave the rest of my planned speech without the assistance of the slides. I refused to unknowingly show another inappropriate picture. I'd already managed to make a big enough ass out of myself as it was; no need to add more fuel to the fire. After finishing the presentation, I hurriedly rushed through saying goodbyes and thank-yous. I gave the excuse that I had a flight to catch. I was just too embarrassed to be in the room with those people for any longer.

I practically sprinted to my hotel room and locked myself in.

I called Amy and left her a very detailed voicemail letting her know the kind of damage she'd just done with that little stunt. I didn't hold back and essentially called her every name in the book while simultaneously threatening to email the entire hospital pictures of her from the work Christmas party last year.

I started to organize the business cards that had been handed to me before I'd speedily left the conference room and notice that at least five of the cards had personal cell numbers telling me to call them.

One in particular stated, "I'd love a personal wakeup call from you."

You have got to be kidding me.

You'd think a room full of hospital officials and prestigious surgeons would have had the decency to act professional, but you show them one picture of yourself scantily clad with a twelve-inch rubber cock and they might as well have jerked one out during my presentation.

Lesson learned. When Amy emails you back and instructs you to *review* the slides one last time, you review the fucking slides.

Better yet, never let Amy touch any slides for any type of presentation ever again.

Chapter Fourteen

"Just remember when you let someone frequent your back door—that back door will start to show the effects of overuse. Then, one day, you might find yourself in the hospital pushing a baby out while a whole staff of 'medical professionals' are looking at you, unable to take their eyes off of your gaping, worn-out back door. Overuse can change that thing from a bank vault to a saloon door in no time."

I'm currently on my third twelve-hour shift in a row and finding it hard to act remotely happy towards my patients. How many assholes are going to stroll into my ER with complaints of sore throats? Does anyone have a primary care physician these days? This shit gets old and I'm wishing someone would walk in with an actual emergency.

Where are the shootings and car accidents when you need them?

Yes, I'm well aware that I'm being an asshole right now.

I know this might come off cold and callus, but I'm slightly jaded these days. Sometimes I wonder if a new job is in order. I haven't seen Trent since our night out at Murphy's Pub, but we've been chatting on the phone and texting a lot. Our schedules just haven't really matched up over the past week since he's had to take over office hours and maintain his on-call surgery schedule. I'm getting kind of angry at myself for falling for a guy so fast. My heart is telling me to jump in feet first, but my brain is telling me to slow my roll and protect myself from getting hurt again.

One of these days, I hope my brain and heart can come to some type of agreement.

Another thing that makes me scared to start dating him is that Trent is only in Charlotte because he is temporarily overseeing Dr. Grey's practice while he is on a medical leave of absence. Dr. Grey was injured several months ago in a car accident. He was hit head-on by a drunk driver and somehow managed to survive. The pictures of the accident itself are completely terrifying, and he is damn lucky to be alive. He sustained several injuries that have required extensive surgery and daily physical therapy sessions, but thankfully Dr. Grey is on the mend. Last I heard, Dr. Grey was doing really well and hopes to get back to his practice in a few months.

This means that Trent Hamilton isn't a permanent fixture in Charlotte.

He is temporary.

Trent is originally from Seattle, and his current plans, that I know of, include moving back there once Dr. Grey is fully healed. So you can see why I'm extremely hesitant to start something serious with him. The heart wants what the heart wants, and I know deep down that my heart wants Trent Hamilton. I'm still trying to deny this fact and would never willingly admit my already strong feelings for him to anyone, especially Amy—or more importantly, Trent.

How long can I keep this up until I get hurt?

That is the million dollar question right now, and I really wish I had some damn answers. I feel my phone vibrate in my scrub pocket, and I glance at the screen to see a text message notification.

Trent: Ellie girl, I hope you're enjoying your day. I went to sleep last night with thoughts of beautiful green eyes, cleavage, and tequila shots.

Sigh. Just one text from him and I'm grinning like a teen mom who's baby daddy just put a ring on her finger.
I quickly text him back.

Me: Dr. Beautiful, my day just got better.

Another text notification causes my phone to vibrate.

Trent: Dr. Beautiful? I guess this means you're going to let me take you out dinner tomorrow night. The only response I will accept is YES.

I'm still grinning like an idiot and quickly text him back.

Me: YES, Dr. Beautiful.
He speedily responds.

Trent: I'll pick you up at 7 pm.

So much for trying to take things slow. I'm practically salivating at the idea of a night alone with Trent. I send another text his way.

Me: I'll be the girl in the black fuck-me heels.

Within a minute, I get his response.

Trent: You're killing me, Ellie girl.

I'm still smiling from ear to ear like a fucking moron, but I can't seem to help myself. Trent is a breath of fresh air; he makes me feel alive. I'm terrified of getting hurt again, but I don't think I can avoid these feelings I have for this devastatingly sexy man. I barely know him, yet he's on my mind constantly.

My heart wants Trent.

My brain wants Trent.

My vagina *really* wants Trent.

Moments like these make me thankful I'm not a guy, because otherwise I'd be sporting some serious wood right now. Not even a half-chub or semi; it'd be full-on boner-time all up in these scrub pants.

Let's face the facts—Trent Hamilton gives me raging ladyboners.

After I manage to pull myself together and focus on work instead of being thrusted by Trent, I head back into bed eight to discharge a patient. I nicely give the elderly lady her discharge instructions so that she can be on her merry way. She has been diagnosed with a very serious condition called *constipation*. Insert copious amounts of sarcasm into that statement.

God damn constipation.

Who comes to the ER for that? I'm pretty sure that shitting is a daily bodily function. If you go seven days without dropping a deuce and you're not alerted by this, then we've got bigger problems on our hands. Don't worry, I've got Mrs. Forgets To Poop covered. I've given her enough laxatives and stool softeners to ensure that she is crapping herself silly by the time she gets home.

After my emergency constipation case ambles out the door, I see a young girl around nineteen or twenty being wheeled in, and it is extremely apparent she is currently in labor. She's screaming, "The baby is coming now!" panting heavily through her contractions, and barely keeping her ass on the wheelchair.

That's a surefire sign of someone who is fully dilated and ready to deliver.

I instruct the transporter to wheel her into bed nine and hurriedly put on gloves because I sure as hell don't want vaginal fluids all over my hands. The last time I saw a patient come into the ER like this, I ended up delivering her baby with my *bare* hands. Lesson learned.

We quickly get her into the ER bed as I continue to do my best to get prepared for a delivery. Since there is visibly no time to get her upstairs to the actual labor and delivery unit, I call their charge nurse and tell her to send supplies and staff down as soon as possible. I ask the patient several questions pertaining to her pregnancy, past medical history, age, and other pertinent information that will allow more insight into what I'm currently facing. Luckily, she has had an uncomplicated pregnancy and her due date is only a few days away. This is a huge relief. It is one thing to do a delivery in the ER, but it is a whole other ball game when you're being faced with a severely premature baby being born without the appropriate staff and equipment.

"Oh my god, get this baby out!!!" She's screaming at the top of her lungs and now beginning to grunt with each contraction. I pull down her already wet pants and underwear, indicating that her water already broke, and encourage her to slowly breathe through her contractions. She's sweaty, panting, and extremely red-faced. I really would like her to hold off on pushing until an obstetrician arrives, but I'm sure this probably isn't going to happen. Regency has an obstetrician in-house at all times. Unfortunately for me, their call room is located upstairs on the eighth floor.

"Screw you! I'm pushing this baby out now!!!!" Did I forget to mention that pregnant women make me *so* happy?

Dr. Simon is our ER physician on staff today, and he wanders into the patient's room as she's screaming, "Ahhhhhh! My vagina feels like it's being ripped apart!" He is visibly taken aback by this, and I'm just holding my breath for his god damn Tourette's to kick into gear. The last thing I need right now is for him to yell, "Pull on my pubes!" to an angry pregnant woman.

I get the patient positioned for delivery. Her hips are close to the edge of the bed, and her two family members are holding her legs. The baby is crowning at this point, and in about two more contractions, her little bundle of joy will be here. Dr. Simon is such an asset to me in this moment. He continues to stand in the corner of the room in shock and not doing a fucking thing to help.

Finally, Amy walks in to assist me. I'm glad she came in, but I know once she gets a gander at what this woman has going on down below, she will barely be able to contain herself. Not only is this chick's vagina spread apart from a giant crowning baby head, but she also has the largest, most gaping asshole I've ever witnessed in my entire life. Yes, this young girl has an unbelievably large asshole, and when she pushes with her contractions, it only seems to double in size.

"Where in the hell is L&D?" Amy asks me as she quickly puts gloves on. She was also present for my bare-handed delivery.

"I don't have a clue. I called them over ten minutes ago," I attempt to tell her over the screaming, grunting, and crying pregnant woman.

Amy comes over to stand beside me, and I know she's already spotted the brown winker because she isn't saying anything. I glance over at her and see her wide-eyed, amused expression. I can practically hear the wheels turning inside of her head. If I had to guess what is going inside Amy's brain right now, I'd lay money on the fact that she's got about ten anal sex jokes lined up and ready. Obviously, a large, gaping asshole is going to lead your mind in one direction—butt sex, butt plugs, anal beads, and in this woman's case, baseball bats.

I'm more than thankful when the OB team arrives and takes over the delivery. Amy and I step back out of the way and let them do their thing.

"So let's talk about that asshole," Amy whispers into my ear.

I just eyeball her and give her a "please shut up" look, because I know I can't encourage her to start telling me ass jokes while we are still standing in bed nine, watching this woman deliver her baby. I'm pretty sure there is some sort of moral code of ethics that frowns up butthole talk while witnessing the miracle of life.

"Is that the baby daddy? Holy balls, he must have a huge cock to do that kind of damage to an asshole."

So much for not encouraging her…

"And how did she get pregnant? Because from the looks of it, he spends most of his time using the back door."

Oh my god, she's not going to stop, and I'm barely able to contain my laughter.

Amy knows I have a serious problem of getting giggly at the most inopportune times, and she makes it a goal to use those times to her advantage. I feel myself start to shake with quiet laughter and have to turn away from the room and act like I'm busying myself with changing my gloves.

I swear she is such a dickhead sometimes.

The young girl delivers a healthy baby boy and everything goes smoothly. Well, as smoothly as pushing a small human out of your snatch can go. Amy and I help our OB team transfer the patient upstairs so they can continue her recovery on their unit. While we are assisting the baby daddy with putting the patient's belongings in their new room, he starts to ask us a few questions about getting around the hospital.

"Thanks again for all of your help, ladies. We used the back entrance when we came into the emergency room. Is it okay if I stay parked back there?" The new dad asks us as he puts his girlfriend's purse on the bedside table.

"Well most people use the *front* entrance, but if you prefer the *back* entrance, I'm sure it's not a problem," Amy manages to say with a straight face. I'm going to smack her when we get on the elevator.

"Oh, okay. Well, I guess since most people don't use the back entrance anyway. I'll just make good use of it," he says with a genuine smile.

Clueless. This guy is so clueless right now.

"Congratulations! Enjoy that new baby boy of yours. He's absolutely precious," I quickly express to the young dad as I drag Amy out of the room by her arm before she can make any more innuendos about back doors or back entrances. That last comment he made left an opening as wide as his girlfriend's asshole, and there was no way in hell I was going to allow her to continue.

As we walk back onto the staff elevator, I can tell she is just dying to start talking assholes. I push the button for the lobby level and lean up against the elevator wall in preparation for some ridiculousness to come spewing out of her mouth. The doors shut, leaving Amy and me alone in the elevator.

"Go ahead. Out with it," I say to her with amusement plastered all over my face.

"Oh my god! Oh my god! Oh my god! Did you get a look at that asshole? I'm pretty sure I could see organs, and it seriously took me a minute to figure out which hole the baby was going to come out of." Amy is practically bouncing up and down with excitement. Her mouth is going a mile a minute, and I'm pretty sure she is speaking some sort of asshole tongues. *Who would have thought one chick's asshole could make her entire day?*

"I know, Amy. I saw it. You saw it. I think the entire emergency department saw it. I don't think it was possible for anyone to miss that girl's pooper."

"How big is her baby daddy's dick to stretch her rectum out like that? And this brings a whole new meaning to the Shocker. Two in the pink and a fist to her stink." Amy is grinning from ear to ear.

"You are hilarious but extremely perverse. You know that right?" I'm barely able to hold back laughter at her new take on the Shocker.

"There is no way that girl ever gets constipated. I bet her shit just falls right out. How many times do you think she's crapped herself laughing?" Amy jokes as the elevator door opens, and an unsuspecting elderly couple overhears her.

"All right, I get it. You've got at least one thousand more random jokes and things to stay in regards to that girl's gaping asshole, but you're going to have to hold it in until we get home. I'm running to the cafeteria to grab a quick bite to eat. I will meet you in the breakroom in like fifteen minutes. Please no more asshole talk over lunch," I beg quietly before walking towards the hospital cafeteria.

"Speaking of holding in it! I bet I know someone who CAN'T possibly do that!" she yells to me as I walk away. I just shake my head and keep walking. I know she's hilarious, but I also know that if I give her an inkling of an idea that I'm finding any of this funny, she won't stop. After seeing Mrs. Forgets To Poop and that girl with the gaping asshole in the span of one hour, my brain is completely over hearing or seeing anything ass related.

The hospital cafeteria is unbelievably crowded because it's exactly noon and everyone, including staff and visitors, are here for lunch. I quickly get in line and grab tray to collect my food. Regency's hospital food isn't all that bad compared to most hospitals. I mean, it's not nearly as good as a nice steak dinner, which I've been craving for the past week, but it's definitely consumable. I order a grilled chicken sandwich and grab a bag of chips.

I'm a freak for honey mustard and make sure to grab a handful of condiment packets. If I could live with only one condiment for the rest of my life, I'd choose honey mustard, hands down, not even a contest. I could eat that special sauce with a spoon. If you know someone who doesn't like honey mustard, don't trust them with anything because they must be certifiably crazy. There is something seriously wrong with a person who doesn't enjoy that tangy, sweet taste of deliciousness.

Honey mustard, have I told you I'm in love with you?

Yes, I'm talking to my condiment packets.

I head back to the emergency department breakroom and am nearly blown away at the surprise visitor I come across. Trent is sitting across from Amy as she animatedly talks about our recent delivery experience today. He gives me a genuine, breath-taking smile when his eyes glance up and see me.

Oh man, he looks good.

Too good.

Trent is dressed in navy blue scrubs, and he still has his surgery cap tied around his head. His biceps are practically bulging out of his scrub top. I can't help but get pulled in by his eyes. They are as blue as the sky with dark lashes framing their beauty. I notice slight dark circles and two-day-old scruff, and I'm assuming he is probably on a twenty-four-hour stretch of no sleep. I know he'd had a grueling call schedule for the past few days, and I have a feeling he has spent most of his time in the OR.

I set my tray on the table and sit down next to Trent while Amy continues to talk all things assholes. He is amused with her enthusiasm and quick wit, every so often giving a husky laugh.

Oh the things that man's deep, sexy voice does to my brain.

As I start to dig into my lunch, Trent grabs the side of my chair and pulls me closer so our knees are touching. He plants a soft kiss on my cheek and whispers, "Hi," into my ear. I look into his baby blues, and the ridiculous grin on my face is probably giving away the fact that I'm thrilled to see him.

"You two are sickeningly sweet together, you know that?" Amy interjects with an amused expression.

I just smile back at her, and I can tell by the look on her face that she is truly happy for me. Amy has seen me at my worst, and I can imagine it's a relief to see someone put a smile on my face the way Trent does. I open at least five packets of honey mustard as I prepare to eat my grilled chicken sandwich. I take a bite and practically moan when my taste buds are bathed in sweet and tangy condiment heaven.

I look up to see Trent intently looking at me.

"You want a bite?" I hold out my sandwich for him.

"Fuck, I thought you'd never ask." He opens another packet of honey mustard and dips my chicken sandwich into it before taking a big bite. "Is there anything better than honey mustard?" he asks me with a grin.

A man that loves honey mustard as much as I do! *Damn, he's perfect.*

"Hands down, the best condiment ever." I open my bag of chips and crunch on a few.

"I'm going to walk in on you two fucking one day and there's going to be honey mustard packets all over Elle's bedroom," Amy declares as she stands up to put her leftover spaghetti in the microwave.

Trent laughs loudly before leaning over and wiping a little bit of honey mustard off the corner of my mouth with his index finger, and then he slides that finger into his mouth to suck the deliciousness off. He wags his eyebrows at me as I shake my head and laugh a little. I'm finding myself *really* jealous of the index finger that just came in contact with his tongue.

Lucky finger.

Trent, Amy, and I talk a little more about his recent OR case. He just finished a six-hour surgery with a man who had been in a terrible accident with a tractor. The surgery sounds like it was brutal and completely exhausting. I don't think I could ever be a nurse in the operating room. Six freaking hours of standing in one place? No thank you.

I feel a vibration against my thigh and realize it's Trent's Blackberry. He sighs loudly as he glances at the screen with annoyance.

"Well, I guess my break is over. Amy, thanks for the laughs," he says as he stands up and puts his Blackberry into the back pocket of his scrub pants. I glance at his tight, toned ass and find myself wishing I was those scrub pants.

Lucky pants.

Trent leans down and whispers into my ear, "Thanks for sharing, Ellie girl. I'll see you tomorrow night." He kisses the corner of my mouth.

"I can't wait. Text me later so I know you made it home, okay?" I motion with my index finger for him to lean in closer and then I softly kiss his cheek when he does.

He smiles happily. "All right, little spitfire." Then he heads out of the breakroom door, leaving Amy looking at me with curiosity in her eyes.

"What can't you wait for?" she asks as she grabs her plastic Tupperware bowl out of the microwave and sits back down in front of me.

"I have a hot date tomorrow night." I can't even try to hide the excitement in my voice.

"You two are going to bang like rabbits and you're going to tell me every single detail," she adds before taking a large bite of spaghetti.

I grin from the mere thought of Trent giving me a good dicking.

"My vagina is praying that you're right," I say before continuing to eat the rest of my sandwich and potato chips.

"Hey, Ellie Belly?"

"Yeah?"

"I'm so happy for you. Let yourself be happy, okay? You deserve it." Amy squeezes my hand and smiles sweetly at me.

"Thanks, Am." I smile back at her. Somehow, this girl just gets me.

Chapter Fifteen

"Vaginas have feeling too."

I put the finishing touches on my makeup and run my hands down my silk, black strapless dress. I'm nervous about my first official date with Trent. I mean, it's kind of crazy that I'm this worked up over it; you would think we've never hung out before.

Trent and I have been talking nonstop since that awesome night at Murphy's Pub. Little text messages here and there throughout the day. Late night phone conversations with Trent while I'm lying in bed and he's at the hospital. This guy is pretty amazing. He's thoughtful and sweet, yet he has this take-no-shit attitude about him. That dominant aspect of Trent's personality has me wondering what he's like in bed.

Oh god, I can only imagine.

I find myself reminiscing about that first kiss we shared in the supply room.

Damn, that feels like forever ago.

Trent had me so worked up with just that one kiss that I know getting naked with him will be nothing short of spectacular. It has to be. And the sexual tension that was blatantly obvious at the bar last week… Well that was intense, potent, and nearly palpable.

I take a deep, calming breath in an attempt to slow my heart rate. Just the thought of Trent naked and inside me has my heart beating like a hummingbird's wings. I feel like a god damn virgin on prom night. No man has ever had me this worked up before, and this foreign feeling is slightly overwhelming.

How can I feel so strongly towards someone I've only known for a short time?

How can one man have this intense of an effect on me?

These are the questions that are running through my mind.

Am I in love with Trent Hamilton?

Just thinking the word love in relation to Trent is completely absurd. I've only known him for such a short time, yet he's made a lasting impression on me. I'm just going to ignore the mere idea of being in love with him already. I can't let myself fall for someone this quickly, and I need to keep reminding myself that Trent is temporary. He has no plans to stay in Charlotte. His home is in Seattle. Not here. Not anywhere close to here. I'm just going to keep things light between Trent and me. Just have fun with him and avoid thoughts of getting serious at all costs. I need to forbid myself from picturing an actual future with him.

How could there be a future?

He's temporary, remember...

I quickly put on my black fuck-me heels and head out toward the living room. Amy is sitting on the couch, watching some ridiculous reality show. She appraises me with a wide smile.

"You look fuckable, Ellie Belly. I'd totally do you." She pats the couch cushion next to her.

I take a seat next to Amy. "Really? You don't think I've overdone it?"

"No, not at all. You look really nervous though." She puts her arm around my shoulder, pulling me towards her.

I place my head on her shoulder and let out a big sigh. "I am so ridiculously nervous. Why am I am so freakin' nervous, Amy?"

"You really like this guy. And don't worry, he feels the same way about you, sweetheart."

"I really hope so, but what's the point of all this? I mean, he's only in Charlotte for a short time." I frown at the thought of Trent eventually leaving.

"You don't know that. You could be the reason he decides to stay in Charlotte." She runs her fingers through my hair. She's doing her best to calm me down, and for that, I love her dearly.

"Let's not get ahead of ourselves. Trent staying in Charlotte for me would be ridiculous. For one, we barely know each other. And two, his entire life is in Seattle."

"Do me a favor and give this guy an actual shot, Elle. Don't put up your walls, okay? Let Trent in and be open to every possibility." Amy is starting to go Dr. Phil on me, and that's when I know she's being completely serious.

I sit up and put up both of my hands in defeat. "All right, all right. Cool it with the Dr. Phil talk. I'll try really hard to just live in the moment with Trent."

I hear a knock at our apartment door and stand up to answer it.

Amy smacks my ass as I walk past her. "Good. Now go have fun with Dr. Thrust Me."

I'm laughing at her nickname for Trent as I open the door. I'm quickly taken aback by the handsome man standing in front of me. He's freshly shaven and his blue eyes are overwhelmingly gorgeous. The deep blue button-up shirt he is wearing seems to make them stand out even more than usual. Trent is smirking at me as I appraise him greedily.

I quickly clear my throat and try to get my mind off of dirty Trent fantasies. "Hi."

"Hi," he says back with a wicked gleam in his eyes.

Oh my.

"Hey, Trent! Take care of my girl, all right?" Amy yells from the couch. She's grinning like a goofball, watching the exchange between us.

Trent takes my hand and kisses it softly. "Don't worry, Amy. I will take *very* good care of her."

We say our goodbyes to Amy, and I grab my purse off of the collect-all table by the door. Trent leads me out with his hand pressed against the small of my back; the heat from his hand is practically scorches me through my dress. If I'm finding myself this worked up over him just touching my back, what in the hell would I feel with a full-on naked Trent pressed up against me?

Again, I'm shaking my head a little in a pathetic attempt to get these wayward thoughts out of my mind as Trent opens the passenger door to his black F-150 truck and helps me in.

A truck? Really?

I expected a surgeon like Trent to be driving a BMW or Mercedes. I'm not judging his choice of transportation; I'm actually fascinated by this.

"Hot shoes," he remarks with a smirk before closing the passenger door.

Trent hops in and starts the engine.

"So you drive a truck?" I ask him as he pulls out of my apartment's parking lot and heads towards the main road.

He chuckles, "Yes, I drive a truck. Were you expecting something pretentious like an Audi or Jag?"

I chuckle at his ability to read my mind. "Yeah, I guess I was. Every surgeon I've ever known has driven some sort of 'pretentious' car." I motion air quotes with my fingers when I say the word pretentious.

He grins widely at me and glances in my direction. "I'm not every surgeon, Ellie girl."

"What's with the Ellie girl? Is that my special Trent-given nickname?" I turn towards Trent in my seat and ask with curiosity.

"You're my Ellie girl. And you look devastatingly beautiful tonight by the way."

He grabs my hand and kisses the inside of my palm then continues to hold my hand in his lap. I sigh with complete contentment at being this close to this perfect man. As much as I want to tell myself that I'm not going to feel serious about Trent, that's what he is to me—one hundred percent perfect.

Trent motions with his eyes for me to choose some music on his iPod. I unwillingly pull my hand away from his and start to scan through his large selection of music. I stop at the one man whose voice nearly makes my panties fall off every time I hear him.

Ray LaMontagne.

Oh my sweet Jesus, I would have sex with his voice, his sexy, too-fucking-hot voice. I choose *You Are The Best Thing* and let out a little squeal of excitement when I hear the raspy, god-like voice begin to play over the speakers.

"A little bit of a Ray LaMontagne fan?" Trent asks with pure amusement in his voice.

"You have no idea! If I could have sex with his voice, I would," I admit as I tap my fingers on the passenger door to the beat of one of my favorite songs.

Trent looks over at me as he comes to a stop at a red light. His blue eyes pull me in, and I'm just looking back at him, letting his eyes wash over me and grab my soul. Normally, this quiet silence would make me feel uncomfortable and awkward, but I relish the opportunity to just take in this moment with him.

We're speaking with our eyes instead of our mouths.

His mouth. Oh, his beautiful, beautiful mouth.

Pink full lips that are just begging my teeth to bite. Because of the intense combination of the sexy voice playing over the speakers and Trent's blue-as-the-sky eyes, I'm feeling seven shades of horny. I can practically hear my vagina encouraging me to straddle Trent's lap and grind myself all over him. He gives me a wicked, seductive grin as he slowly pulls his eyes away from mine and pushes on the gas when the light turns green.

"I'm a little jealous right now." Trent's truck starts to accelerate onto the highway.

"Jealous?" I'm extremely curious and secretly enjoying the idea that Trent is jealous.

"Yeah, babe. I'm jealous that another man's voice has that effect on my Ellie girl."

I like the idea of being his far too much. The sixteen-year-old girl in me is scribbling "I love Trent Hamilton" in big fat bubble letters with corny hearts all over her girly notebook as we speak.

I'm left a little dumbstruck at his recent declaration of being his.

I'm internally beaming as I continue to sing the lyrics to one of my favorite Ray LaMontagne songs. This song is the absolute sweetest—a man declaring that a woman is the best thing in his entire life.

What girl wouldn't love the idea of this?

This is the ultimate fantasy, perfect dream, and wish come true for every girl out there, no matter how much she denies it. This song is hands down the best declaration of love anyone could hope for. I picture John Cusack standing outside my window with a stereo blaring this song. This song is like The Notebook, Say Anything, and Sixteen Candles combined into one perfect, lyrically beautiful track.

Trent and I talk about my love for Ray Montagne and specifically this song. I give him a little insight into how amazing I think the lyrics really are. I tell him that it's every girl's dream to have a guy feel about her the way *You Are The Best Thing* describes. It paints the perfect picture of love, friendship, and fairytale happiness. Trent seems to find my keenness for one single song "adorable"—his word not mine.

I know I'm making it blatantly obvious that, although my heart was broken not too long ago, I'm still a romantic deep down. I still want to find the one guy to sweep me off my feet. My knight-in-shining armor, my prince on the white horse, my "You had me at hello" perfect man. Now, I know this isn't completely realistic, and I definitely don't want perfection. I just want someone who will love every part of me, including the obnoxious, sarcastic, and often times awkward Elle. And although I'm desperately trying not to admit it, Trent is looking more and more like this guy every moment I spend with him.

"Are you going to tell me where we're going?" I ask him as I look around at my current surroundings.

"Nope." He looks over at me with a sweet smile and warmness to his eyes.

"You're killing me, Casanova. *Killing me.*" I continue to browse through his music selection and choose another big favorite of mine. The soulful voice of Van Morrison starts to fill the air as he sings *Brown-Eyed Girl*. I quickly roll down my window and turn off the air conditioning. I turn up the music and start to loudly sing along with one of the all-time greats. I let the warm breeze of the summer air wash over my face and long, auburn locks. This song is downright lovely, and it soothes my soul into utter contentment. *Brown-Eyed Girl* reminds me of summer and sunshine and young love.

Trent starts to sing along with me, and I'm not going to lie, his voice isn't perfect, but the huskiness definitely has a sultry sexiness. I could quite honestly listen to him sing to me every single day of the week. Trent rolls his window down and we continue to sing along to *Brown-Eyed Girl* together as we head down one of Charlotte's main highways.

I'm pleasantly surprised when Trent pulls off of the highway into downtown Charlotte. He obviously took the very long way in order to keep me on my toes. We head into Uptown Charlotte, a really nice part of downtown. The real estate in this area is extremely expensive. I'm expecting him to take me to dinner at a nice restaurant but realize that he's got a whole different type of date planned.

"So I'm making you dinner tonight," he reveals as he pulls in front of a very upscale and modern looking building.

"Oh. Is this your place?" I'm definitely surprised.

"Yeah it is. I hope you're in the mood for steak."

Can he read my mind?

Wasn't I just thinking about how I've been craving a nice steak for over a week now?

He gets out of the truck and opens my passenger door. I know I'm staring at Trent with an odd expression on my face, but I'm a little freaked out that this guy might have some weird mind-reading super power that I'm not aware of.

Oh my god! What if he can hear everything I'm thinking at this very moment? Or all the times before this when I've stared at his pants and tried to telepathically take them off!

"Elle, are we going in or just going to stay here and stare at each other? I've got no problems with either choice." Trent is grinning from ear to ear, and those heavenly blue eyes are filled with mirth.

"Tell me what I'm thinking right now." I'm looking back at him seriously.

Don't think about his cock. Don't think about his ridiculously hot body.

"Uh, you're really hungry for steak?" He guesses questioningly.

I pull him by the shirt so he is standing between my thighs and I stare directly into his eyes.

"Are. You. Sure?"

Trent attempts to hide his amusement at my unexpected display of weirdness, but I can still see a small grin on his lips. "I'm. Not. Sure.*"*

I nudge his chest a little with my hand and laugh. "Stop fucking with me. I feel like you're always reading my mind, and I'm just trying to make sure you're not hiding some Hamiltonian super power from me."

Trent softly kisses my lips and pulls me out of the truck. "I promise I can't read your mind, but now you've got me really curious about what's going on inside that adorable head of yours."

"Believe me, you do not want to know what's going on up here. All kinds of crazy!" I tap the side of my head lightly.

"Come on, Ellie girl, bring those fuck-me heels and get your sweet ass into my apartment."

He grabs my hand and pulls me towards the entrance of his building.

We make our way up to his place, and I'm utterly impressed. Large pillars, gleaming hardwood floors, and arched ceilings frame the open living area. The entire apartment is done in warm, neutral hues. The kitchen is state-of-the-art with stainless steel appliances and beautiful marble countertops. The apartment has a modern yet elegant feel to it.

"Your place is gorgeous, Trent," I tell him as I stand in front of the floor-to-ceiling window looking out onto a balcony that gives a nice view of downtown Charlotte.

"Thanks. I honestly could see myself living here for a long time." He opens a bottle of Merlot and hands me a glass. I try to ignore the idea of Trent living in Charlotte permanently. I just don't want to allow myself to get my hopes up.

"When is Dr. Grey due to be back from his medical leave?" My mouth sputters out, and now I wish I could just take back that stupid question. I don't really want a timeline I can obsessively watch like a hawk.

Trent's look is pensive, relaxed. "The last I heard, he is due back around the second week in October, but no exact date is set. I'm in no rush though." His treacherously sexy smirk is nearly knocking the wind right out of my chest.

There's your fucking timeline, you idiot.

My brain is already trying to mentally count the days.

STOP. Don't do that. Don't make yourself crazy counting down. Just live in the moment, enjoy the fact that this undeniably amazing guy is here, and for some reason, he wants to spend time with you.

Sometimes I really wish I could take the advice my subconscious gives me...

Trent takes a plate of steaks out onto the balcony and puts them on the grill. I follow him out and lean my back against the railing, facing him. He tells me about his family in Seattle. His parents have been married for over thirty years and his dad, also a physician, just recently retired and sold his family practice. I can tell Trent is extremely proud of his father, and it's very apparent that his dad was a huge inspiration for him to finish medical school and become a surgeon.

His mother stayed at home with Trent and his two older siblings. She seems lovely, and Trent's adoration for her is undeniably cute. His brother, Josh, and sister, Leah, both reside in Seattle and are happily married. Leah has a four-year-old daughter named Mia, and Trent is completely in love with this little girl. His parents seem utterly delightful and are currently enjoying time together, road tripping to various tourist spots across the country.

"So tell me about cute little Mia. I can tell you adore her." I swirl my wine around in the glass and take a sip.

"My Mia is the cutest four-year-old you will ever meet. She has me wrapped around her little finger and I love every second of it." He smiles over at me as he flips the steaks.

"I bet you're an awesome uncle and spoil her rotten. Do you miss her?"

"I make a point to bring her a new Barbie doll every time I see her, and yes, of course I miss her, but I'm extremely happy about what Charlotte has brought me." He waggles his eyebrows and grins devilishly.

Good god, he's this irresistible combination of charming and sexy. This combination is lethal and dangerous, yet I just want to dive head first with my tongue.

"That's freakin' adorable, Trent. I would love to meet her someday." I let that little statement leave my lips before thinking about the fact that I'm openly admitting to wanting some sort of future with him.

Son of a bitch.

"Elle, I would love for you to meet Mia. Honestly, she's a lot like you. She's adorable, yet she has this sarcastic quick wit to her that keeps me laughing constantly. My sister Leah wants to strangle me most of the time because I seem to encourage her precocious personality."

He gives a sexy wink before turning his attention back to grilling the steaks.

I tell Trent about my family in Louisville—my wonderful parents and older sister, Elizabeth. My parents own a small diner that's conveniently located near the University of Louisville's campus. I tell him about my waitressing days, and he seemed to get a kick out of the idea of me in an apron. I still talk to my mom and dad daily but haven't really spoken with Lizzy in a while. She's married to a successful lawyer and always seems to have a benefit or charity function to attend.

Lizzy is six years older than me, and although we are similar in looks, we are *complete* opposites. She's conservative and, in my opinion, a little uptight. Lizzy worries about appearances and strives for nothing short of perfection in everything she does. I'm more of a free-spirit, fly-by-the-seat-of-my-pants kind of girl. I'm spontaneous and seem to make a career out of being found in embarrassing, ludicrous situations. Lizzy hates spontaneity, and I'm sure you can see why we're not as close as most sisters. Despite our differences, I still love her and would do anything for her. I would just rather do it from a distance in order to avoid her judgmental attitude. Because that's just Lizzy; she can be a little pretentious at time.

"I'd really like to see the two of you interact together," Trent says with a grin. Yeah, that's probably not going to happen anytime soon. The next time I see Lizzy will be when I head home for Thanksgiving in the fall.

We take our conversation into the dining area, and Trent refuses to let me help with anything. He grabs me by the shoulders and leads me towards the dining table when I attempt to help him with dinner.

"*I'm* making *you* dinner tonight, so sit your cute ass down and relax."

Once dinner is ready, Trent refills my glass of wine and sets my plate in front of me before sitting down at the table. My mouth is watering at the sight of this delicious meal. New York Strip, asparagus, baked potato, and bacon-wrapped-scallops. I take a bite of my steak and moan out loud with appreciation.

Holy shit this guy can cook.

Our dinner conversation is easy, relaxed. There are never any awkward silences or uncomfortable small talk, and I find myself wondering why I was even nervous about this date.

Trent continues to make me laugh about stories of him and his brother getting into trouble growing up. It sounds like his mother had her hands full with those two boys together. They are only eighteen months apart, and if Josh is anywhere near as good-looking as Trent, I bet they had quite the female fan base in Seattle. I share a few stories of my own about Elizabeth and me. Most of my stories end up with me making an ass of myself and Lizzy being pissed. Trent finds this extremely sidesplitting. I'm glad I'm not the only one who finds her dramatic reactions comical.

I once dressed up like Lizzy for Halloween when I was eleven. I wore pearls, my grandmother's cardigan set, and a hideous pencil skirt. Let's just say her reaction was less than enthusiastic. She was furious. The costume was pretty damn accurate though, if I do say so myself. Lizzy never left the house in anything but conservative cardigan sets and prim-and-proper skirts.

I'm not really sure how she landed her husband. I guess he gets off on the Lizzy-look. It's a cross between "my husband is running for a presidential campaign" and "I'm the school librarian." It's hard to believe a sixteen-year-old girl was dressing like that in high school, but that's honestly Lizzy. Conservative, prim-and-proper, prudish Lizzy. If my parents weren't so head-over-heels in love with each other, I would strongly entertain the idea of me being the mailman's kid.

We move our conversation to the comfy leather couch in front of the ginormous flat screen television. I'm a little buzzed from the wine and can feel my face flushing as I register the fact that I might get into Trent Hamilton's pants tonight.

"What's with the blush, babe?" Trent puts his arm around me and pulls me closer to his side, rubbing his thumb across my cheek.

I let out a nervous laugh. "Uh…I'm not blushing. I think I'm just warm from the wine."

Or maybe it's because I keep staring at your crotch and wondering how big your dick is.

"I was hoping you'd say it was from me and the dirty things you're thinking about doing to me," he says with a wicked grin.

I playfully roll my eyes at him and shake my head.

"Are you sure, Ellie girl?" He's persistent and continues to gaze at my lips.

"No." I bite my bottom lip and my breath hitches.

"You weren't thinking about doing dirty things to me?"

He leans in closer, his breath warm on my mouth. He places his hand underneath my chin and brings my eyes up to his. His stare is heated, passionate, and it's practically burning me. I have no words. Literally, I have zero words to say. I'm speechless and dive lips first towards Trent's mouth.

Our kiss is hot, rough, and desperate. I've been thinking about kissing those lips again for far too long. Our hands are everywhere, all over each other, as his tongue slides against mine. His taste is sweet and devastatingly delicious. He roughly grabs my hips and pulls me onto his lap, my legs straddling him. I let out a breathy moan as he continues to kiss me deep and strong. His mouth is unrelenting on mine and his hands are in my hair, pulling me close, my breasts pressed against his chest. He trails kisses down my jaw and then his tongue is on my neck.

Oh fuck.

I moan loudly as my head falls back and I start grinding into his arousal.

He pulls the top of my strapless dress down, freeing my breasts. My nipples are hard and begging for his touch. Trent leans down with a groan and sucks me into his mouth. I'm writhing against him with desire and the intense, overpowering need to feel him inside of me. I vaguely hear my phone ringing in the background, but my brain just continues to ignore it and live in this moment with Trent. While he's licking and suckling at my breasts, he slides a hand up my thigh and under my dress. I feel his large, warm fingers slide my panties to the side and begin to rub soft, smooth circles against my clit. My hips jerk at the penetrating feeling that radiates up my spine.

"You're wet. So fucking wet," he says as he slides a finger inside of me.

I hear my phone ringing again, but my vagina is calling the shots at this point, and she doesn't give a shit about a phone call. Getting thrusted is her priority—her *only* priority right now—and I'm practically begging Trent to put his cock inside of me.

"Please...*please*...Trent, I need you inside of me."

He continues to slide his finger through my wetness as he brings his mouth to mine and kisses me with a fierceness that has me involuntary clenching.

"I want to feel you do that around my cock. Fuck, I *need* to feel you do that," he moans into my mouth.

"Yessss... Harder, Trent!" I yell out, my voice breathy and thick with wanton desire.

I'm grinding myself down onto his hand and practically riding his fingers. His continued assault on my clit has me panting and nearly screaming his name.

"Oh god, yes!" I moan, before his lips crash into mine.

"God I want to taste that sweet pussy, baby."

And that little line of dirty talk has me clenching his fingers tightly and coming with an intensity I didn't know was possible with just Trent's hand alone.

Oh holy orgasm.

I think I may have just had some type of unintentional spiritual awakening. What's going to happen when he thrusts inside of me? Death by motherfucking orgasm, that's what...and I will for sure rest in peace.

Trent takes his fingers that are drenched in my arousal and rubs them across my breasts, coating my nipples with my slick wetness. He gazes at me with hunger in his blue eyes and says, "I can't wait to taste you." And then he leans forward and sucks my nipple into his mouth.

Fuck, that's a hot move.

He's sucking and licking at my breasts like he can't get enough, and I feel him huskily moan into my chest. "Elle, your pussy is perfect. I want to bury my face between your legs all night, just to keep your taste on my tongue."

I think I just came again.

I start to unbuckle his belt so I can finally see that gorgeous cock I've been dying to feast my eyes on. And again I hear my phone ringing followed by several text message notifications. A large sigh escapes me, and Trent rests his forehead against mine.

"I think you need to answer that, babe."

In my head, I'm screaming, "God dammit! Can't a girl get finger-banged without being interrupted?"

I quickly get up off the couch and grab my phone from my purse. I see several missed calls and text notifications—all of them from Amy. The last text message she sent gives me pause.

Amy: Emergency. Call me back ASAP. Lizzy is here. She's shitfaced and crying.

What in the hell? Lizzy? My sister Lizzy?
I call Amy and I'm surprised to find out that my sister Lizzy showed up at our apartment with several suitcases in tow, saying she left her husband. Apparently she's drunk and sobbing. My heart breaks for her, but I'm not going to lie, I'm pretty pissed she decided to show up on this night *of all nights.*
And why is she running to me?
The last time I spoke with her was weeks ago. I tell Amy that I'll be home shortly and to keep Lizzy away from our liquor cabinet, because it's one thing to ruin your sister's chance of getting dicked by a hot, sexy guy, but it's a whole other thing to drink her alcohol supply. Alcohol that I'm most likely going to need tonight…
I also think my sister just gave the greatest unintentional cock-blocking performance of all time. She's now the MVC. *Most valuable cock-blocker.*
As Trent and I head out of his apartment, I think I can quietly hear my vagina crying as she puts Celine Dion on her iPod and calls it a night.

Chapter Sixteen

"Once you hit the age of fourteen, you should not have a day-of-the-week reminder on your snatch."

Trent and I walk into my apartment to find an annoyed Amy and *extremely* drunk Lizzy. I don't recall a time where I have ever witnessed my older sister this intoxicated. She puts new meaning to the term intoxication. Her bags are strewn across my apartment as she rummages through her largest suitcase, throwing random items of clothing out onto the living room carpet. She's disheveled and her lack of clothing has me slightly concerned about what I'm going to face tonight—and more importantly, for the next few weeks.

Lizzy's auburn hair is stacked in a messy bun on her head, and her mascara seems to be attempting to make a great escape to her neck. She's stumbling around in an old t-shirt, and her pants have yet to make an appearance to this little party.

Her white cotton panties say "Thursday" across the front. Unfortunately, it's not Thursday. It's actually Friday, and the Lizzy I know would have never let a travesty like this occur. She's normally organized and has every detail planned to perfection, including her day-of-the-week underwear, which I'm a little shocked to see she still wears. I feel like once you enter adulthood, day-of-the-week panties should be pulled from your wardrobe. Lizzy is thirty-four years old. I'm pretty sure she doesn't need a reminder on her snatch to figure out what day of the week it is.

"Hey! It's my sister! My Ellie Jelly Belly!" Lizzy nearly tackles me in the kitchen with a sloppy hug.

"Hi, Lizzy. I'm a little surprised to see your face tonight."

I attempt to disentangle myself from her vice-like grip around my neck. I settle myself against the counter, crossing my arms over my chest. Trent is sitting across from me at my kitchen table. He's leaned back in the chair, hands behind his head, and a perfect picture of relaxation. I'm glad someone is relaxed.

I, on the other hand, am far from relaxed. I've got a drunken sister who resembles a hobo traipsing around my apartment like she owns the joint, and my juice-box is pretty angry she didn't receive a good screwing tonight.

"I fucking hate my husband. Matt Montgomery 'the third,'" She attempts to use finger quotes to accentuate her comment. "He's a tool. A stuck-up momma's boy." I'm going to have to work with her on better insults. Later of course, once she's sober enough to comprehend English.

"I get that you're pissed at Matt, but what made you come all the way to Charlotte? Not that I'm not thrilled to see you, but this seems a little out of the ordinary for the Lizzy I know."

I need to figure out what in the hell has caused my sister to drive over seven hours and throw herself on my doorstep. The girl that is stumbling around in front of me is a chick I've never met. This isn't Lizzy, not by a long shot. Lizzy is prissy and conservative, and she always has everything in its perfect little place. This chick is drunk and obnoxious, and she has a serious issue with wearing pants.

"He doesn't care about me. He cares about his lame job and stupid car and golf clubs," she slurs out, before opening the fridge in search of something, most likely more booze.

"Does Matt know you left him, Lizzy?" I'm obviously getting now where fast with this conversation tonight. She's too befuddled to give me an inkling of an idea of what caused her to drive to Charlotte and unload this shit storm on my doorstep.

"Nope." She pops the 'p' loudly with her lips and then takes a seat next to Trent, giving him an interesting facial expression I can't really distinguish. I'm thinking it might be an attempt to be sexy, but I'm not really sure.

"What about Mom and Dad? Do they know you're here?"

"Nope. I just packed my bags and *blew* that popsicle stand." She attempts to seductively accentuate the word blew as she stares intently at Trent.

God, first this bitch strolls into my apartment drunker than Snooki at the Jersey Shore house, interrupts my finger-banging session, and now she's trying to flirt with Trent. This entire situation is comical. I look back and notice Amy watching the entire spectacle go down from her cozy spot on the living room couch. Amy just grins back at me and I flip her the bird. She laughs loudly before giving me a sympathetic smile, indicating she realizes how hard this entire ordeal is going to be.

"Well how about I go ahead and call everyone, let them know where you're at, and then you can sleep in the spare bedroom tonight."

"I don't want to go to sleep right now. I want to meet your friend." She's still staring at Trent, who is currently looking back at me with an amused grin.

"Well my *friend*—" I start to say but then I am abruptly cut off by Trent.

"*Boyfriend.*" He's smiling warmly at me, and I can't help but return the smile.

"Lizzy, this is my *boyfriend,* Trent Hamilton." I'm shocked that he's already prepared to call himself my boyfriend. We haven't even banged it out for fuck's sake, but I can't deny the fact that I love the idea of Trent and me together.

"Oh. He's *your* boyfriend? Shit. Where did I go wrong? He's fucking hot." She appraises him greedily with drunken eyes.

After hearing Lizzy say the word fuck for the fifth time in the last fifteen minutes and eye-fucking Trent for another fifteen minutes, I realize my top priority is to get her boozed-up ass to bed.

"He's all right, but I think it's time for him to leave. He probably has to be up early tomorrow." I'm attempting to discreetly hint to Trent that we need to cut my sister off from conversation for the rest of the evening.

"Elle is right. I've got an early surgery schedule tomorrow. Nice meeting you, Lizzy." Trent stands up from the kitchen table and gestures for me to follow him to the door.

"Surgery schedule? What the fuck? You're hot and you're a fucking doctor! Well fuck me sideways and call me Sally. My little sis has hit the jackpot! I'm so fucking jealous of you right now!" Lizzy slurs.

Then she proceeds to pull out a frozen pizza from the freezer.

"I'm fucking hungry! Pizzzzzzzzaaaaaaa. I want pizzzzzaaaaa." She tears open the cardboard box and throws the frozen pizza into the oven, which is still currently off. "I can't wait to eat this shit." Lizzy plops herself down and rests her head in her arms on the kitchen table.

Fingers crossed she passes out.

"I got this, Elle. You go ahead and tell Trent goodnight." Amy walks into the kitchen and takes over drunk-girl babysitting duties.

"Let me walk you outside. I'd like to say goodnight to you without my sister screaming out about your hotness." I smirk at him as we walk towards the front door.

Trent places his hand at the small of my back and leads me towards the elevator. We make our way downstairs and outside to his truck. He walks around the back and drops the tailgate down so he can sit on it. Trent wraps his arms around my waist and pulls my body between his thighs.

"Come here, little spitfire."

I make myself cozy in Trent's embrace and wrap my arms around his neck. He's warm and comfy, and I wish I could stay tucked in his arms for the rest of the night.

"Thanks for letting me off the hook tonight with the boyfriend comment. I think that was the only way Lizzy was going to stop being so relentless in her drunken pursuit of getting into your pants." I laugh into his chest.

I feel Trent take a deep breath, and strands of my hair blow out past my face. "You really don't get it yet, do you? It's okay. I'm a patient man. I have no problems with waiting until you catch up."

"Catch up? What are you talking about?"

"When the time is right, we'll have this conversation, but now isn't the right time because right now, I'm going to kiss you."

Trent gently lifts my chin so I'm looking up at him. His eyes are piercing yet tender. He softly presses his supple lips to mine and proceeds to give me the sweetest kiss I've ever received.

"Ellie girl, tonight was amazing, and I'm one lucky son of a bitch for having a beautiful girl like you agree to have dinner with me."

"You're crazy, but I'll take the compliments. And I had a wonderful time too. I'm sorry our night was interrupted." I look down at his hands placed on his lap and start to trace small circles with my fingers on his palms.

"No worries. I'm glad I got to meet your sister Lizzy."

I raise my eyebrows and give him a look of disbelief. "What? Now you're being really ridiculous. Lizzy is completely shitfaced and not at all like the Lizzy I know."

"She thinks I'm really hot." He's giving me a shit-eating grin.

"Yeah, yeah, yeah. Lizzy thinks you're one sexy piece of man-meat." I poke his chest and give him an annoyed expression.

He pulls me close and places his hands on my cheeks, cupping my face gently.

"You know I'm just messing with you. Yes, your sister was shitfaced, but she's still *your* sister, and I am happy I got to meet her. Anything that has to do with you, I want to be a part of. Now come here, little spitfire, and give me another kiss goodnight." He places his lips on mine and gives me the most perfect kiss goodnight a girl could ever ask for.

Chapter Seventeen

"A good sister will eventually understand and forgive you for the moments when you're being a total asshole, even when you cock-block her from getting her bang-bang on with a hot surgeon."

I wake up to a loudly groaning Lizzy in the bathroom. She's obviously feeling the effects of the copious amount of alcohol she consumed last night. I groggily head out into the kitchen and find Amy sitting at the table, smiling big while looking down at her phone.

"What's got you all smiley?' I ask Amy as I pour a cup of coffee. I'm going to need a lot of caffeine to get me out of this tired state.

"Nothing," she replies as she quickly types something and then sets her phone on the table. "Sounds like Lizzy is praying to the porcelain gods. She must have a lot of sins to repent for." Amy smirks at me with amusement.

"Yeah, she should be asking for forgiveness for cock-blocking her sister last night." I sit down at the table and add some French vanilla creamer to my coffee.

"So you didn't get to make bang-bang with Dr. Thrust Me?"

I hang my head down in frustration. "Nope. My juice-box only got finger-banging action last night— *fantastic* finger-banging action though." I look up and grin at Amy.

"Nice! Sounds like your meat wallet had a good time." Amy takes a sip of her coffee and grins widely at me.

We continue our discussion of my and Trent's date last night. I tell her every last detail at her persistence and even disclose the hot little move where Trent licked my arousal off of my tits. Just the thought of his lips lapping up my cum off of my boobs has my snatch nearly wetting herself.

"All right, I can't take any more details of Trent and his hot moves or else I might start dry humping the leg of this table."

I laugh loudly and make a mental note to keep his hot moves to myself. Our table is already on its last leg.

"Ellie Belly, I'm really happy for you. Keep letting Trent in, let him love you, and before you try to give me some bullshit line about it being too early for talk of the 'L' word, Trent loves you. He really does, and it's apparent every time you two are together." Amy reaches out and grabs my hand, giving it a tight squeeze.

"I think you're being a little overzealous with the whole idea of Trent being in love with me, but I appreciate everything you just said." I smile back at her.

A few hours later, Lizzy strolls out into the living room to find Amy and me laughing our asses off at a trashy reality show. I glance up and pat the couch cushion next to me, encouraging Lizzy to take a seat. We've got a lot to chat about.

Her husband Matt was pretty upset when I called him to let him know Lizzy had made a surprise appearance at my apartment. He gave a little insight into the situation when he told me they'd had a huge fight, but Matt still seemed shocked that his wife had just up and left him.

He was persistent in his attempts to find out what had spurred Lizzy's great escape from Louisville. I didn't mention that she was talking divorce or the fact that she seemed pretty convinced things with her and Matt were through. I sugarcoated most of the situation and just told him that she seemed upset. I gave him the impression that she made the trip to Charlotte so she could have some time to herself—time away to think about everything.

"How ya feeling, drunky?" Amy leans past me to give Lizzy a big grin.

"Ugh. I feel like death. I'm so sorry for just showing up unexpectedly last night. My plan was to get a hotel after I chatted with you, Elle, but I started drinking wine while I sat in your parking lot. Then next thing I knew, I was drunk, crying my eyes, and knocking on your apartment door." Lizzy sits down next to me, and I wrap my arm around her shoulder.

"What's going on, hun? What caused you to make a seven-hour trip to Charlotte to see me?"

Tears begin to slowly fall down her cheeks as she starts to explain everything that is going on with her. "Things with Matt and me aren't good, Elle. We've been fighting more and more over the past few months. He's so involved in his law firm, and I just feel like I'm slowly losing a part of myself every day. I'm tired of being the perfect little wife who sits around, waiting for her big shot husband to give her the time of day. I'm thirty-four years old and I don't feel like I know myself anymore. Over the past two years, we've been trying to have a baby, and I found out that I have some serious fertility issues. We've tried *everything*. Matt makes me feel like a disappointment, a complete and total failure for not being able to conceive. He refuses to give adoption a try, and I'm left feeling completely helpless. He's not the man I married six years ago. He's different. He's distant, cold, and I just can't do it anymore. I can't be Elizabeth Montgomery." Lizzy leans forward and places her elbows on her knees and her head in her hands.

I can see she's shaking with heartache. I can't believe things have gotten so awful for her and Matt. I'm shocked and honestly a little hurt that she didn't let me in. That she didn't come to me before now. Before everything was at its absolute worst. I gently rub her back and look over at Amy to see what's running through her head. Her expression is purely sympathetic. I can tell she feels as terrible as I do—terrible that my sister has been going through all of this alone.

"Well, I say that you move your ass in here, give yourself some time to think, and work through some things before you make your final decision," Amy generously offers to Lizzy.

I'm going to be indebted to my best friend forever for being so damn amazing.

"You just took the words right out of my mouth. I agree with Amy. Move in with us for a little while and take time to get your head straight. It'll be nice to have my only sister so close." I continue to rub her back.

Lizzy looks up at both Amy and me, and it's the first time I've seen her *really* smile since she made the trip to Charlotte. "Are you guys being serious? You're really okay with me staying here with you for a while?"

"Yes, we're one hundred percent serious. We've got a spare bedroom and you're just the girl to make use of it." I pull Lizzy in for a tight hug and feel Amy wrap her arms around both of us.

"Lizzy, you have kitchen duty today," Amy whispers quietly while we're all still wrapped up in each other's arms. Lizzy laughs loudly and my heart smiles at the sound of my sister's happiness. Although, we are complete opposites and have had our fair share of fights in the past, Lizzy is my sister. She's family, and I will always do anything for my family.

Chapter Eighteen

"My 'I give a fuck' actually gives less fucks than your 'I don't give a fuck.'"

Today is Regency's annual golf event, and Trent is waiting patiently downstairs for Amy and me to get our asses in his truck. He volunteered to be our driver for this wonderful Saturday afternoon. Little did he know that Amy and I make a tradition out of taking a few shots before heading out to schmooze it up with Regency's finest physicians and hospital administrators. Yeah, I know. This is quite the dangerous game we play, but this is Amy and me we're talking about here. Our "I give a fuck" actually gives less fucks than most people's "I don't give a fuck."

Lizzy has been moved in with us for a week now. She seems sad at times, but I'm hoping this period away from her life in Louisville is giving her time to think things over. I know things with Matt haven't been the best over the past several months, but I would just hate for her to throw her marriage of over six years away. There was a point in time when Matt and Lizzy were blissfully happy, and I feel like if they really worked on things, they could find that happiness again.

I've been doing my best to take time to spend with my sister. I begged her to go to this charity event with us, but she was insistent on staying in for the day. She has a phone call planned with Matt later this evening when he's home from work. From what Lizzy's told me, Matt isn't really taking things so well either. He's immersed himself even more than before in his job, which explains his weekend hours. I just hope he can pull his head out of his ass and realize he's about to lose the best thing that ever happened to him.

I urged Lizzy to call me if she needs anything and even encouraged her to stop by the charity event later after she and Matt talk. I know she most likely won't show up, but I just want her to realize that I'm here for her always. No matter what, I will always have her back.

Amy and I are officially four tequila shots down and feeling really good.

A little too good, actually.

Skipping breakfast was probably not the best idea. I grab my purse, straighten my adorable golf skirt, and strut my slightly tipsy butt out the door. Trent is on his Blackberry, finishing up a call as Amy and I hop in the passenger side of his truck. He's all kinds of cute with his bright blue eyes shining like diamonds. The combination of his jet-black hair and white oxford polo seems to make his eyes stand out even more. He's watching me climb into his truck with a gorgeous grin spread across his full, soft lips. I fold the center console up and slide into the middle seat next to my devastatingly handsome...boyfriend?

I guess that's what Trent is to me.

That's what he's been calling himself for the past week. I really want him to be my boyfriend—shit, I want him to be my *everything*—but I'm well aware that he is not going to be a permanent fixture here in Charlotte. I bet y'all are tired of hearing me say this, but I can't help myself. Crazy does what crazy wants, and I'm not ashamed to admit that I've got a little bit—okay, a lot— of crazy inside of me.

You know what else I want inside of me?

Oh my god, I'm hopeless!

It's like I can't go thirty seconds in Trent's presence without automatically thinking about the D. Yes, his dick. I'm practically orgasming at the thought of Trent sliding his manhood inside of my vagina. Ha! You know I'm tipsy when I'm thinking words like *manhood*. Either that or I've been reading too many Harlequin Romance novels…

"So, Ellie girl, whatcha been drinking, sweetheart?" Trent winks at me as he sets his Blackberry back into the cell dock on his dashboard.

"Uhhhhhh. Tequila?" I say with a kittenish expression.

"Don't play coy with me, drunky. I could smell the booze on you two when you hopped in my truck. I see how it is. You agreed to ride with me to the charity event so that I could be *your* D.D." He's grinning at me with those beautiful blue eyes, and my drunken brain is completely lost.

Speechless.

I've got nothing, nada, zip.

You get the idea.

"Oh dear god, please stop making fuck-me eyes at Dr. Thrust Me." Amy whines as she fakes a gagging noise from the back of her throat.

Trent is practically crying from laughing so hard. "What did you just call me? Dr. Thrust Me?" He holds up one finger, attempts to hold back his laughter, and asks, "Who came up with this nickname?" He raises an eyebrow at us.

Amy and I both point to each other and Trent starts laughing again.

He is shaking his head at us as he pulls out of our apartment complex and onto the main road.

"I was hoping my Ellie girl was the one who'd come up with that awesome nickname, because I would have had to thank her *personally*." He glances my way and gives a sly smile.

Amy starts cracking up and says, "Oh fuck me, that's hilarious! I'm the one who came up with that nickname, by the way. Are you going to thank *me* personally, *Dr.* Thrust Me?

Bitch!

Cunty McCunterson!

Loose-Lipped Labia, Sloppy Pussy Pudding, Cum Twat!

"Loose-Lipped Labia, Sloppy Pussy Pudding, Cum Twat?" Amy asks in amusement.

"Shit, did I just say that out loud?" I look back and forth between them and notice Trent is nearly shaking with hilarity.

"Uh huh, you sure did, dickhead." Amy pinches my thigh with her fingers and I yelp from the combination of shock and stinging pain.

"Ow! Fucko! That hurt!" I yell back at her.

"You deserved it!" She sticks her tongue out at me.

"Girls! Settle down before I have to pull this truck over and spank both of your asses." He grins wickedly at us.

"Yes, please!" Amy and I say simultaneously, and this causes us to both to start giggling uncontrollably. She snorts, and I nearly piss my pants from hysterics. After we manage to calm ourselves down, I tell Amy I'm sorry for calling her a cum twat, even though it was quite obvious she deserved it. You heard her flirting with my man! She knows the rules, and I'm well aware she gets a kick out of getting me riled up.

"Holy shit, Elle, isn't that Frank?" Amy is looking towards the sidewalk only a few blocks from our apartment.

I squint my eyes, attempting to make out the disheveled man despite the bright sun filtering in through the windows. "Oh my god, yeah, that's definitely Frank."

"Who's Frank?" Trent asks as he puts his turn signal on to switch lanes.

"He's a psych patient that frequents the ED all the time," I tell him.

"He's creepy. *Super creepy,*" Amy explains with wide eyes.

"I don't like the idea of him walking around so close to your apartment. I get the positive side of being within walking distance of Regency, but I'd say this right here would definitely be a negative." Trent squeezes my thigh and gives me a concerned look.

"Let's not get all serious, now. I've got a buzz to keep." I place my hand on Trent's and give him a reassuring smile.

Trent's husky laugh fills the truck. "God forbid you lose your buzz, sweetheart."

"Labia face is right. No more creepy patient talk." I give Amy a pointed look and she just responds with blowing me a kiss.

She is such a sarcastic cunt.

The drive to Centennial Golf Club is an hour from Charlotte, and Trent pulls over at a nearby gas station to fill up before we make the long trek. Amy nearly sprints inside to use the restroom, and I lean up against the bed of the truck to watch Trent pump gas. He swipes his credit card and sets the gas nozzle up to pump automatically before standing in front of me with a huge grin on his face.

Grabbing my hips, he spins us around so his back is leaning up against the truck, and I'm standing between his legs. He pulls me in for a tight hug and kisses my forehead softly. I feel him brush my hair behind my ear.

He whispers, "I missed you." He presses his nose into my hair and inhales deeply. "I missed my little spitfire and her delicious strawberry shampoo."

Trent seems to be obsessed with the fact that my shampoo is strawberry scented, and honestly, I love that he notices something as simple as the scent of my hair products. It really proves just how sweet and thoughtful of a guy Trent Hamilton truly is. I hug him back tightly and nuzzle my face into his strong, muscular chest.

"I missed you too, Casanova. I really missed you too."

Just being near this man puts a huge smile on my face. I probably look like I'm high off of Prozac, but I can't help myself. He just has that effect on me.

"You're killing me in this skirt, sweetheart. Fucking killing me." I feel him slide his hands down to my ass and give each cheek a squeeze. I giggle in response and tilt my chin up to look at him. His blue eyes shine down on me, and I'm lost in his stunning gaze. He leans down and kisses my lips softly, affectionately. The kiss is sweet and delicious, and it feels like home.

Home? Oh man. I'm a lost cause.

"Come on, dickheads! Enough dry humping! We've got places to be!" Amy yells as she opens the passenger door. I can't believe I was so lost in Trent's kiss that I didn't even notice Amy was already back from the bathroom. Trent smiles against my lips and gives my nose a small peck before I turn away and walk towards the passenger door of his truck. He pinches my ass and I squeal a little at his adorably crass behavior.

We're about twenty minutes away from our final destination and I can't believe Trent hasn't strangled us yet. Amy and I have alternated playing DJ and completely monopolized his iPod. Our song choices have varied from Rihanna to Nine Inch Nails to Salt-N-Pepa. Our rendition of *Closer* by Nine Inch Nails could quite possibly make someone's ears bleed. Neither of us can sing worth a damn, but that doesn't stop us. Trent just seems to find us humorous and is content with just holding my hand in his lap as we cruise down the highway.

How much longer can I deny the fact that I'm in love with this man?

"Okay, Destiny's Child, let's take an intermission for a minute here." Trent takes the iPod from my hands and turns down the music. "So how often do you two golf?" He asks us with a questioning gaze. Amy and I immediately start laughing, and Trent raises both eyebrows at our reaction to his question.

"Um, well…We don't really golf…at all," I answer with slight hesitation.

Amy laughs at me and says, "Yeah, we blow donkey dick at golf. It's a miracle they asked us back after last year."

Oh, here we go…

"Last year? I have to hear this story," Trent says before he takes the exit for Centennial Road.

"Ha! Oh. My. God. Last year, Elle hit the CEO in the back of the ass while she was attempting to practice her 'swing.'" Amy motions air quotes with her fingers.

"Like you should talk, dick! You nearly drove the golf cart into the pond!"

She really did almost sink one of the club's golf carts on hole twelve. Her lack of driving skills is still a mystery to me.

"Hey! It wasn't my fault the brakes went out! I was lucky I came out of that alive!" Amy shouts back at me.

"The brakes did not go out. You pushed the gas instead of the brake and—"

"Enough. Agree to disagree. I don't want to talk about this anymore." Amy turns her head away from me and looks out the window. I can barely hold back my smile; she just makes it too damn easy.

I glance over at Trent and he smirks at me, which causes my shoulders to shake with silent laughter. I can barely contain the giggles that want to spill out of my mouth. I tightly clamp my hand over my lips and try like hell to keep my amusement to myself.

"I know you're over there quietly giggling like an idiot." Amy spats as she continues to stare out the window.

I wrap my arms around her shoulders and hug her tightly. "I'm sorry. Please don't be mad at me." I give her my best pouty face and see the corners of her mouth turn up into a smile.

"Alright, fucko. I forgive you."

We manage to make it to the golf course in record time, and Trent starts getting his golf clubs out of the bed of his truck. I notice that he not only pulls out one set of clubs but actually pulls out two more.

"Three sets of golf clubs?" I look at him curiously.

"Well, there are three of us, and I would have put money on the fact that you two didn't have clubs." He raises his eyebrow mischievously at me as he signals for one of the club's workers to help carry our clubs in.

An adorable young kid who isn't a day over eighteen heads towards us. He is all baby-faced and bright blond hair. If I were eighteen years old, I would be practically drooling over this little cutie.

I notice Amy giving him a nice, long once-over. She's obviously satisfied with what she sees. I elbow her in the side so she'll pick her jaw up off of the ground.

"Cut it out, pervy," I sternly whisper to her.

"Ow! That hurt!" she says far too loudly. Trent and Jailbait glance over at us with curious expressions.

"She stubbed her toe. She's fine, just a little dramatic."

And for that comment I get a swift elbow to the tit.

"God dammit!" I whisper through clenched teeth.

Amy just grins back at me like an asshole. "Elle, I'm gonna go find Tony before we tee off. I'll meet you by the first hole." Amy makes an obscene gesture with her fingers, indicating her dirty thoughts regarding any talk of holes.

"All right, labia face, I'll see you in a few." I give her a slight wave.

"Peace out, cum twat!" Amy's voice is far too loud for a public charity function. I blush beet red from the intrigued stares that look my way, and Amy finds this every bit of hilarious.

Trent makes arrangements for our clubs to be delivered to the first hole of the course, and I happen to notice him slip two one hundred-dollar bills into Jailbait's hand. The kid's smile is wide and he's more than appreciative of this generous gesture. I have a feeling we'll be seeing his face later. He'd be an idiot not to attempt to offer more services if Trent is going to tip him that well. Trent puts his arm around my shoulder and pulls me close as we walk into the clubhouse.

"Hey, you. That was quite the generous tip you just handed that kid." I kiss him on the cheek.

"Ellie girl, I used to do that very same job when I was in high school. Every summer, my brother Josh and I would work our asses off being golf caddies and doing other odds and ends at the course. It's really hard work, and I am more than happy to make his life a little easier with extra cash flow."

God I love—I mean adore—*this man.*

He could be such a pretentious dickhole with all that he's accomplishment, but Trent Hamilton is one of the kindest, most considerate guys I've ever met. He's completely selfless, and I just adore him.

Yes, I'm completely head over heels in adoration for Trent Hamilton.

As he smiles down at me with those big blue eyes that nearly leave my heart in my throat, I know that I'm falling hard and fast for Trent Hamilton, and I'm well aware that there isn't a damn thing I can do about it.

"What's with the goofy grin?" He asks as he discreetly pinches my ass.

I giggle and shake my head a little. "I'm not telling you. That is top secret information, Dr. Hamilton, and you are not privy to it at this moment. Maybe someday though." I give him my sweetest smile and he abruptly stops to pull me in for a tight hug. My feet aren't even touching the ground as he crushes me to his chest, and I'm sure there are tons of people staring at our very public display of affection.

He kisses the tip of my nose and says, "I would give my left nut to know what's going on inside that pretty little head of yours. But I can tell you, whatever you're feeling right now, I'm feeling it too." He kisses me gently before slowly putting me back on my feet.

I'm just standing in front of him, slightly shell-shocked at his little admission.

Does he know that I'm pretty much in love with him?

I place my hand on his cheek and smile at him. Our eyes meet and we seem to communicate so much feeling, so much emotion without even saying anything.

Trent grabs my hand. "Come on, sweetheart. Let's go see what you can do with a club." He flashes his pearly whites before leading us towards the check-in area for the charity function.

We sign up, get our nametags, and make our way towards the course. Trent is stopped several times by some of Regency's higher-ups and successful physicians. He kindly introduces me to the ones I don't already know, and it doesn't go unnoticed that he continually uses the word girlfriend. I guess Trent Hamilton really does consider me his girlfriend. I know we've only been out on one official date, but I'm not complaining— not one bit. I'd give my left tit to be with Trent Hamilton forever.

Did I just use the words forever and Trent Hamilton in the same sentence?

Fuuuuuuuuck, I'm definitely a lost cause.

This year's charity function is raising money to update Regency's oncology unit with new state-of-the-art equipment to assist our cancer patients in receiving some of the best treatments available. I'm really excited about this cause, and I found out from Trent that this cause hits very close to home. His mother is in remission from breast cancer. She's a survivor, and Trent is extremely proud of his mother's strength through her terrifying fight with cancer. Five years ago, she was diagnosed and had to go through several rounds of chemotherapy and radiation along with a total mastectomy of her right breast. The woman is a fighter, and I find myself hoping to have the opportunity to meet her someday.

Our foursome includes yours truly, Trent, Amy, and a newer surgeon who specializes in orthopedics, Dr. James Williams. He's tall, with a broad, muscular chest, dirty blond hair, and green eyes that would make any woman swoon. He's kind of a dreamboat in the looks department, and I have a feeling that Amy is dying to get her fingers on him. James is extremely nice with a fantastically dry, sarcastic sense of humor that compliments Amy's ill-timed outbursts perfectly.

This round of golf should be nothing but tremendously entertaining.

Amy and I are sitting in the golf cart as James and Trent tee off. The mid-July air is practically melting my skin, and I relish in the nice shade the golf cart is providing. Why in the hell does Regency choose to do these big golf charity events in the middle of summer? The heat is downright blistering and I can already feel sweat dripping down the nape of my neck.

Amy and I are staring unabashedly at Trent and James's tight asses and laughing despite ourselves. The two of us are savoring our ice-cold beers and an occasional swig of tequila from the flask she snuck into the event. We're on a one-way trip to Sauced-ville and I'm already feeling a little tipsy.

"You're up, Ellie girl!" Trent calls over to me.

"Good luck, idiot," Amy tells me sarcastically as I strut towards Trent. I discreetly give her my favorite finger from behind my back before standing near Trent, ready to tee off.

"Are you just going to sit there and stare at me while I make an ass of myself?" I'm attempting to practice my swing as Trent watches me with a face full of enjoyment.

"I'll definitely be staring at your ass, crazy." He waggles his eyebrows up and down like a complete weirdo.

My weirdo.

I stick my tongue out at him and he gives me serious, determined eyes. "Keep that tongue in your mouth unless you're planning on doing dirty things to me with it."

I roll my eyes and laugh at his obscene tongue gesture. "Stop it or else everyone at Regency is going to think we're kinky assholes!"

"We are kinky assholes, babe. And I haven't even had the chance to get my cock inside that tight little pussy of yours yet." I hear James choke out a laugh from behind me and I blush cherry red at the realization that he's heard our back-and-forth sexual banter.

"Oh my god! You're incorrigible! And no more cock talk until we're somewhere where you can actually do all these things you've promised me." I smirk at him before putting my ball down in preparation to tee off.

I awkwardly swing my club and completely miss the ball on my first try.

"Son of a bitch!"

Trent laughs at my amateur display of terrible golf skills and attempts to help me with some "hands-on" assistance. He is standing behind me with his chest to my back, his hands over my hands, as I grasp my golf club. He's giving me step-by-step instructions of the proper way to hold a club and all I'm thinking about is him pressing his cock into my ass.

"Are you even listening to me right now?" He whispers roughly into my ear.

"Uh, no. I'm completely distracted by the close proximity of your dick," I whisper back to him with my eyes closed. Trent grabs my hips and pulls me tighter against his body and I nearly shiver at the feel of him pressed hard against me.

"*This* is distracting you?" I can hear a smile in his voice.

"God dammit, Casanova. Now *you're* killing *me*." He throws his head back in riotous laughter, which only causes him to press his pelvis into my ass even harder.

"All right, Dr. Thrust Me. You have to stop this or I'll make you finger-bang me out here on the golf course in front of everyone." Now Trent and James are both laughing at my absurd outburst about inappropriate public displays of affection.

Trent steps back from me and instructs me to do my worst, which I do.

"FOORRRRRRE!" All three of us yell as my ball heads towards a small group of spectators standing off to the side of the course.

"Nice work, asshead!" Amy shouts from the golf cart.

"Come on out here and show us your spectacular golfing skills!" I roar back to her.

Amy attempts her first round and, to my extreme satisfaction, screws up just as badly as I did. Trent and James are seriously in for it. Trent might be willingly cutting off his left nut just to put himself out of misery by the end of this.

We continue on to the next several holes with James and Trent neck and neck. Surgeons are notoriously competitive, and I'm coming to find out that this even includes golf charity functions. Amy and I, on the other hand, are lucky if we keep the stupid ball on the course. We decide to take turns yelling, "Fore!" for each other, since it's become that much of an occurrence.

I'm generally competitive and get extremely frustrated when I'm not doing well at something, but the combination of beer and tequila has made me completely carefree. I'm taking the fact that I blow ass at golf quite well, considering that I would normally be screaming profanities at this point in the game. Trent and James keep us laughing with hilarious sexual innuendos and highly inappropriate banter. *Constantly*.

I think Amy may have met her match with James. He's sarcastic, hilarious, and as quick-witted as she is. They seem to be getting cozier together by the minute. As I head to tee off for the ninth hole, I notice James put his arm around Amy's shoulders and whisper something into her ear. She giggles loudly and can't contain the huge grin on her face. That's when I know he's got her. Whenever Amy starts giggling around a guy, she wants that guy. This is her tell, her little sign of approval when she is attracted to someone. No one else would probably pick up on it, but I know my Amy almost as well as I know myself, so I definitely do not miss it.

"Are you going to tee off or just watch those two flirt with each other?" Trent asks with a smirk and a raised eyebrow.

"You were noticing that too?" I set my ball on the tee and prepare to showcase my horrible swing.

"I am, and honestly, I think they'd be perfect for each other."

"Shhhhhhh!" I whisper-yell to Trent as I prepare to tee off. "Can't you see the soon-to-be professional golfer preparing to stroke her ball into that pond over there?" I grin at him and then prove that professional and golfer will never be used in the same sentence to describe me.

"I'll give you something to stroke, smartass." Trent takes my club from my hands and wraps his arm around my waist as we head back towards the cart. I attempt to give Trent a serious look of disapproval, but my mouth betrays me. I can't help the chuckle that escapes my throat and the look of amusement that shines from my eyes. Trent is a pistol, and his sense of humor is something I truly enjoy. There really is nothing like a man who can make you laugh, and Trent Hamilton makes me laugh. All. The. Time.

James and Amy are quite the comfy little pair in the cart, and I grin at her like a lovesick idiot.

"Stop smiling at me like that. It's creeping me out." Amy is curiously gauging my reaction to her and James sitting next to each other. He's holding her hand and gently rubbing his thumb along her knuckles as they talk quietly about something. She looks so happy in this moment. I just slightly shake my head and chuckle at her before taking my place in the front seat next to Trent as we head over to the next hole.

We're finally nearing the end of our anything but ordinary golf outing. Amy and I have consumed enough alcohol to tranquilize an elephant.

Does that make any sense?

Sure it does. Everything makes sense after you've been drinking for several hours straight. Trent and James were tied throughout most of the game, but my sexy man managed to pull out the win by a few strokes. Amy and I demanded that they stop keeping track of our scores because it was a huge waste of time. She quit after the ninth hole, and I managed to lose a disturbing amount of golf balls throughout the course. My voice is actually hoarse from yelling, "Fore!" after every shot.

I'm definitely more of a mini-putt kind of girl.

Trent and James take us back to the country club where we will have a nice sit-down meal with everyone at the event. Amy is overwhelmingly giggly and clingy at the moment, and I'm concerned of the possible scenarios that could occur during this meal. My fingers and toes are crossed while I simultaneously pray that she manages to keep her shit together and not act like a boozed-up idiot in front of our coworkers. This, I know, is a shot in the dark, but I'm trying to keep a positive perspective on the situation. Luckily, James seems to be handling her pretty well at the moment. He keeps her laughing while concurrently managing to keep her from yelling drunken obscenities at everyone we pass. That's kind of her thing—the "I'm going to yell incomprehensible words of drunkenness at you" thing. Don't ask me why. It just is.

"Trent, I'm going to head to the restroom for a moment. Mind keeping an eye out?" I nod my head towards an unsuspecting Amy. Trent just gestures a *yes* in return as he asks that adorable boy from earlier, Jailbait, to put the clubs in his truck.

As I walk under the elegant awning that encompasses the clubhouse, I notice my ex-fiancé, John, standing near the front doors. He's having an animated conversation with Veronica. Yes, *that* Veronica, or Loose-Lips McGee as I warmly enjoy calling her.

Normally this situation would have my chest hurting and bile rising from my stomach, but I'm relieved to not feel overwhelmed by those feelings. The feelings of heartache and anger—the very feelings that nearly ate me alive only a few short months ago. I know that this has everything to do with Trent. He's been more than just a pleasant surprise; he's the surprise of a lifetime. He's like the winning lottery ticket, Olympic gold medal, and Nobel Prize wrapped up in one beautiful package with a giant red bow.

Can I pass that last comment off as the alcohol?

Yeah…didn't think so.

The feelings I have for him are overwhelming but in a wonderful, amazing, fan-fucking-tastic kind of way. Am I getting close to being able to say I'm in love with him? Maybe. The only thing that is holding me back is the fear I have. The fear that I'm falling too fast. The fear of letting myself jump head first and him not being able to catch me. What John did to me was devastating, heart-crushing even, but what Trent could do to me… I don't think I could survive something like that.

I continue to walk past John and Veronica, and I can't help but notice their discussion is actually an argument. This argument seems to be slightly heated for this type of occasion. I'm surprised that John is even allowing this conversation to occur and risk other people overhearing them. He is all about appearances and maintaining a perfect persona.

I feel his eyes on me as I head in towards the bathroom but maintain my composure and avoid making eye contact. I know this is for the best. Maybe someday I'll actually be on speaking terms with him, but we are a long way off from that. Our best bet is to continue living our lives and moving forward. We are no longer a part of each other anymore.

As I'm washing my hands and attempting to fix my hair a little in the mirror, I see Veronica burst in through the bathroom doors and lock herself in one of the stalls. Tears were streaming down her face and she was visibly upset by whatever conversation had occurred between her and John. I feel a little bad for her—*just a little*—but I really don't think it's my place to ask her what's wrong. I figure I'll let one of her close friends know she's in here and encourage them to go check on her.

I mean, at least I'm nice enough to do that, right?

It's not like I owe her anything. She did bang my fiancé—in my bed. I think that kind of gives me a free pass in terms of not being responsible for giving her a shoulder to cry on.

I walk out of the restroom and notice John leaning against the wall with an annoyed look on his face. He looks stressed and slightly older. His eyes aren't as bright as they used to be. He starts to smile at me but then thinks better of it.

"Hey, Elle. How are you?" He is looking at me with caution, almost like he's afraid I'm going to go off on a rampage.

"Hi, John. I'm great. How are you?" I lean on the wall next to him and give him a friendly smile.

"You look great, Elle. Really, you do. I've been better." His expression is sad and slightly off. His attempt at showing happiness isn't all that successful.

"Thanks. You look stressed. I hope your night gets better." I pat him gently on the shoulder and realize that touching him no longer evokes any type of intimate feelings within me. Contact with him doesn't seem to bring out any type of emotion from me. Being close to him, talking to him doesn't remind me of the past. It just allows me to open my heart up to the future, to the possibilities of finding the right relationship, the right person to spend the rest of my life with.

"Thanks." He hesitates for a minute, looking down at his shoes, and then glances back up at me. "So you're making a go of it with Trent?" He's waiting for my reaction. He's trying to figure out just how serious Trent and I are.

"Yeah, I guess you could say that. Trent and I are definitely making a go of it." I can't help the grin that spreads across my face with the mention of Trent's name from my lips. John frowns slightly and runs his fingers through his tousled brown hair, frustration radiating off of him.

"That's really great, Elle. I guess it's time I started to move on, huh? I guess it's time I realized that I made the single biggest mistake of my life and there's no way you'll ever take me back." He pauses for a moment and takes a shuddering breath. "Ellie, I just want you to be happy. I really hope you're happy." John's eyes are filled with tears as he steps toward me and kisses my forehead softly before walking away.

I let out the breath I didn't realize I was holding and lean back against the wall.

Did I just hallucinate that entire conversation?

I'm unknowingly shaking my head and sighing in what seems to be relief. Relief that John has realized it's time to move on, relief that we were able to have a civil discussion without one of us yelling, and most of all, relief that even with his admission of still wanting me, I am one hundred percent certain that I am over John Ryan. He no longer owns my heart.

Someone else has my heart now. Someone who walked into my life at a very unexpected yet perfect moment. Someone who makes me laugh and smile, and someone who has my pulse racing at just the thought of his lips pressed against mine. Someone who embraces me for everything I am—even the flaws. Trent doesn't put me down or try to change me. He seems to like Elle just the way she is.

I lightly touch my lips with my index finger as I reminisce about the last time Trent kissed me; I can still feel his warm, supple mouth on mine.

My face is beaming as I glance up to see Trent walking towards me. His blue eyes are tender and taking me in. His demeanor is sweet and loving as he flashes a grin in my direction. Trent comes up beside me and pulls me in for a gentle hug. My cheek is pressed against his chest as I inhale his scent. He's sweet and spicy with an undertone of sexiness. Like ginger, cedar, and clean laundry all rolled into one.

"Are you sniffing me?" Trent laughs into my hair.

"Yes, I'm sniffing you. I could just sit here and sniff you all day long. You're like a combination of Christmas, sex, and rugged, manly hotness."

Trent starts to laugh harder as he pulls me in tighter.

"God, you crack my ass up, little spitfire." He leans back and looks into my eyes, gently brushing strands of my auburn hair out of my face. "Do you realize how much you make me laugh? You're so damn adorable and yet, you manage to be ridiculously sexy at the same. Do you even know how much you turn me on? I've been walking around in a constant state of blue balls since the other night when our date was interrupted."

I stand up on my tiptoes and press my lips to his. "You're making me fall in love with you."

Did I really say that? Fuck, I said that, didn't I?

I close my eyes in anticipation of Trent's response. Alcohol sure has a way of making me lay out all of my feelings.

Fucking feelings.

Stupid, fucking feelings and my stupid emotional inner monologues…

"Open your eyes, Ellie." Trent's husky voice and sweet breath washes over me. I slowly open my eyes and the expression on his face nearly knocks me on my ass.

He's beautiful.

His face is warm and embracing every part of me. He's drinking me in with every blink of his eyes, almost like…like he feels the exact same way. He looks like he's falling hard, too—falling faster than he has ever fallen before.

"I'm falling in love with you too, sweetheart. I know you're scared, and I know the shit that dickless douchebag put you through has you doing everything in your power to never go through something like that again, but I'm not him, baby. Don't run from it. Fall with me. Be with me, Ellie. I want to give you every part of myself. I want to be the reason you wake up every day with a smile on your beautiful face. *God, Ellie.* You own me. You fucking have me by the balls and I don't even care."

No one has ever said anything to me like this. Trent just laid everything out there.

All. Of. It.

He just jumped. Put himself out there without even knowing how I would take his words. The words that just took a giant piece of my heart and held it hostage. The words that just sealed my fate. The very fate that includes loving Trent Hamilton, because right now, I do…

I love Trent Hamilton.

I grab Trent by the back of the neck and sharply crash my lips to his. He pulls my hips closer as our tongues entwine. I'm attempting to show him just how much he owns me through this kiss, because Trent Hamilton owns me. He owns every single part of me, and I don't think I'll ever recover from this. I know there are unknowns about our future. Trent is just supposed to be temporarily in Charlotte, but I just can't seem to find the strength to care about this huge dilemma. I'm melting into this kiss, this wonderful, awe-inspiring, toe-curling kiss.

Trent pulls back, trying to slow his breathing. "Ellie, Let's go. Let's get out of here. I can't wait a second longer to be inside of you."

Yes, let's go. Right. Now.

And with that statement, I grab Trent's hand and quickly pull him back into the clubhouse that is already set up for a nice dinner. A dinner that Trent and I will most definitely not be attending. I walk towards our assigned table and see James and Amy sitting down, still visibly enjoying each other's company.

"Hey, James, I need you to take Amy home tonight, okay?" I ask, unable to ignore the ridiculous grin that is spreading across Amy's face.

"Yeah, no problem." James slides his arm around Amy's shoulder.

"What's got you two kids in a big rush? You heading home to play hide the salami?" Amy questions unabashedly. I hear Trent chuckle behind me and feel him pull my hips back toward him. He is harder than stone and causing my body to tremble from his close proximity. My panties are already wet at the feel of his cock against my ass.

"Don't worry, Amy. Ellie and I are going to do more than just play hide the salami. I'm taking her back to my place tonight and you probably shouldn't expect to see her until late tomorrow, if not the day after that." My insides clench at the mere idea of having more than twenty-four hours to be with a very naked Trent.

"Bye, Amy! Bye, James!" I yell behind me as Trent hurriedly escorts me out of the clubhouse and toward his truck. He quickly helps me inside and practically peels out of the parking lot.

Oh hell yessssssssssssssss.

Chapter Nineteen

"When a hot guy instructs you to lie naked and spread-eagle on his bed, you follow those orders without a second thought and let him give your vagina some good old fashion face-time."

We manage to make it to his apartment in record time. I swear Trent was driving over ninety miles per hour the entire way, swerving in and out of traffic like a man on a mission—a one-man mission straight to my cock-pocket. I kept attempting to unzip his pants so I could feel him hard in my hands, but he put the kibosh on that.

"Don't even think about getting my cock out before we get home or else I'll pull over and fuck you in the bed of this truck, and I won't give a shit who sees us."

If that doesn't make you cream your panties, I'm not sure what would. Trent kept sliding his hand up and down my thigh, brushing his fingers over the apex of my sex, and then rubbing soft circles on my clit through my panties.

We're in the elevator now, and my back is pressed against the wall, my hands clenched tightly together. I'm struggling to be a good girl and wait until we make it inside his condo before I start attacking him like a sex-starved woman.

"Ah, fuck it," Trent says before quickly pushing the stop button on the elevator and tenaciously pushing himself against me. "I can't wait another minute. I have to be inside of you. *Right. Now.* I need to feel your tight, wet pussy around my cock more than I need my next breath." He makes quick work of his zipper and has my skirt around my waist faster than I could say, "Thrust me hard, Dr. Hamilton!"

He slides my panties to the side as he wraps my legs around his waist and plunges himself inside of me. He is thick and hard and deep—oh so deliciously deep. His hands are gripping my ass, and I clench tightly around him. Within an instant I'm lusciously full. I'm dripping wet from my arousal, and this only spurs my instinctual sexual desires to take over. My hands are frenzied, grabbing him, touching him, running my fingers all over his body.

And then he stops. *Stops moving*. Stops his delicious rhythm inside of me.

"FUCK," Trent groans out and his eyebrows pull in. "Ellie…" He takes a choppy breath. "I can't believe I started this without a condom." He rests his forehead against mine in frustration.

"It's o-okay," I pant against his mouth. "I'm on birth control. Have been for years." I urge his hips closer to mine with my heels.

"Fuck, Ellie. You make me crazy. You make me lose all control. I've *never* not used a condom, and yet with you, I just completely forgot…about everything. All I could think about was getting inside of you." His eyes are remorseful, almost as if he feels like he's betrayed me.

I place my hand on his cheek and lock my gaze with his. "You make me crazy, too. And I've never been *with anyone* without a condom— even my ex. I can't believe you can get me so worked up that all rational thought just leaves the building." I grin at him and rub my nose against his. "So uh…how about we get back to the crazy…*you're still inside of me*…and *I'm still wet*…so please…*please* keep fucking me."

Trent lets out a rough growl as he slowly pulls out a few inches and then slams back inside of me, my back roughly hitting the elevator wall. And with that, my hands are all over him again, grasping every inch of his muscular body as he kisses up and down my neck. His breath is hot in my ear, causing delicious shivers up my spine.

Oh god yes.

Deeper. Harder.

Trent's large hands tightly clutching my ass as he continues to push inside of me, getting back that lusciously perfect rhythm. Each thrust brings me closer to climax. Each thrust has me moaning and panting and nearly screaming his name. My breathing is embarrassingly loud and echoing throughout the small elevator cart.

"Trent! Yes! Oh yes! Right there! Oh my god, right there!" I moan out with a raspy voice. My lips are pressed against his shoulder and I fight my urge to scream by roughly biting him through his shirt. My hands are tightly clasping his neck and I'm scratching my nails down his back from the intense feeling of his cock filling me to the hilt. He's stretching me, filling me, urging me closer with each thick penetration.

"Better than I could have ever imagined. Being inside of you, feeling you scratch your nails down my back and tremble in my arms is the best fucking thing I've ever experienced," Trent groans into my neck before using his teeth to pull down my shirt past my bra then doing that same sexy move to slide my bra down past my breast, exposing my pebbled nipple to his lustful eyes. He slides the flat part of his tongue across my nipple, swirling the tip. Around and around… My full breast fills his mouth, his tongue working me over.

My hips jerk involuntarily, and I'm whimpering into his neck as Trent sucks me hard into his mouth and proceeds to drive himself in and out of me at a feverish pace.

A devastating pace.

A pace that has me screaming his name. He quiets me by bringing his lips back to mine and nipping my lip with his teeth. I roughly suck his tongue into my mouth at the same rhythm that his shaft is moving in and out of my sex. I'm so wet, so pleasurably wet. My arousal is dripping down his balls as he continues to slam into me, his sac smacking against my ass.

The sound of skin against skin fills the small space. The scents of Trent and me, sex, and sweat fill my nose as I try to breathe in deeply. I'm trying like hell to hold back my impending orgasm, to prolong this intoxicating moment. My climax is so close; I'm nearly falling over that bliss-filled abyss toward that beautiful moment when your orgasm takes control. The moment when you're shuddering and trembling and you can't form coherent thought. When your eyes roll back and your lips part as screams of desire escape your throat.

I can feel the delightful tingles starting from deep within and working upwards toward my spine. I clench tightly around Trent and he brings his eyes to mine, looking deep, so deep, like he's claiming my soul with just one look.

He owns me. He fucking owns me.

"You fucking own me. God, I'm so close, Trent. I don't want to come yet," I rasp with desire.

"You're mine. Don't hold back, Ellie. Come for me. Let me feel that sweet pussy clench around my cock and your cum dripping down my thighs. Let me hear you, baby," Trent says into my lips.

My eyes involuntarily close as my head falls back against the elevator wall.

"*Open.* Keep them open. Let me see you. Let me see how beautiful you look when I'm making you come."

I open my eyes and stare into Trent's as my orgasm washes over me. My lips are parted, breasts heaving up and down, as I pant through each euphoric wave of passion that rolls through me. Trent's eyes are locked on mine as he fills me deeper and deeper, pushing my orgasm past the brink of control, urging my mouth to scream out his name.

"Trent! Yes!" I'm yelling out incomprehensible things as Trent slides his thumb down my stomach and starts to rub smooth circles around my clit. He crashes his lips to mine as he prolongs my climax with each thrust, each soft circle on my clit, and each lick of his tongue inside my mouth.

Whatever I imagined sex with Trent would be like for the first time is not even close to the kind of un-fucking-believable type of experience he is giving me right now. I have never been ravaged and fucked so perfectly by any man before, and yet, somehow, Trent manages to do this while still making love to me. Because that is what Trent Hamilton is doing to me right now. He is fucking and making love to me.

Fucking making love to me. Making fucking love to me.

You get the idea.

Trent stills inside of me and he is still hard as steel. He has yet to come and slowly sets me down on my feet and adjusts my skirt before tucking his still-hard cock into his pants. I'm looking at him curiously as he gets the elevator to start moving again and we reach his floor.

"Don't look at me like that, sweetheart. We've got a long night ahead of us. A *long* night that includes us naked and my cock, buried deep inside of you for *hours.*" Trent looks at me seductively before wrapping his arm around my waist, leading me out of the elevator and toward his apartment.

I can't help but giggle a little at the giant tent he has on display. I could use his cock for a coat rack right now.

"You think this is funny?" He glances down at his crotch before opening his apartment door with his keys.

"I'm finding your situation extremely funny. I think I could hang my purse from that thing."

And with that, I attempt to dangle my purse from Trent's ever-apparent erection. He laughs a little as he steps back from me before swiftly spanking my ass.

"Hey!" I yelp. The sting of his hand on my ass has my vagina already dripping with need. My snatch is nearly creaming herself at the thought of Trent's hard cock thrusting vigorously. My inner sex-goddess does a little happy dance of excitement because she knows that tonight... *It's fucking on.*

"Get that sexy ass naked and lying spread-eagle on my bed. I'm starving and I know just what's on the menu." He winks at me before spanking my ass again, and I pick up the pace to his room. I'm good at following orders, especially when my pussy is on the to-be-eaten menu.

And tonight, my pussy is the appetizer, entree, and dessert.

Chapter Twenty

"When you say 'Let's christen the kitchen,' my only response will be, 'Where shall we start? Appliances? Counter tops? The kitchen table?'"

My eyelids flutter at the feel of warm sunlight across my face. I feel someone let out a sigh of contentment next to me as he wraps his arms around my waist, pulling my back against his chest. I inwardly beam as memories of last night flash through my mind. Trent and I spent hours getting acquainted with each other. He turned me inside out with the most incredible sex I've ever experienced. His mouth and tongue found their way to every single part of my lust-filled body, and he showed me that he is not only skilled in the OR. Trent Hamilton's mouth has the ability to bring me to several orgasms in record time. I'm not sure how he acquired his mad oral skills, but I should probably send a thank-you card to someone, because seriously, Trent Hamilton is incredible. And as far as the sex goes, he deserves a lifetime supply of blow jobs for the dicking he gave me last night.

"Are you awake, Ellie girl?" Trent whispers sleepily in my ear and then kisses my neck tenderly with his full, soft lips.

"Mmmmmm," I moan quietly. The feel of his lips on one of my most sensitive erogenous zones has me craving more of his touch.

"Is that a '*Yes I'm awake, Trent, so please keep kissing on me*'?" He leans up and puts his chin on my shoulder, gently rubbing his lips against my bare skin.

"Mmmmhmmmm." Chill bumps immediately spread across my naked body.

"Are you speechless, little spitfire, or just too tired from all the sex I gave you last night to give me actual words?" I can feel his mouth grin against the back of my neck as he delicately rubs his nose back and forth, causing more chill bumps to spur.

"Mmmmmhmmmm." I attempt to hide my smile.

"I think you need some help waking up. I think…" Trent quickly moves his hands to my sides and starts to tickle across my rib cage.

"Ahhh! Stop it!" I'm trying like hell to squirm out of his touch, but his muscular arms have a vice-like grip around me. He's relentless in his pursuit as he continues his tickle assault all over my body.

Trent releases his hold on me and gets up on his knees, straddling my hips with both thighs. He is deliciously naked, and seems *really* excited to see me. "Let's see… Where are my Ellie girl's most ticklish spots?" He explores my body with his hands, gently tickling his fingers in random areas, making me fidget and squirm.

I'm wiggling around, desperately trying to move out from under him, because I've always been extremely ticklish. I once tried to get a massage at a local spa and had to end the session early because I could not stop squirming and laughing every time the masseuse put her hands near me. I should make it clear that she ended the session, promptly giving me a refund, and demanded that I *never* schedule another massage with her again under any circumstances.

"Okay! Okay! I give up! What do I have to do to get you to stop before I piss all over your bed?" I giggle out in a breathy voice.

"Piss all over my bed?" Trent immediately stops tickling me and begins shaking with laughter. I can't help but notice that his dick is still hard and bouncing up and down against my stomach. My eyes are locked on his beautiful shaft, and I feel a rush of excitement wet the tops of my thighs, which are now tightly pressed together.

Trent clears his throat and I pull my gaze back to his.

"You hungry for something, sweetheart?" His brow is arched; his smile is laced with a cross of amusement and lust.

A laugh bubbles up from my belly and escapes my throat. "I think I am, Casanova." I squelch the laughter and give him a serious, determined look.

"Mmmm, I like that look." He leans down and grasps my face in his hands, pressing his mouth to mine, probing his tongue past my lips. Our tongues entangle, and Trent grinds his erection against me through the sheets. I spread my legs, giving him better access.

"Turn over, sweetheart." Trent kneels above me, giving me room to follow his command. I promptly turn over, leaving my ass uncovered from the sheets. He grabs each cheek with his strong, muscular hands and massages my ass with deep, smooth strokes. "Your ass is fantastic. Tight, soft, and just enough curve for me to grab on to."

"I'm glad you approve." I turn my head to the side and peek back at him.

"I more than approve. I fucking worship your ass." He stops

moving his hands and gazes at me.

"Please, don't let me interrupt the worshipping. Carry on." I gesture with my hand.

Trent laughs huskily at my demands. "Carry on? My little spitfire is bossy today." Smirking back at me, he spanks my ass hard and then hops up off of the bed.

"Hey! Where in the hell are you going? I was enjoying that!" I turn around on my back and unabashedly watch his sexy ass strut around the bedroom, grabbing a pair of boxer briefs. He leans down and slides them on, the lean muscles in his back stretching and rippling.

God, his body is ridiculous.

"You said you were hungry. I'm headed to the kitchen to make you something to eat." He winks at me and then heads for the door, walking out of the bedroom and into the hallway.

"I'm not hungry for food! I'm hungry for your cock!" I yell out to him, my voice echoing throughout the apartment. I hear Trent chuckle, and his footsteps continue to work their way toward the kitchen.

"Rise and shine, baby! My cock is in the kitchen now!" Trent shouts back to me, laughter lacing his voice.

Well, shit. I guess it's time we christen his kitchen. I decide that this idea is the best idea I've had since I woke up this morning and hop out of bed, jogging into the hallway naked. My boobs are bouncing up and down as my feet make their way to Trent's kitchen. He is standing at the island, cutting up fruit, and his eyes find mine when he sees me heading towards him. His eyes go straight to my breasts; he seems to be enjoying their current active state.

"Nope! One more lap around the apartment!" Setting his cutting knife down on the marble island, Trent motions for me to turn around and continue jogging around naked.

I laugh and continue moving towards him.

"You *would* want me to keep running around this apartment with my tits bouncing all over the place, pervy."

I hop on Trent's back and wrap my legs around his waist. He turns his face back to mine, giving my lips perfect access to dive into his mouth. I savor the lovely taste of strawberries on his tongue.

"You taste good, baby. I just want you for breakfast." My lips quirk up in a devilish grin.

Trent takes a few steps back and my ass bumps against one of his spacious kitchen counters. I lift up a little and sit down, my legs dangling down, feet tapping against the bottom cabinets. He turns around and stands between my naked thighs.

"I think I want to enjoy you right here on my kitchen counter. This kitchen is due for a good christening." Trent wraps his arms around my waist, pulling me flush against his cotton brief-clad pelvis.

"Due for a christening? Are you saying, 'Since you're a woman and I haven't fucked anyone on this counter, I think you'll work for this occasion'?" I raise an eyebrow and wait for his response.

"No. I'm saying that you're *my* woman, my *only* woman. The woman I'm head over heels for. The woman who's got me tied up in knots and I love every fucking minute of it. The woman who owns me. The only woman my cock is aching to christen this kitchen with."

Oh my.

I abruptly grab his face and pull his lips to mine. My kiss is desperate, deep, rough, and begging for him to fuck me right here on this kitchen counter. I pull his boxer briefs down, his cock springing free. Wrapping my hand firmly around his shaft, I start to stroke him leisurely, enjoying the feel of him in my grasp. He groans into my mouth and nips my bottom lip with his teeth. Moving his face away from mine to nuzzle my neck, Trent starts sucking and nibbling my earlobe, causing a shiver to rush through my body. He presses open-mouth kisses all along my jaw line as he lightly thrusts his now *very* hard cock in and out of my grip with short, smooth movements as I continue to caress him with my hand.

I quiver at the feel of Trent's lips and tongue on my collarbone. My body is trembling in frantic need for his touch. I want his hands on my breasts, my pussy, and my ass. I want his mouth kissing my lips, rubbing across my nipples, suckling at my clit. I want him doing a thousand different things to me all at once. I want him everywhere, on me, in me, behind me, over me, under me...

I start to lick and caress my way down his chest. Sexy, firm pectoral muscles and rippled, washboard abs. I trace my index finger of my other hand over the V muscle that my tongue craves to lick for hours. Lustfully gazing up at Trent, I continue to slide my tongue along the muscular contours of his body. "Mmmm I love the taste of your skin on the tip of my tongue. It's absolute heaven." Trent growls at my words.

I watch with euphoric eyes, my hand moving up and down on his length. I'm craving to put my mouth on him and find myself pushing off of the kitchen counter and getting on my knees.

"Wha...What are you doing?" Trent is looking down at me with surprise.

He shudders when he feels my tongue, mouth, and hands moving down his body. His cock twitches against my breasts with each long, torturing swipe of my tongue as I move southward.

"Shit, Elle," Trent groans.

I lick my lips at the sight of him. "I'm going to fuck you with my mouth." I say each word slowly, with absolute precision.

My eyes pierce his as I slip the tip of his cock into my mouth, slowly swirling my tongue around. He jerks at the feel of my lips around his length. "Mmmmmmmmmmmm." I hum around his shaft as I slowly take him entirely, engulfing him with my willingness. My willingness... and my want—my *need*—to pleasure him, to bring him to climax, to watch him come inside of my mouth.

"Ah, Elle..." Trent slides his hands into my hair as I continue to take him deep. I feel his hands start to clench tighter into my hair as I continue to suck him to the back of my throat and then slowly pull away. I hear his breath hitch and I feel a gush of arousal touch my thighs.

I glance up and see Trent's eyes nearly roll into the back of his head when the tip of his shaft hits the back of my throat. I continue to bob my head up and down on his entire length while stroking his balls with my hand. I'm undeniably turned on by the sight of Trent's enraptured expression. The pleasure I'm giving him, bringing him closer to euphoria, is so hot. I insert two fingers into my slick heat; I'm swollen and dripping wet.

Trent watches me with a heated stare, and his eyes lock onto the two fingers sliding in and out of my aching core. He attempts to push his hips away from me, but I quickly take my hands and grasp his ass, firmly pressing his cock past my lips.

"Elle, baby, I can't take much more."

I pull back so my lips are still wrapped around the head of his shaft. "Come in my mouth, Trent. I *need* to taste you."

"Oh, god! Ellie...I'm so close!" he hisses through clenched teeth, and I feel the tip of his cock get even harder, letting me know he is almost there.

I purr at the sight of Trent crying out in ecstasy. I vigorously suck him while involuntary mewling sounds escape my throat.

"Yes!" His head falls back and his hands clench tighter into my auburn hair. I swallow his cum greedily as Trent continues to spurt his seed. He stares down at me as he continues to make small, slow thrusts, and it's the hottest thing I've ever seen.

Moaning, shuddering, lips parted, breathing heavily and eyes filled with rhapsody. I smile around him and lick every last drop of cum from the tip.

"God, you're amazing." Pulling me up by my arms and hugging me tightly to his chest, Trent leans back and looks deep into my eyes before placing tender, reverent kisses on my lips.

"I think I'm in love with you, beautiful girl."

I smile against his insistent mouth.

"I think I'm in love with you too."

I can't ignore the rush of fear that fills my gut when those words slip past my lips. I'm scared shitless.

Scared and happy.

Afraid and excited.

Worried and overjoyed.

My mind and my heart might as well be at war with themselves.

Before any more thoughts or emotions cross my mind, Trent hurriedly kisses the worry, the fear, and the nearly overwhelming anxiety away. He pushes all the negativity out of my head with the feel of his lips against mine, his warm hands embracing me.

Chapter Twenty-One

"Superhero cocks don't fuck around. They mean business."

I'm sitting on Trent's kitchen island, my legs crossed, dressed in one of his old college t-shirts and pair of black cotton panties. My hair is a disaster—evidence of the hot, vigorous sex Trent and I have engaged in all morning. A strand of my auburn locks falls down across my face and I try to blow it out of the way, failing miserably. Trent chuckles at my laziness as he uses chopsticks to dig into one of the many Chinese take-out containers strewn across the granite marble counter top. I roll my eyes as I languidly tuck the errant hair behind my ear.

Sitting on one of the wooden barstools with his shoulder leaning against my leg, Trent might as well be a god damn cover model. Sometimes I wonder if he realizes how fuckable he looks on a daily basis. Right now, Trent Hamilton is *fuckable.*

So fucking fuckable.

He's dressed in only a pair of grey boxer briefs, and his hair is still damp from the quick shower he took after round…four, I think? I've honestly lost count of how times my O-face has made an appearance today.

I'm starting to develop a habit of licking my lips whenever Trent's sexy ass is strutting around. He's downright delicious and he seems to cause my brain to malfunction, turning me into a twenty-eight-year-old with constant ladyboners and a propensity for licking her lips like she's a fucking dog watching its owner eat a giant, juicy cheeseburger.

Note to self: Buy Chapstick.

I think he might make me a drool a little bit, too. Not one hundred percent certain of this, but wait, let me check… Yep, I'm officially drooling on myself.

Add extra paper towels to my grocery list.

I discreetly wipe the small dribble that is hanging off of my lip and pray that I manage to do this without Trent noticing. I peek over at him out of the corner of my eye and thankfully he's still savoring his Kung Pao chicken. Seriously, this man is consuming my head and turning me into a lick-lipping, ladyboner-sporting, mouth-drooling, cock-craving, bumbling idiot. I'm blaming this on him.

Trent Hamilton and his Hamiltonian Effect.

Yes, the Hamiltonian Effect. This is an actual thing. At least it is now, and I know this from experience because I got the full Technicolor experience last night. And let me tell you, Trent is hands down the best sex I've ever had. He puts new meaning to the phrase, "Take me to Pound Town."

After eighteen straight hours of getting *acquainted* with him, I've come to one conclusion. His cock is a superhero. That mind-blowing piece of equipment deserves its own secret headquarters, cape, covert car, superhero side-kick, and independent wealth to purchase the giant mansion with a cave that he can fill with all of his superhero gadgets.

"What has your mind so entertained right now?" The sound of his voice encourages my eyes to wander towards his as I take another bite of chicken fried rice.

"Huh? What makes you think my mind is *so entertained* right now?" I place my chopsticks down next to me and my arms rest in my lap.

"The small smirk you keep flashing. What filthy thoughts are rolling through that head of yours?"

"I have a suspicion that your cock is a superhero." My face is blank, giving him zero inkling of my actual intent.

"My cock *is* a superhero." Trent has his poker face on, which only encourages me to continue this conversation further.

"Yes, I know your cock is a superhero. What's your superhero cock's name?"

"Dr. Hammer." He's still straight-faced and doing one hell of a job at hiding his satisfaction regarding the whole superhero-cock topic.

Dr. Hammer? Really?

I mean, it's so lame yet so awesome at the same time.

"What's Dr. Hammer's superpower?" I challenge him with a quirk of my eyebrow.

"He's a take-action kind of guy. A doer, so to speak. Dr. Hammer has no qualms with thrusting himself into dirty situations, and his superpower is *satisfaction*. Dr. Hammer can one hundred percent ensure one hundred and ten percent of the time that he always gives *satisfaction*. No matter the job, no matter the task, Dr. Hammer will leave you satisfied."

"Seriously? Did you seriously just come up with that on the fly or have you had that stocked away somewhere?"

"What can I say? I'm quick on my feet." He finally drops the poker face and gives me a wicked grin. "Are you satisfied with Dr. Hammer's superpower?"

"Nope. I think Dr. Hammer is a fucking liar. He should be satisfying me right now and yet, there he sits, not satisfying." I flick my wrist toward the crotch of his boxer briefs.

Trent abruptly grabs my feet, pulling my legs to the edge of the kitchen counter. He licks his lips at the sight of my legs spread open and black panties visible to his sensual gaze. I quickly smack his hands away from my thighs. "I'm kidding! I'm kidding! My vagina needs a break. You've been pounding her all day." Trent's husky laugh vibrates from his chest as he swiftly moves his hands away from my persistent smacks.

"Just so we're clear, Dr. Hammer is going to make you pay for that little joke later."

I laugh at his ridiculous threat. "Okay, weirdo. Give my pussy like an hour and I'll be ready for the wrath that is Dr. Hammer and his satisfying superhero cock powers."

We continue to dig into our Chinese food, giving each other small bites here and there. I'm enjoying his company immensely. I love the easiness of our relationship. Our conversation always flows, and we seem to savor the occasional silences together. Being with Trent just seems to come natural for me. There's no pressure to be someone I'm not. No pressure to put on a perfect appearance or stress over saying the wrong things. Trent makes me feel like I can just be me...*Ellen*.

Taking the last bite of my chicken fried rice and swallowing it down, I tap Trent on the nose with my chopsticks and ask him a question I keep forgetting to bring up. "How old are you?"

"Thirty-four."

"Shiiiiit, you're thirty-four?"

"What the hell is that supposed to mean? You say that like it's really old. I'm not old. I'm a young, hot surgeon you can't seem to keep your hands off of." He smirks at me before standing up and cleaning up our take-out containers.

"Well...thirty-four is *kind of* old, but it's okay. I think your ego more than makes up for the old age and wrinkles."

"Shut up, smartass." His back is to me as he tosses our silverware in the kitchen sink, washing them off before placing them in the dishwasher.

"Aren't you going to ask me how old I am?"

"Twenty-eight." He closes the dishwasher and turns towards me, leaning against the counter, crossing his arms across his chest while a smug grin consumes his face.

"Uh, how did you know how old I am? Have you been snooping through my purse? Stalking me? Following me? Which is it? Do I need to call the police?" My eyes dance with hilarity.

"I stalked you when I first started at Regency. I *had* to know who the hot nurse with the fuck-me heels was in Nashville."

"What do you mean you s*talked* me?"

"I got your manager Shirley to dish some dirt on you. Your age, work schedule… You know, all the important stuff so I could begin my seduction of *The Infamous Ellen James*."

I laugh a little at the way he says my name as if I'm some sort of enigma instead of just a boring ER nurse with a proclivity for smut novels and hot surgeons with superhero cocks.

"How in the hell did you get Nurse Ratchet to give you details about me? Did you flirt with uni-brow, Trent Hamilton?"

"Yes, yes I did, and I'm not the least bit ashamed of it. I'm blaming it all on the sexy little nurse with perfect tits and that ability to wear a twelve-inch strap-on like no one's business."

"You're never going to let me live that one down, are you?"

"Nope, never, and it doesn't help that I snapped a picture of that slide with my phone and I can look at it whenever I want."

"What?! You have a *picture* of that picture?"

He nods his head yes.

"Oh my god! Give me your phone. We are deleting that right now!" I hop off the island and stalk towards him, frantically grabbing around the back of him where his Blackberry is sitting on the kitchen counter and charging.

He quickly snaps the phone out of the charging dock and holds it above his head.

"Hey! Give that to me! Give that phone to me now!" I'm jumping up and down in an embarrassing attempt to grab the phone from his hands. Trent is standing his ground, holding his Blackberry high in the air while laughter is bursting from his lips. I decide that tickling is my next approach. I speedily place my hands on his ribcage and begin furiously tickling his sides.

"Shit!" Trent squirms out of my reach and tosses his phone on the counter. Then he grabs me before I can manage to get my hands on it. His arms have me in a firm grip and I'm struggling to break free.

"I think it's time your pussy gets ready for Dr. Hammer," he hoots before grabbing my waist and throwing me over his shoulder.

My head is pressed against his back and my legs are firmly in his grasp. He smacks my ass and then heads towards his bedroom, striding through the hallway with purpose.

"I hope you're ready to be satisfied," Trent says and smacks my ass again.

"Oh my god! You're so lame! Enough with the Dr. Hammer and satisfied talk!" I yell as I continue to hang off of his shoulder, my boobs pressed against his back.

Trent chuckles loudly, smacks my ass for a third time, and walks into his bedroom.

He tosses me on the bed and traipses towards me like a predator—a predator that's ready to fuck his prey into a god damn coma. My pussy clenches at the sight of his strong, precise movements, and his eyes have my nipples harder than I ever knew was possible.

"We're not leaving this room until I've fucked you senseless and you have to tell me to stop making you come. Because that's what I'm going to do. I'm going to make you *come* and *come* and *come*… and when you don't think it's possible to have another orgasm, I'm going to eat that delicious pussy like it's my last fucking meal and make you come again."

Ohhhhhhhh, I think Dr. Hammer just gave me a lifetime guarantee.

Chapter Twenty-Two

"If your friend is going through some guy problems, always make sure you gauge her level of anger with this: 'On a scale of 1 to Adele, how pissed off are you at this guy?' If she says, 'Adele,' go ahead and take the matches from her and proceed to drive far, far away from that guy's house…immediately."

Sitting contently in Trent's truck as he's driving me home, I turn down the music that's blaring through the speakers so I can actually manage a conversation with him.

"You can turn on whatever you like." He glances at me out of his periphery as he accelerates onto the highway toward my apartment.

I've been holed up in Trent's apartment for the past thirty-six hours, enjoying his company among many other things. I begrudgingly let him drive me home only because I have to work a night shift in the ER tonight.

"Tell me about the first time you had sex."

Trent sputters a little as he lets out a choking cough, obviously surprised at my request. "You want to hear about when I lost my virginity?" Turning his head towards me for a brief second, he allows me to see the curious amusement in his eyes.

"Yes I do. How old were you? Who was it? Where were you? Tell me everything." I tap my fingers lightly on the passenger door, grinning at him.

"I'll share mine, but only if you share yours." His eyes are back on the road, switching lanes on the highway and passing a slow-moving sedan.

"Deal."

He clears his throat and then begins to tell me all about Tammy, the girl whose vagina stole his virginity. "I was seventeen, and like any teenage boy, I had sex on the brain constantly. My girlfriend's name was Tammy. She was cute, too nice for a horny kid like me, and her father was a pastor. We were alone at her parents' house on a weeknight. I think they were busy at a church function. I'm pretty sure we were supposed to be working on some school project together, but one thing led to another…and then Tammy was lying naked on her bed, nervously ready to have sex. Hell, I was nervous too. Seventeen and not a clue what in the hell I was doing. The sex wasn't the best, being it was our first times, and I came in under a fucking minute, but it's what happened after the sex that makes this story so interesting…"

"Oh I have to hear this!" I turn in my seat so that I'm facing Trent, all ears, ready to listen to whatever comes out of his mouth.

"Well, right after I finished, Tammy's parents came home—"

"What?! Did they walk in on you two? Oh my god, did the pastor find you with your dick out in his daughter's room?!" This story is getting better by the second.

"Not exactly. I had time to throw on my pants, but I was so nervous that I forgot to take the condom off—"

"You left the condom on? The condom that was filled with your teenage spooge?!"

He lets out a husky laugh. "Uh, yeah, I had a very uncomfortable thirty-minute conversation with her pastor father about random bullshit that I can't even remember, and the condom that was in fact filled with my teenage spooge was still on." He looks over at me and smirks.

"Oh my god! That is hilarious!" I'm laughing at the mere idea of this entire jizz-filled condom fiasco.

Shaking his head and running a hand through his hair, he says, "Yeah, I know. Not one of my best moments, yet I can definitely see the hilarity in it. That condom stayed on until I got home. *After* I ate dinner with my parents."

Laughter is bursting from my lips; I clutch my stomach in pure merriment.

Trent gives me a minute or two to calm my jovial ass down before saying, "All right, all right. Enough laughter at my expense. Let's here yours." He gets off at the exit that leads to my apartment.

"Oh god. Mine might be worse."

"Then I definitely need to hear this," he demands with an intrigued tone to his voice.

"Okay." I take a deep breath and then tell him all about Billy…

"I was sixteen and it was prom night. My boyfriend's name was Billy. Things were getting hot and heavy in my friend Tonya's room. We were spending the night at her parent's house. They were, of course, out of town. Cliché I know, but I was sixteen. So I was all prepared to let Billy pop my little cherry and then we realized we forgot one very important thing—*a condom.*"

Grinning over at Trent, I continue on with my story. "Billy drove us to the nearest gas station. It was when he started to get out of the car that I realized he was only wearing boxers, a t-shirt, and socks. No shoes, no pants…" Trent starts chuckling. "I sat in the car patiently like any teenage girl who's waiting to get thrusted for the first time would, and I waited and waited and *waited.* Fifteen minutes went by, and I started to get a little concerned. How damn long did it take to purchase condoms? What in the hell was he buying in there? Then Billy came sprinting out of the gas station, tossed the box of condoms to me, and hopped his shoeless ass in the car, peeling out of the parking lot like a mad man. I remember sitting in the car thinking, *What the fuck is going on?* So I asked him why he was driving like his dick is on fire and he said it was because he'd forgotten his wallet…"

Trent glances over at me and raises his brow. "Forgot his wallet?"

I sigh and finish the story. "Yeah, he forgot his wallet, so he stole the condoms."

"He stole the condoms! Let me get this straight. He had no shoes, no pants, and he STOLE the condoms?!" Trent's chortles are now full belly laughs.

"Yes." My face flushes a little with embarrassment. "You have it straight. That was the infamous night that Ellen James lost her virginity."

"Holy shit! Yours is definitely worse than mine." Trent pulls into the parking lot, still laughing like an idiot, now at my expense.

"All right, all right. That's enough. I'm well aware that is one of the most ridiculous virginity loss stories ever." I give him a pointed stare, letting him know to knock off the laughter.

He winks at me and pats my thigh. "I'm done…for now. I can't make promises that I won't laugh about that one later."

"Preferably when I'm not around," I say with a roll of my eyes.

He parks the truck in a designated spot in front of my apartment and cuts the engine. "You want me to come inside or do you have to get ready for work?"

"I wish I could take you to work with me." I unbuckle my seatbelt and scoot closer to his side. "But you might as well just go on home. I have to get ready for work, and I'm sure Amy is going to berate me with questions about our weekend."

"A fucking fantastic weekend." He brushes the hair out of my eyes and places his palm on my cheek. "Thanks for staying with me."

"Thanks for having me. And I agree, we had a fucking fantastic weekend. Emphasis on the fucking." I give him a sarcastic smile.

"Yes, smartass, a whole lot of emphasis on the fucking." He laughs lightly before leaning in and giving me a sloppy, wet kiss that ends with him licking the side of my face.

"Oh my god! Stop licking me, weirdo!" I act exasperated, but I secretly enjoy his sense of humor and ability to constantly make me smile.

"You love it." His grin is as wide as Texas and I can't fight the urge to smile back at him like an infatuated idiot.

"Yeah, yeah, yeah. I love it. Give me some more sugar, Casanova. This time no licking." I pucker my lips and he gently places his lips to mine, tenderly kissing me.

"Have a good night at work, Ellie, and text me later if your night isn't too busy. I'm on call for the rest of the week so I'm sure we're going to cross paths at Regency at some point."

"Okay." I give him a swift peck on the cheek before hopping out of the truck.

As I head to the lobby door of my building, I notice a disheveled and very dirty-looking man walking out of my apartment's parking lot and toward the main road. His back is to me, but I'd know that man anywhere. That's Frank. ER frequent flyer Frank. I'm praying he didn't see me getting out of Trent's truck, and I have a feeling that I'll probably be seeing him in the ER very, very soon. This poor man has had a lifelong battle with mental illness, his primary diagnosis being paranoid schizophrenia. He's definitely made me feel uncomfortable at times, and he can come across as a total creep, like Amy would say, but I really do feel bad for him. No one should have to suffer through a life that's a constant battle of trying to keep your foot in the door of reality's house while crazy town is constantly trying to pull you right back out to Never Never Land.

As I unlock my apartment door, I can hear Adele's *Rolling In The Deep* blaring from the stereo. I am little concerned about what this could mean. Amy and I have specific music that we play when we are pissed off about a guy. Rihanna when we're slightly pissed off; think angry texts and phone calls. Taylor Swift when we're definitely pissed; think egg his car or toilet paper his house. And Adele, well, she's the big guns, the "I'm going to rip his balls off, make a nice slow cooker meal with them, and then shove said ball-roast down his throat" kind of pissed. Yes, we totally go Hannibal Lector.

Nice Chianti and some fava beans, anyone?

So you can see my concern when not only is Adele blasting from the speakers in my apartment but *Rolling In The Deep* of all songs is playing.

I hesitantly head into my apartment, finding Amy and Lizzy sitting on the living room couch, eating ice cream. Amy is belting out the lyrics of the song like she's singing for a crowd of thousands into her giant ice scream scooper that must be serving dual purposes—spoon and microphone. My sister is just sitting next to her, digging into her pint of chocolate chip cookie dough, seeming to enjoy the impromptu concert that's taking place in my living room. I walk towards the stereo and pause the music.

"*WE COULD HAVE HAD IT*.... Hey! What the hell, Elle?" Amy scowls at me.

"What's going on?"

"Nothing is going on. Lizzy and I are just enjoying some ice cream while we listen to Adele." She avoids my eyes and dips her scooper into the gallon tub of Rocky Road ice cream that is sitting in her lap.

"Don't be an asshole. I know you. And I know what Adele means. Lizzy has plenty of reasons to listen to Adele, but you, I need to hear your reasons." I point my finger at her as my voice raises.

"Stop pointing at me, dickhead!" Amy shouts with a mouth full of ice cream.

"Seriously, what's going on?" I look at Lizzy.

"James pissed Amy off—" Lizzy starts to say before Amy throws a pissed look her way, promptly causing her to shut her mouth.

"What happened with James?" I look back to Amy, impatiently tapping my foot. I need to hear this story and I only have a short time before I have to get ready for work.

"James... Nothing happened with James. Let's hear about your night with Trent! Did he bang your brains out?!"

"Yes, he did, in fact, *bang my brains out*, but you're not off the hook. Spill it, Amy, or else I'll be worrying about you all night when I'm at work." I'm trying to use the guilt factor to entice her into telling me what in the hell happened with James. I mean, it seemed like she was really hitting it off with him.

Amy sighs heavily and looks down at her ice cream, stirring her scooper through the melted cream on top. "He's an asshole, all right? A total dickhead douchebag and I don't ever want to speak to him again. He turned my pussy down! My pussy! My perfectly groomed, hot, sweet, tight—"

I cut her off before she starts to give me exact measurements of her labia. "He turned you down?"

"Yeah, Dr. Limp Dick turned me down. I basically threw myself at him, and he just dropped me off at our apartment." Oh god, she's already nicknamed him. This is worse than I thought.

"I don't get it. You two seemed like you were hitting it off before Trent and I left the country club." I'm definitely taken aback by this, but I feel like there's a piece of this story that's missing.

"Yeah, apparently my vagina was too drunk for his liking. Fucking dickhead…" Amy grumbles into her ice cream, and now I just got that missing piece. I swear, sometimes Amy just can't seem to grasp the big picture, especially when it comes to men. She's pissed off at James for refusing to have sex with her because she was too intoxicated. I think I just gained a hell of a lot of respect for that man. If I had more time, I'd sit down, chat with Amy, and try to get her to open her fucking eyes, but work calls.

"Can we finish this conversation tomorrow? I have to get ready for work."

"Sure. I can't wait to rehash how some guy refused to make boom-boom with my so-called 'drunken vagina,'" Amy rolls her eyes dramatically as she uses her fingers for air quotes.

Looks like I'm going to have my work cut out for me with this situation.

Chapter Twenty-Three

"My bright idea came to me one night, deep inside my rectum...said no one ever."

"Ellen, I just placed a patient in bed two," Trudy says as she sets the chart down in front of me. "I should warn you... It's Katy." I sigh heavily before grabbing Katy's giant chart and glancing up at Trudy. She's one of our emergency room registrars, and the fact that even she knows who Katy is should tell you that the ER might as well be this woman's second home.

Katy Parson is a thorn in my side. A raging yeast infection inside my snatch; a cluster of hemorrhoids in my ass. No joke. She's a thirty-year-old woman whose presence of facial hair and absence of proper hygiene has a strong resemblance to Chewbacca. She frequents my ER because she has an obsession with anal fixation and a strong proclivity for sticking random household items up her ass. Last week, it was a tube of toothpaste, and the week before that, it was an aerosol can of air freshener.

I'm cringing at what she may have stuck up her ass tonight.

The list of possibilities is endless...

"Thanks, Trudy," I say before standing up and walking toward bed two. This is one of those moments where I ask myself, *Why in the hell did I choose nursing as a career?*

"Well what brings you in tonight, Katy? I feel like I just saw you in here the other day with... What was it? A bottle of Febreeze trapped in your rectum?" I've lost my patience with this girl, and I'm more than aware that sarcasm is leaking from my voice like a faucet.

"I was changing my light bulbs and one accidentally got stuck..."

Seriously? A god damn light bulb?

I roll my eyes in annoyance and set her chart on the bedside table.

"An *accident*?" My look says *You're full of shit, and I know it.*

"Yes, an accident. I just don't know how I keep getting myself into these situations." She laughs nervously as she awkwardly adjusts on the bed. I grab my phone and call the nurse's station, telling our hospital secretary to put a call out to the first surgeon available and notify X-Ray that I need them up here right now. The fact that she has a glass light bulb lodged in her rectum has definitely met the requirements for emergency surgery, and I can tell by the way she's barely sitting on the bed that she's telling the truth.

"Throw this gown on and just go ahead and stand for the time being. The last thing we need is for the light bulb to burst while it's still inside of you. X-Ray should be up shortly. This *accident* is most likely going to require emergency surgery." I set a patient gown on her bed, get supplies to begin drawing blood, and start her IV.

"Emergency surgery?! Oh my god! Can't they just pull it out? I mean, it went in pretty easily…" Her eyes are wide as the entire situation registers in her mind.

"Uh, yeah. Light bulbs are *glass*, therefore, the only way to remove it safely from your rectum is to have you under sedation and in the operating room." I place the tourniquet around her arm and start perusing for a good vein. I can see she's starting to get scared at the mere idea of going into surgery, and a small part of me is sympathetic for her, but the other part of me, the part that's seen her continuously mutilate her asshole with her sick obsession, is extremely aggravated.

This woman is now starting to put her life in jeopardy and I'm not sure how much further she can take this. We've tried everything to get her into counseling, therapy, anything to help her work through her questionable mental state, and she continually refuses our supportive resources. The entire situation is frustratingly exasperating. How do you help someone who doesn't want to be helped? And even more importantly, how do you get someone to stop heaving random objects up her butt?

Who wakes up and says, "Hmmm, I think I'll make my coffee, read the newspaper, and maybe attempt to put this coffee pot in my ass"?

A crazy person, that's who; a crazy person who is otherwise ignorant to the fact that she may quite literally die with cleaning supplies hanging out of her rectum. And why doesn't she just buy a dildo, a vibrator, or a butt plug? Even anal beads might do the trick! She obviously prefers things that are, in fact, quite large, and I know from experience that you can purchase some extremely hefty dildos.

An X-Ray technician arrives in the room after I've managed to draw blood to ensure she's stable to go under anesthesia and started an IV with fluids now running to get her well-hydrated for surgery. I walk out to the nurses' station and sit down, waiting for X-Ray to finish and a surgeon to arrive. I'm charting my current assessment for the obsessive anal fixator and glance up to see Trent strolling through the ER doors. I can't help but grin as he walks toward me, still dressed in the clothes he was in earlier today when he dropped me off at my apartment.

"Oh thank god! Dr. Hamilton is here to save the day!" I act overly excited and he shakes his head, laughing at my sarcasm. Trent sits down next to me just as the X-Ray tech drops off Katy's films. I slide them over to him and give him a huge smile.

"Here you go. She's all yours."

Trent pulls the films from the giant yellow envelope and his eyes go wide at the sight of a perfectly intact light bulb lodged inside someone's anal cavity. "Are you joking with me right now? I got called in for this." He runs his hand through his hair in irritation.

"Definitely not joking with you. Your patient Katy *accidentally* fell on this light bulb and now it's lodged inside of her ass."

"Wow. That is the most ridiculous story I have ever heard. Is this the same Katy that Dr. Mitchell had to remove an aerosol can from of last week?" He flips to the next slide, an even closer view of the problem he's just been hired to fix.

Not your brightest idea, Katy.

"Yes, that's her. The obsessive anal fixator." I click through her electronic chart, pulling up the files I know he will need to look through, labs included. "Here you go. This is everything you'll need. Her labs look fine, and I've got her in bed two standing straight up. I refuse to let her sit down on my bed. I'm not in the mood to deal with shards of glass and a hemorrhaging asshole tonight." He chuckles and slides his chair closer to me, glancing through Katy's medical history.

"You know I wasn't even first call tonight, but I agreed to come in when they called and said it was you who was requesting a surgeon. Now I'm rethinking my decision." He winks at me before standing up and heading towards Katy's room.

"Aw, you're the sweetest, Dr. Hamilton! I owe you big time!" I yell over to him as he walks into bed two.

Trent peeks out from behind the curtain. "I'll remember that, and I'll make a list of all the ways you can make this up to me!" He calls back with a wicked grin.

Trent saves the day and successfully removes the light bulb from Katy's ass. She's now in recovery and doing fine. I really hope this girl will get some help, because her anal fixation is starting to put her life at risk.

Death by anal fixation.

Don't feel bad. I'm laughing my ass off, too.

I have another patient in bed three and start scrolling through the chart. My eyes immediately grow wide when I see his name… *Frank*

Dubussy. The paranoid schizophrenic who frequently forgets to take his medication. The same man I've now witnessed twice walking the streets near my apartment. My gut told me I would be seeing him soon in one of my ER beds, and it looks like my instincts were spot on.

My heart goes out to this man; really, it does. His mental illness takes a toll on him daily, and his quality of life is truly questionable. I quickly call one of our psychologists on staff and request that he sees Frank immediately. Then I ask Tony to walk into his room with me. There's one thing I've learned from working in the ER for as long as I have, and that's to *always* bring a strong man into an already established crazy patient's room with you. You just never know what could happen, and it's best to have another person there to help if they get violent. Frank has never gotten violent with me, but he's been extremely inappropriate before, making sexually explicit suggestions that made even me feel violated and uncomfortable.

Tony and I walk in to find Frank pacing back and forth in the room, his hands furiously grabbing handfuls of his greasy, dirty hair. He's sweating, panting heavily, visibly anxious, and frantically talking to himself in hushed tones. He doesn't even notice our presence in the room, and I'm thankful I grabbed a syringe of Haldol. This medication is an anti-psychotic that I will be more than willing to use on him if he starts to get violent.

Paranoid schizophrenics are extremely difficult to deal with when they're in a mental state like Frank currently is. He's too far gone from reality, and rational thought is not even capable at this point. Tony and I try to wait for one of our psychologists to get in the room before we confront Frank, but he notices us standing in the room. Tony has leather restraints in his right hand, which are securely behind his back, out of Frank's view. We have both had intense confrontations with this man and are all too aware of what he is capable of.

Lucky for us, Frank is nothing but cooperative tonight. He sits down on the bed when instructed and lets us administer the injection of Haldol when the psychologist gets in the room. These types of situations always wear on my nerves. Psych patients are loose cannons, so you honestly never can predict what they are going to throw your way. I'm thankful that tonight was anti-climactic; Frank didn't give us any problems. We were able to quickly get him transferred to Regency's psych unit, where they will assist him with getting back on his medications, and hopefully, he gains back some semblance of reality.

At around three a.m. I feel my phone vibrate in my pocket. I glance down at the screen and see that Trent has sent me a message.

Trent: Next time you have another bright idea about needing a surgeon, warn your surgeon boyfriend that is on call what type of situation he may or may not be walking into...

I laugh and quickly text him back.

Me: My apologies. Thanks for lighting up my night with your beautiful smile and ability to remove light bulbs from rectums. Enjoy your sleep while your nurse girlfriend slaves away in the ER.

My phone vibrates again.

Trent: I'll be dreaming of you, Ellie girl. Have a safe drive home in the morning. Text me when you get to your apartment. Night, baby.

Chapter Twenty-Four

"Sometimes you just gotta take the man by the balls and make your fantasies come true."

Trent is busy playing Dr. Trauma Surgeon in his office today, so I decide to surprise him with lunch. I stop by my favorite deli just outside of Charlotte and pick up their famous Reuben sandwiches. This delectable sandwich is always their spotlighted August special, and I'm excited for Trent to taste the scrumptiousness. I'm sure he's been busy all day with patients and barely had any time to eat. I head to his office and send Amy and Lizzy a short text telling them I picked up an extra shift tonight in the ER. We had plans to go see the newest Ryan Gosling film, but my manager called and practically begged me to work a night shift. The promise of double-time and Saturday night off might have made the extra shift a little too good to resist. I pull into Trent's office and stroll in with our hot sandwiches from Mabie's Cafe in tow. I see Beverly, his receptionist, at the front desk, and she gives me a bright smile.

"Well, hello there, stranger! I haven't seen you in ages. How are you doing, sweetheart?" Beverly says in a cheerful, perky voice. Beverly is in her late fifties, and her positive, upbeat personality is infectious. I used to work with her in the ER at Regency, until she took this office job. She's one of the nicest people you will ever meet. Her hair and makeup always look immaculate, and she just has this motherly aura about her. She was one of the first coworkers I became close with when I started working at Regency as a brand new nurse. I was just a baby at the ripe old age of twenty-one and probably had the deer-in-headlights look for the first six months.

The personalities that are present in the ER are nothing short of aggressive and would have most new nurses running for the hills—or at least a job in a medical office. Being the new girl in an area of the medical field that is known for "eating their young," I was more than thankful to meet someone like Beverly, who always went out of her way to make everyone feel welcome.

"Hey, Bev! It's been too long! How are you? I miss seeing your smiling face around Regency!"

"I've been good. Dr. Hamilton temporarily taking over Dr. Grey's practice has definitely kept me busy, but I've enjoyed the distraction and extra money. My husband Bob had back surgery a few months ago and has been unable to work. "

"Oh no! I'm so sorry to hear that. Please send him my best and let me know if there is anything I can help you guys with. I hope Dr. Hamilton is treating you well," I say with a questioning grin.

Beverly laughs and nods her head yes. "Of course he has, but if anything changes, I'll let you know. I hear the two of you are an item these days. I noticed an adorable picture of you on his office desk."

"Oh god, I can only imagine. I better go check this picture out for myself." My cheeks flush a little with embarrassment in thinking that Trent has a picture of me on his desk. We've only been dating for a few weeks, and I don't recall any photo ops.

"Well Dr. Hamilton is back in his office. I think he's on a conference call with Dr. Grey right now, but I'm sure he'd love to see your cute butt stroll in."

"Thanks, Beverly! We need to do lunch sometime soon and catch up on old times."

"Of course, sweetheart! I would love that!"

I head back to Trent's office and hear his deep, husky voice on the phone when I approach his closed door. I slowly open the door and his blue eyes immediately glance up at me from behind his desk. He looks downright edible and undeniably fuckable. His black and grey pinstriped tie is loose, the first two buttons of his white oxford collared shirt are unbuttoned, and his sleeves are rolled up to his elbows. He smiles back at me, and I don't miss the fact that his eyes peruse my body from head to toe.

I'm a little dressed up for the occasion in my newest pair of heels, a pencil skirt, and a fitted, pink button-up blouse. My attire is a little on the sexy side because I planned to tease him, but seeing Trent sitting there looking sexy as sin has me thinking that this visit is going to turn into something hot. I've had a specific office fantasy with Trent in mind and decide that now is the perfect time to turn my dirty thoughts into reality.

I quietly shut the door and ensure the lock is secured. After tossing the bag with our sandwiches on the brown leather couch that lines the wall across from his desk, I seductively saunter in his direction. I walk around his desk and he slides his chair back to make room for me. Trent gestures for me to sit on his lap while he finishes up his conference call, but I decide that I will start my seduction of him in hopes that he will agree to play a starring role in my office fantasy. I stand between his thighs and proceed to slowly kneel down in front of him. He's watching my every move as he continues his current phone conversation about boring insurance premiums.

Sliding my hands up his thighs, I stroke him lightly through his black dress slacks. He's already hard, indicating he is well aware of my intent. I unzip his slacks and pull his cock out from his grey boxer briefs. His erection has my mouth watering as I use my hand to caress him in smooth, soft motions. Trent's breath hitches as he starts giving curt, short responses to the other party on the phone.

I lean forward and begin to use my mouth on him. I run my tongue up his shaft and around the tip as I grasp his sac with my right hand. Making eye contact with his hooded stare, I suck him to the back of my throat and find a rhythm that he seems to be enjoying.

He is still on the phone...

This is only making me hotter, more turned on by the idea that we're doing something forbidden, something that's completely spontaneous.

He clears his throat and gives a breathless *yes* into the phone. I'm assuming he is answering a question, but maybe he's just too turned on by my performance. I reach up and place my index finger in his mouth. He sucks on my finger then releases, providing delicious lubrication for my already aching core. As I continue to do unspeakable things to him with my tongue, I slide my skirt up to my waist and push my white silk panties to the side so I can begin to relieve the deep throb between my legs.

"Y-Yes. No, it's f-fine." Trent is still attempting to sound professional and serious while I continue to blow his mind. "Of course. N-No need to worry. We'll fix...it." He's starting find it difficult to maintain his current phone conversation while I'm on my knees with him in my mouth. "Let's resume this discussion tomorrow. Something has uh...has, uh, come up." His inability to stay focused has my lips quirking up into a smirk.

Trent clumsily hangs up the phone, quickly ending his conference call. A loud moan escapes his throat as he places both of his hands in my hair. He begins to thrust up into my mouth as I continue to take him deep.

"Fuck. Fuck. Fuuuuuuuuuuuck."

I look up at him with desire flooding my eyes, heat filling my veins as I watch him get pleasure from me. "Do you like this?"

"Yessss. I love this." He lets out a pleasurable groan that causes me to feel a deep, delicious clench, and I begin to slide two fingers in and out of my pussy.

He allows me to continue for another few minutes before he grasps my hips and pulls me up so that I'm straddling his lap. He crushes his lips to mine and kisses me with deep, hard thrusts of his tongue. His yearning for me is evident, and I being to grind my wetness along his hard shaft. Using his right hand, he slides my panties back to the side and quickly pushes himself inside of me.

Fast and deep.

"Oh yes, Trent. God, yes," I moan breathlessly into his mouth.

"Elle, you feel so good. *So. Fucking. Good.* There's nothing better than this."

I begin to increase my pace as I ride him in desperation…in *need* of reaching orgasm. His office chair begins to squeak and roll around on the hardwood office floor as we continue to fuck each other senseless. Trent grasps my hips and quickly stands up, placing my bare ass on the smooth wood surface of his office desk. I wrap my legs around his waist and grab his taut, toned ass while he pushes inside of me, plunging hard and deep.

Oh, fuck… fuckity fuck.

My orgasm is imminent, euphoric tingles racing up my spine. My entire body flushing with insane pleasure, causing several loud moans to escape from my lips.

"I'm so close. Keep going, Trent. *Right there,*" I say a little too loudly for an office setting.

He kisses me deeply again in attempts to keep the office staff from hearing us. Trent bites my bottom lip, tugging back roughly as I begin to clench down around him in rhythmic waves.

"Come for me, Ellie. I want to see that look on your face when your pussy comes all over my cock." Trent is breathing raggedly as he continues to bring me to climax.

I come fast and hard, and I am barely able to contain my need to yell out unfathomable things. My body is trembling and my breath is shaky, the intensity of my orgasm causing uncontrolled whimpers to leave my lips. Trent drives deeply a few more times before I feel him come inside of me. He presses his face into my neck and his moans are muffled by my hair. I hug him tightly as we both attempt to catch our breath. I can feel his heart pounding against my chest. My limbs are jelly, and I'm riding out the endorphin high his dick just gave me.

Trent leans back and kisses my forehead. "You never cease to amaze me, little spitfire."

"I just planned on surprising you with lunch, but when I got here, you just looked too fuckable. I couldn't resist." I smile at Trent and take in the way in looks right now. Messy hair, my red lipstick all over his face, he is sexily disheveled and downright irresistible.

"Good thing you're not on staff here. I could file sexual harassment charges against you," he teases with a big dimpled grin as I rub my smeared lipstick off of him.

"I'm pretty sure it's not sexual harassment when both parties participate willingly." I pull his face to mine and playfully nibble on his lip.

"I welcome Ellie's stealthy attack on my cock with open arms. Any day of the week."

I giggle into his mouth and kiss him softly, letting my lips linger on his for a long pause. We're still wrapped up in each other's arms, my legs still around his waist, and I'm enjoying every moment of our sweet embrace.

"So, lunch? I brought sandwiches from my favorite Charlotte deli."

"Let me get this straight. You come to my office, surprise me with a blow job and incredible sex, and now you're going to feed me? You're perfect." Trent places sloppy kisses all over my face, which leaves me laughing at how adorable he can be sometimes.

I glance to the left of me and find the picture Beverly mentioned. I grab the frame and take a closer look while Trent nuzzles my neck. The picture is actually from my apartment. It's a ridiculous beach photo that Amy took last year when we vacationed in the Bahamas. I'm standing near the ocean in my red bikini with my sarong tied loosely on my hips and my hands are on top of my head, holding my floppy straw hat in place. I'm visibly laughing in the picture probably from something sarcastic Amy said.

"Hey, when did you take this picture from my apartment?" I'm definitely flattered at the idea of him having a permanent reminder of me on his office desk.

"The night your sister cock-blocked me. You look so damn perfect in that picture and I couldn't resist. Forgive me?" He gives a small pout and his version of puppy-dog eyes.

How could I ever be pissed at him with that look on his face?

I place the picture back on his desk and give his lips a soft peck. "All right, charmer. You're forgiven. Now let's eat our no-longer-hot Reuben sandwiches from Mabie's!"

After we disentangled ourselves from each other and enjoyed the lunch I hand delivered, I make a few mental notes.

Trent loves Reubens from Mabie's Cafe.
Trent loves blow jobs. Better yet, I love blowing Trent...a lot.
Office sex with Trent is even better in reality.
I must have office sex with Trent again.

Chapter Twenty-Five

"A true best friend will watch you masturbate without criticism."

Ugh.

I'm uncomfortably horny and finding myself getting aroused at weird places, like the grocery store or gas station…or work. I think it's from all of the crazy, hot sex I've been getting from Trent over the past month and a half. That and I think someone might have spiked my birth control pills with ecstasy.

I'm standing in my kitchen, contemplating whether or not I could orgasm from rubbing myself up against the fridge.

I think I could climax right next to the Christmas cards that are hanging by the flip-flop magnets.

I'm ignoring the fact that Trent only has a month and a half before he's no longer needed to run Dr. Grey's practice and just focusing my energy on how I'm going to get my rocks off. Trent has been working nonstop the past few days, and I'm badly in need of some good, hard thrusting.

The superhero cock thrusting.

I'm one vagina clench away from finger-banging myself in the living room. I head into my bedroom and shut the door, throwing myself down on my bed, my face coming in contact with the pillow Trent sleeps on whenever he stays over. I'm sniffing myself into a pathetic one-woman show of foreplay.

Mmmmmm. His cologne. His vagina-arousing cologne.

Trent promised that he was going to head straight to my apartment after his last case in the OR, but he has been delayed due to an unexpected emergency surgery. So here I sit, jonesin' for an orgasm. My snatch is twitchy and aching and clenching involuntary at infomercials for P90X. Shit, I can't hold out any longer. I'm going to have to take things into my own hands…

I glance at the clock and see that Amy isn't due home for another hour, and Lizzy is out working off her frustrations with her new personal trainer, who's not a day over twenty-four and sporting some serious V muscles.

Ohhhhh, Trent's V muscles. His sexy, sexy V muscles.

I decide to settle on the next best thing—my vibrator. This little baby has seen me through some rough times and can work my clit like no one's business. Yes, this is the same vibrator I now fondly call Trent Hamilton. And boy oh boy can Trent Hamilton magically work my juice-box until I'm squirting like a Capri Sun. I grab T.H. from the nightstand and get myself comfortable on my bed.

My panties are off, and my tits are pulled out of my bra, showing my seemingly ever-present hardened nipples. I turn T.H. on and spread my legs wide, ready to get this party-of-one sex show going. I slide it along my folds, the tip of the vibrator already glistening with my arousal. I turn up the speed and push those vibrations along my sex, running smooth circles around my clit, causing my legs to tremble in anticipation.

Oh yes. I need this.

My right hand strokes my breast, tweaking my nipple, as my left hand works my snatch over with T.H.'s euphoric sensations. My eyes close and my lips are parted as waves of pleasure build deep inside.

Yes. Work my clit, Trent. Work my fucking clit.

I'm fantasizing about Trent taking me roughly from behind, his hand grasping the back of my neck as he pushes me on to my bed, plunging inside of me.

Right there… Oh yes, right there!

I slide T.H. inside my pussy and my walls tighten automatically. The rhythmic vibrations send shockwaves throughout my body, building my climax to immeasurable heights. My mind is still off with the real T.H., getting fucked from behind with a possessive fervor. He's got my ponytail wrapped around his wrist and he's pulling my hair in sync with each thrust.

I'm so close! Oh yes! Keep going, Trent!

A faint giggle pulls me from my thoughts and my eyes jerk open just in time as crashing waves from my orgasm start to pull me under. I'm in full climax mode as my eyes are locked with…*Amy.*

Fucking fuck! God dammit, Amy!

My mind and vagina are on the complete opposite spectrum. I'm trembling and shuddering and quietly moaning while my mouth is agape, looking at Amy in complete shock. My jaw has nearly dropped to my chest and I'm clutching my vibrator like I'm going to use it as a weapon.

I'm going to vibrator-whip Amy.

"What in the hell are you doing?!" My voice finally squeaks out once my vagina comes down from her O-induced high.

"Well…" Amy clears her throat and leans against my doorframe with a cheeky grin on her face. "I came in here to let you know that Trent called. He's on his way, and I just wanted to see what you were up to." She shrugs her shoulders innocently.

"You didn't think that knocking was an appropriate choice in this situation?" I spat with fury all over my face. "Or maybe, I don't know, getting the hell out of my room when you saw me in here…"

"Diddling your skittle? Fluffing your muff? Shucking your oyster? Beating your—"

I cut her off brusquely as I clutch my sheets to my chest. "God dammit! I just came while I was looking at your face! This is seriously deranged. Are you not seeing how completely fucked up this entire situation is?"

"I think it's kind of sweet actually." She smiles widely at me. "I mean, we just took our friendship to the next level, Ellie Belly. You just put me in your spank bank rotation!" She holds her hands up to her chest in glee like she just won first runner-up at a beauty queen pageant.

"Remind me why we're friends again?" I close my eyes in exasperation and take a deep, calming breath in a weak attempt to hold myself back from smacking her across the face with my vibrator.

"Because you love me and now you love diddling yourself to my pretty face."

I clench my vibrator in my hand, and then, before I can bring myself back down from my irritation, I launch T.H. across the room, smacking Amy right across the face and leaving a glistening hint of my cum on her forehead.

Amy is frozen from shock as she stands in my doorway. She's looking back at me with determined eyes as her fingers touch her forehead, feeling the already light red spot my vibrator placed there.

"And we're friends because you love me and now you like when I put my cum on your forehead."

Amy dives toward my bed in a fit of rage, jumping on top of me and wrestling me to the floor. The sheet is no longer covering my nearly naked body as we continue to roll around on my hardwood floor, screaming, pulling hair, and smacking each other in frustration.

"Cum twat!"

"Obsessive masturbator!"

"Loosey McLabia Face!"

A hard knock on my door and a husky voice clearing its throat stops us mid-wrestle. We both look up to see Trent grinning back at us. He's standing there in all his physician glory with his surgery cap still tied on his head, and his muscles are bulging through the perfectly snug navy scrubs he's wearing.

"So this….is interesting." Trent is glancing back and forth between us, trying to piece together the puzzle of why there's a vibrator lying on the floor near my bedroom door, why Amy is on top of me, and why I'm pretty much naked, wrestling with my best friend.

"Uh yeah, about this…" I motion my hand between me and Amy, who is still lying on top of me like a god damn idiot. "Can we just write this off as something that just can't be explained?" I say like I'm asking him a question, because really I am. I'm asking him to forget this entire scenario even occurred. "And you can get your scrawny ass off of me now!" I glare at Amy, who winks at me before grabbing my boob and then running out of my bedroom.

"Add that to the Amy section of your spank bank album!" She yells as she sprints down the hallway.

I jump up and start to rush after her, but strong arms grip my shoulders and pull me back inside my bedroom, promptly shutting the door behind us.

"I just worked twenty-hours straight, sixteen of which were spent in the OR, and I came home to find you rolling around naked with your best friend like you were wrestling in a pool of Jell-O in front of an entire house full of frat guys. My dick is now hard, and you're still naked, so you're most definitely not leaving this bedroom until we settle a few things." He winks at me before pulling his scrub top over his head and making quick work of his pants and shoes. He grabs my waist and tosses me onto my bed like I weigh ten pounds and proceeds to climb on top of me, sliding his erection against my thighs.

Oh my.

Trent stops as his body is hovering directly over mine, his eyes are curious as he glances down at me. "Before we settle a few things"—his eyes motion towards his very apparent hard-on—"is there anything you need to tell me?" His tone is light and teasing.

"I didn't get it on with my best friend." I sigh loudly. "She walked in on me while I was enjoying a little time with T.H."

"T.H.?"

"My vibrator…T.H." My face flushes red with embarrassment.

"What does T.H. stand for?" His eyes are beaming, and it's apparent his mind has already put it together.

"You're going to make me say it, aren't you?"

He nods his head and grins widely at me, his pearly whites in full view.

"I call my vibrator Trent Hamilton."

He fist pumps in the air and starts to playfully rub himself up against me, dry humping my leg like a horny dog. "Fuck, that turns me on." He's still smiling and laughing a little as I roll my eyes skyward.

"Just kiss me and stop gloating."

Trent leans down, sucking my bottom lip into his mouth, and then lets it loose with a loud pop. "Just so you know, I used to be in a fraternity in college and I'm *really* good with Jell-O…so if you want to get Amy back in here…"

I smack his chest hard, the sound of my hand hitting his skin echoing in my bedroom. "You're such a kinky bastard."

He grips my thigh tightly and presses his face into my chest, my breasts vibrating from his husky laughter. "You love it, and for that, I'm going to show you just how much of a kinky bastard I can be."

Chapter Twenty-Six

"Sometimes the best sex isn't even in the comfort of your own home. Sometimes it's the rush you get from spontaneity, the excitement from being somewhere you're not supposed to be that makes it even more pleasurable."

"Oh shit," Trent says as he slides my scrub pants down and finds a tiny scrap of lacy, red material. His eyes are flaring wide with lust, with want, with pure carnal need. I admit this thong is a little on the small side, but it's actually laundry day and I'm running low on my usual work-appropriate cotton panties. I decided to harass Trent on my lunch break. I know, this is not nearly an appropriate setting for making boom-boom with your boyfriend, but I can't help myself. Trent and I haven't really seen each other since the T.H. vibrator fiasco a few days ago. I'm dying to feel his hands on me, to feel him inside of me. He's fueled a desire that has bloomed from my core, and all rational thought has left the building.

Leaving a very turned-on Elle and her very horny vagina.

"How am I supposed to scrub into the OR and actually attempt to concentrate after finding out you're practically wearing nothing underneath those scrubs?" His gorgeous baby blues are smoky, filled with undeniable heat.

I lie back on the small call room bed with Trent's hands caressing up my thighs, causing my body to involuntary tremble with desire. "I don't know, Doc, but I've been a really bad girl today. I think I need to be fucked. Rough and hard." I'm baiting him at this point. I've found that Trent goes insane for the bad girl talk.

I coyly smile up at him and his eyes lock with mine. His look is almost predatory. My nipples harden and I feel a gush of arousal wet my panties. After tossing my pants and thong across the room, he roughly takes my scrub top and bra off then unties his scrub pants and pulls his hard, rigid cock out. I'm mesmerized by the sheer beauty of him. He's silky and hard. Soft and rough. He has the most beautiful cock I've ever seen and I'm nearly panting for it. I slowly get down on my knees and beg him to let me put my mouth on him. I've never really been a girl who's had gusto for blow jobs, but when it comes to Trent Hamilton and his superhero cock, I want to suck on that beautiful shaft like a Charms Blow Pop.

"Trent, let me fuck you with my mouth," I plead while looking into his eyes and slowly rubbing the tip of him around my lips, savoring the taste of his pre-cum that has now reached my tongue. His eyes darken, those blue orbs catching fire. He nods, and I can tell he is so turned on at this point that he probably can't form a coherent thought much less answer me.

I slowly take all of him in my mouth until I can feel him tap the back of my throat. I make a little humming noise just to drive him a little closer to the edge. His cock jerks and Trent curses under his breath.

Damn, I love getting to him like that.

I continue my assault on him and do not leave an inch untouched. I lick and suck and stroke him into a fucking frenzy. Before I can finish him off, he grabs my hips with insistent hands and throws me onto the bed. This seems to be a theme between us—him tossing me around, taking charge of the situation.

Boy oh boy do I enjoy this take-charge Trent theme.

Our eyes catch as he kneels between my legs. Just looking at him, Trent in all his erotic beauty, something opens wide and deep inside of me. It's a feeling that is slightly familiar, yet so unfamiliar at the same time. A feeling that nearly grabs my heart out of my chest.

I love him…I love him…I love him.

My chest hurts from fear that this man will be my undoing. That Trent Hamilton could destroy me. The thoughts that fill my brain are quickly pushed to the side when Trent thrusts inside of me, wild and hard. My body trembles from the feel of him, the feel of his cock rigid and insistent, pressed deep inside my core.

My panting and whimpering only seem to fuel his lust further, encouraging him to take me, mark me, make me his. He fits against me, inside of me, like my missing puzzle piece.

My perfect mate.

Trent pulls out and stares down at me, his face straining, delaying his orgasm.

"Ellie," he mutters under his breath, teeth clenched, neck muscles flexing.

"Now, Trent. Now. Please, I need you inside of me." I'm moaning and clutching at his arms eagerly. My heels dig into his backside, pushing him closer, showing him what I want, what I need, what I can't live without. He slides back inside of me, achingly slow, forcing me to feel every inch of him. I'm panting like a whore in church and whimpering involuntarily. He plunges and thrusts and reaches a depth that has the pressuring building inside of me.

Building and building...

My vision blurs, my body flushing with heat, my nipples hardening against his chest. I fist my hands into his stiff scrub top as shivers roll up and down my spine. A soft murmur escapes my lips. A murmur of inescapable pleasure, of inexplainable arousal. My lashes sweep down as my eyes squeeze tightly shut, my climax starting to take hold and pull me under. I grasp his shoulders and run my nails down his back. I'm clutching to him in desperation. Desperate for my release, desperate to feel him come inside of me.

And I crashed....

Crashed into an ocean of euphoria while the most beautiful eyes were locked on mine, watching me fall apart at the seams. Watching me shudder and scream in undeniable pleasure.

Pure ecstasy.

I'm high as a kite off of my release, nearly fucked into a stupor. A delightful stupor at that. Trent's pace increases, plunging farther, stroking himself with my core. His expression is fierce as he nears that pivotal point—the point of no return, the point where he falls into a bliss-filled abyss of never-ending desire.

My entire world vanishes as I luxuriate in the feel of him, the beauty of him over me, inside of me. There are only two people left. *Trent and Ellen.* He is the focus of my world. Everything. Nothing else even comes close to being important in this moment. There's an intangible connection between us. A connection so strong, so deep, so unexplainable, nearly taking my breath away.

My back arches as his gaze sweeps over my body, lighting every inch on fire. My breathing is uneven, fast, and gasping. Another rush of pleasure is building inside of me, tingling up my spine, and causing my muscles to contract, clenching him tight as another orgasm threatens to plow through me.

"You. Feel. So. Good. *Perfect.*" He moans into my mouth as his lips crash into mine, his tongue matching the thrusting rhythm of his cock. "That's it, baby. You are so tight. So wet. Just for me. I love being deep inside of you, feeling you...all of you."

"I'm so close. Come with me. Come. Now. Trent." My body shudders wildly, my orgasm bursting through me and making me scream his name.

"Oh fuck!" Trent's growls as his spine straightens, his back arching with his thrusts, his hands clenching my hips as he empties himself inside of me. *Marking me*. Making me his.

"Best sex I've ever had at work," I hoarsely say to Trent while trying to catch my breath. I'm lying next to him, breathless and sated. My bones have turned into jelly, and I think I might have to call someone to bring a wheelchair to get me back to the ER.

"I hope it's the only sex you've had at work," he says as he glances over at me and smirks.

"This is definitely a first for me," I say, beaming at him.

Trent abruptly pulls me back over on top of him and kisses me passionately, his lips searing while his large muscular hands grasp my ass.

"I love you, Ellie. I love you so god damn much that I feel like I can't breathe sometimes," he whispers into my mouth while resting his forehead on mine. His eyes are fathomless, causing emotion to clog my throat. His gaze engulfs me, consuming me whole. His eyes are so expressive, so full of emotion. I can see the small gold flecks sprinkled throughout the ocean blue. When I look into his eyes, I feel like I've been blind for thirty years and can finally see the sun for the first time. Trent's eyes are my safe place, my home.

This man is everything.

I softly kiss his lips and fight the tears that are stinging my eyes, threatening to spill over. "I love you too, baby."

Trent crushes me to his chest and I relish in the strength and comfort of this wonderful man. In an instant, he took me from lusting over his cock to emotionally breaking my soul open and stealing my heart.

I spot the calendar hanging on the wall across from the small call room bed.

September.

I feel like time is slipping away. The past month and a half feels like it's passed by at warp speed. Forty more days and Trent Hamilton won't be in Charlotte anymore. Forty more days and I will be faced with the huge dilemma of…*where do we go from here?* In true Elle fashion, I do what I always do with difficult situations—I squash that shit down as far as I can, desperately trying to avoid it, avoid the mere idea of Trent walking away from me, leaving me in Charlotte, while he goes back to Seattle and lives his life.

Shit.

I know. I know you're thinking, *Why are you being so frustrating? So utterly annoying? Why don't you just talk to him about it?* I wish it were that easy. I really do. I wish I could just beg him to stay and not hold any sort of guilt for holding him back in a career he's worked his entire life to achieve.

Trent Hamilton is a trauma surgeon first and foremost. He's giving up so much of his life just to be in the position he is in right now. I'm not sure what Seattle is offering him. I know they want him back; I also know that they are one of the most renowned trauma surgery centers in the country. So now let me ask you this. How in the hell do I ask him to give up everything for a girl he's known all of two months? How can I do that and actually live with myself?

I can't and I won't. If Trent Hamilton stays in Charlotte, it needs to be on his own accord. I'm not going to beg him or make him feel guilty. I'm going to let him make that decision for himself, and I just hope I can survive the aftermath.

Chapter Twenty-Seven

"Never shun the strippers. You never know when you're going to have a shirt full of cranberry and vodka and need to borrow some clothing. The moral of this story is… Strippers are nice and you should go ahead and take an additional hundred bucks out of that ATM to tip them generously."

In celebration of Tony's upcoming nuptials to his beautiful fiancée Rachel, Amy and I planned a fantastic bachelor party for him. We refused to take no for an answer and pretty much forced him and his beautiful bride-to-be to attend a night of shenanigans with us. I know he just proposed to her like a month ago and their wedding isn't for another six months, but we were just too damn excited to wait any longer!

We're driving around in a party bus decked with a stripper pole, neon flashing lights, an ungodly amount of alcohol, and of course, a few inflatable naked girls. This bus is filled with ten of our closest friends from work, including my wonderful man Trent. Seeing as we have now made our relationship "work official," I'm ecstatic to enjoy a night with him where we don't have to worry about prying, curious eyes trying to figure out our current status.

You can imagine the gossip that has stirred since Trent came to Charlotte. The questions, the knowing glances that have been sent my way. I've been the center of far too many conversations since my breakup with John, and the relationship that's blossomed between Trent and me, well, that only created more curiosity for my coworkers.

Everyone knows.

Everyone is aware.

And hopefully they can just get over it and stop trying to meddle their nosy faces in my business.

Amy and I have taken an unhealthy amount of Jell-O shots, currently finding ourselves becoming more obnoxious by the minute. I'm sitting on Trent's lap as Rihanna's *Cockiness* starts to blare over the party bus's speakers.

"Holy shit! Get your little ass over here, Elle! Come dance with me!" Amy is now standing near the stripper pole and shaking her hips. Everyone on the bus starts to cheer her on.

Oh lordy. The last thing that girl needs is encouragement.

"Yeah, *Elle*. Get your little ass up there and dance with your friend," Trent whispers in my ear before biting my earlobe.

This man can get me hot and bothered like no other. I groan and squirm a little in his lap, trying desperately to relieve the deep, delicious clench between my legs. He laughs a little at my expense, obviously getting a thrill from getting me riled up.

Jerk. Sexy, too-hot-for-my-own-good jerk.

"I know what you're trying to do here, and I can promise you, payback is a bitch."

My look is telling despite my light and teasing tone. I stride over to Amy and then look back at Trent to find his blue eyes smirking at me. I wink at him and he immediately starts laughing. Trent calls my attempts at winking "adorably awkward." Honestly, he's one hundred percent right. My inability to wink has made me the brunt of many jokes, but Trent seems to embrace my awkwardness with open arms, which makes me dig him even more. I start dancing with Amy to the sensual voice of Rihanna as she sings explicit lyrics about licking and sucking. I shake my hips seductively and see Trent watching me with hooded eyes. I grin and, unfortunately for everyone on the bus, attempt a sexy wink again.

"What is wrong with your face? You're a weird cross between constipated and ready to have a seizure!" Amy hollers over the music. I flip her off, which only spurs her to throw more sarcastic jabs my way.

"Seriously. This is what you look like." Amy shakes her hips a little and then does her best "Elle winking" impression. Honestly, it's the most ludicrous thing I've ever seen, and I start laughing...hard. Tears streaming down my face, bent over and clutching my abdomen, I can't help but laugh at how hilarious she looks.

"You're such a cunt! Stop making fun of me!"

"I can't help it! You attempting to wink has to be the funniest thing I've ever seen!"

"Amy, I love you, but seriously, you're a cunt!" I shout back at her before, leaving her to dance to Rihanna by herself. I stride back over to Trent and sit on his lap.

"You're so fucking adorable, it's making my dick hard." He wraps his hands around my waist and chuckles into my neck.

"You're getting a hard-on from my being cute?"

"Yes, and from the fact that you look sexy as hell shaking those little hips of yours." He practically growls into my ear.

"Dr. Hamilton! I'm appalled at your crass behavior!" I put my hand to my chest and feign offense.

He starts to tickle my ribs a little, which only makes me scream out in laughter and wiggle around in his lap. "Stop! Okay stop! Please stop!"

Trent holds me tight to his chest and rains playful, sloppy kisses all over my face. I don't think anyone has ever made me as happy as he does. Somehow, he just gets me and seems to embrace every single part of me, gracelessness and all.

"Stop it, weirdo! You're practically slobbering all over my face!"

"I'm your weirdo. Deal with it," he says with a big grin on his face.

"Click," I say out loud as I take a mental picture of him in this moment to keep on file in my head.

"Click?"

"Yeah. *Click*. I just mentally took a picture of that ridiculous dimpled grin of yours and added it to my 'Trent Album.'"

His grin gets wider. "You have a Trent album? How many mental pictures do you have stocked away in that funny, little brain of yours?"

"Wouldn't you love to know, weirdo?"

"I bet you've got some kinky ones in there. Kinky pictures of me doing delicious, sexy things to that hot little body. Kind of like the other night…"

I smirk and shake my head at him. "All right, cut it out. We will resume this discussion later. Much later. Like when I have you naked…in bed."

He puts his hand behind my neck and crushes his mouth to mine. He is practically swallowing my face whole with this intense, mind-blowing kiss. I immediately melt into him and allow him to continue his sensual assault on my ever-willing lips. The way Trent kisses would make any woman's toes curl. His mouth is firm and demanding, yet soft and sensual. It's absolute perfection, and I find myself wishing I could kiss him for the rest of my life.

"Hey! Get a room, you two!" Amy yells over to us.

I could honestly care less that my best friend is hurling obscenities our way. Trent's mouth on mine is the only thing my brain is focusing on in this moment. I can vaguely hear the rest of the bus heckling us, and then I feel an odd sensation of plastic being rubbed against my back. I pull away from Trent and peer back only to see Amy pretending to dry hump a naked inflatable doll, which is now sandwiched between her and my back.

"You and your new girlfriend are being fucking cock-blockers right now," Trent voices to Amy with a laugh.

"God I love this guy, Elle! Can we keep him forever and ever?"

"Yeah, Elle. Will you keep me?" Trent's blue eyes are expectant, with an ever-so-slight hint of amusement laced in.

"Eh, I guess so. At least for a little awhile." I simper back at him. God yes, I definitely want to keep this one. I know that in order to do this I may have to become a psycho-stalker and follow his ass to Seattle. And well…I think I'm actually entertaining this idea.

"Hopefully it's going to turn out better than that time Elle decided to get a cat!" Amy bellows loudly.

"Shut up, labia face! Leave Bea Arthur out of this!" I flip Amy off with both hands.

"Bea Arthur? As in Bea Arthur from the Golden Girls?" Trent grabs my chin and pulls it toward his face so I am looking directly in his eyes. He's visibly holding back laughter.

"Yes as in Bea Arthur from the motherfucking Golden Girls!"

"I need to hear this story, babe."

"No way. No how. You are not getting the cat story out of me. At least not tonight. Definitely not tonight!" My cheeks flush a little with embarrassment, and I'm just going to blame it on the alcohol and not the fact that the Bea Arthur story is one thing Trent will never let me live down. Amy still brings the cat story up to this day, and I wouldn't be surprised if her drunk ass spills the beans about it at some point during this night of debauchery.

Basically, Bea Arthur was an asshole.

That cat wreaked havoc on my life for three straight weeks before I finally threw in the towel, and decided I'm not a cat person. Bea Arthur seemed to find enjoyment out of knocking random shit over at the most inopportune times. She also loved to hide out underneath my bed so she could attack my legs while I was getting ready for work. That cat scared the shit out of me and I'm pretty sure she was possessed. Bea Arthur was judgy, neurotic, and had a propensity for shitting outside of her litter box. And that's just the summarized version of the hellish period that Bea Arthur lived with Amy and I. I'm not even going to get into the fact that she managed to sneak into my Amish neighbor's apartment and attack his goat…

Needless to say, that goat ambush was the very last straw for the feline bitch that was Bea Arthur. Don't worry, I was nice enough to find Satan's spawn a nice home with a family who could handle her judgmental attitude. And to answer the question that's probably on your mind right now, *yes*, my Amish neighbor may or may not have a goat that lives with him part-time. That's a whole other story for an entirely different day.

After bar hopping around Charlotte, the party bus pulls up to our final destination, Trixie's. This is one of the best strip clubs downtown

Charlotte, North Carolina, has to offer. When Amy and I planned Tony's night of shenanigans, we knew this party wouldn't be complete without a trip to a strip club. Tony looks over at me and Amy with shocked delight. I'm not sure why he's surprised; he should have expected nothing less from the dynamic duo.

"Have I told you girls how much I love you!" Tony grabs Rachel, Amy, and me into a tight hug. We're all shitfaced and practically falling over each other at this point. I giggle into his chest as Amy professes her vagina's undying love for Tony and Rachel. I'm not sure why that's another one of her drunk things, but it happens far too often. Amy loves to profess her vagina's undying love for people whenever she gets hammered. And her vagina apparently isn't biased upon gender—she's loves both men and women alike. Her vagina likes food, too. I once saw her make a drunken vagina profession in the middle of Taco Bell. She animatedly told the girl at the counter about her vagina's love for Cheesy Gordita Crunches. Then she proceeded to call her snatch Cheesy Chalupa for the rest of the night, telling everyone in a ten mile radius that she was extra juicy and her special sauce tasted like nacho cheese. Things got a little more than bizarre and uncomfortable that night…

We stroll into Trixie's and see scantily clad waitresses taking drink orders near high top tables across from the main bar. This strip club is small, intimate, and it only has one main stage with a single stripper pole. There are several open seats near the main stage so we immediately head that way. Trent sits down, grabs my hips, and immediately pulls me onto his lap. I look over and see Rachel and Tony sitting close, visibly enjoying their party. I swear those two are going to be together forever. The moment Tony introduced me to Rachel a little over a year ago, I knew she was the one for him.

An extremely attractive cocktailer heads our way to get our drink orders. She's decked in perfect strip club attire: fishnets, booty shorts, and a tight corset that leaves very little to the imagination. She seductively looks at Trent and asks him what he would like to drink. He orders two beers for us and proceeds to nuzzle into my neck, holding me tight. I hate to compare Trent to John, but this is a perfect example of how different the two of them are. John would have flirted back with the cocktailer, eating up every moment of her obvious flirtation that was directed at him. Trent is so different and it's unbelievably refreshing. He was curt but polite to her while still making sure she was aware he was here with me. How could I not be in love with him for that? Still, thinking the words love and Trent in the same sentence is a little overwhelming, but fuck, it's the god damn truth. I'm seriously in love.

After the devastation John put me through, I wasn't sure if I would ever love anyone again. My feelings for Trent are different. They feel more real, more desperate, and undeniably passionate. This man makes me feel things I have never felt before. It's like he's made me come alive, and I relish in the idea of spending more time with him.

More time?

Shit, we're talking a little over a month and he's going to be heading back to Seattle.

Push that shit down. Way, way down.

We watch as the next dancer comes out onto the stage. She's absolute female perfection. Blond hair, long legs, lean body, huge tits, and an ass most women would kill for. Her stripper heels and suggestive attire only accentuate her irrefutable attractiveness. She begins to sway her hips to the pounding bass of a song I've never heard. She heads over to the pole and begins to prove why her body is so perfectly toned.

"God, I need to put a pole in my apartment so I can see your hot little body give me private dances." Trent's breath is hot on my ear.

I glimpse at Trent to see him staring back at me with hooded eyes. "Mmmm, I'd love to do that for you. But…this is me we're talking about here. I'd end up in the ER with some sort of weird muscle pull to my vagina." Trent laughs, and then his eyes get serious again, intensity radiating from them.

"How about you get some money out of my pocket so I can watch you pay compliments to this hard-working girl?"

I start to reach towards his pockets, but he pushes my hand away. "No, baby. I want you to kneel between my legs and get this money out of my pockets with your teeth." He gleams wickedly at me.

Oh. My.

My buzz from the alcohol is nothing in comparison to what this man does to my head. He makes me practically euphoric and fills me with overwhelming lust. I'm already wet from hearing him growl dirty things into my ear. His hooded eyes and provocative grin are only spurring my desire for him into an uncontrollable need. I have the urge to straddle his legs and ride his cock right here in front of the entire club. I slide myself off of his lap, making sure to rub my ass on his ever-present arousal for me. I turn to face him and slowly kneel between his thighs. I place both of my hands on his hips and dip my face low, rubbing my mouth right over the very visible bulge of his jeans. I peek up at him as I make my way back over to his right pocket.

"The other pocket," he says breathlessly.

I lock eyes with him and unhurriedly move from his right pocket to his left, paying special attention to the visible strain on his zipper.

"Fuuuuuuck, Ellie," he groans under his breath before he adjusts a little in his seat.

When I reach his left pocket, I notice that he's already got a wad of money sticking out of his pocket. Obviously, this scenario was premeditated.

"Oh my, Casanova. I guess you came prepared." I grab the wad of money out of his pocket with my teeth and deliberately slide my body back up his, pressing my breasts tightly against him. When I'm level with his beautiful blue eyes, I pull the money from my mouth and hold up it for him. He grabs a few bills from the folded wad and hands the rest back to me. I sit back down on his lap and he adjusts my hips so that my ass can feel just how hard he is.

His cock is like steel. Dr. Hammer better give me full satisfaction tonight...

I wiggle my ass a little and feel him groan into my neck.

"Stop that or I'll fuck you right here in front of everyone in this club."

"Promise?" I wiggle my ass again against his straining erection and smile back at him.

"I swear to it. You keep that up and I'll pull your panties down from underneath that skirt and fuck you senseless." His eyes are unwavering and stern with an underlying intensity seeping through.

"What if I'm not wearing any panties?" I softly place my lips on his and then gently nip his bottom lip with my teeth.

He looks at me questioningly before slowly sliding his large hand up my thigh as he proceeds to discover that I am, in fact, not wearing anything underneath my skirt. With his hand tightly grasping my thigh, he swipes his thumb through my folds. I let out a breathy moan and lean my face down into his neck as he begins to rub my clit with small, demanding strokes.

Thank god this club is dark and everyone's current attention is focused on the awe-inspiring pole acrobatics of the current spotlighted dancer or else I'm pretty sure it would be quite obvious that Trent is currently working me over. My breath is coming in short bursts, and my nipples are so hard they are practically poking holes through my bra.

"What are you trying to do to me?" I whimper into his ear.

He growls. He fucking growls in my ear.

"I'm not sure how much more I can take," I whisper as I feel pleasurable clenches with each of his circular strokes on my clit.

"Stand up. Follow me. *Now*," Trent demands as he pulls his hand out from under my skirt and guides my hips to a standing position. He grabs my hand and quickly leads me toward the doors that lead out of the club. I make eye contact with Amy, who is standing near the bar with a few of our coworkers. She grins at me and waggles her eyebrows like a fucking idiot, and I can't help but to smile back at her.

I'm sure she probably witnessed our little display of public affection…and I'm well aware that's putting it mildly. I follow Trent out of the club and toward the party bus that is parked in front of the strip club. He whispers something in the driver's ear and hands him the money he originally pulled out from the wad of cash I played Go Fish with from his pocket. The driver nods and quickly steps off of the bus before Trent ensures the doors are closed tightly.

"Lie back on that couch and let me taste that perfect pussy of yours."

I shudder involuntarily as I lie back on one of the couches that line the party bus. Trent quickly kneels between my legs, pushing my skirt up past my waist and lifting each of my knees up so they are resting on his shoulders. He starts slowly licking up and down my hot core before placing a light suction on my clit. My breathing is heavy and my moans are becoming loud as I feel him bringing me closer to orgasm. He slides two fingers inside of me as he continues to use his mouth on my sex. Delicious tingles rush up and down my spine as I focus on the orgasm that is building deep within.

I suck in a breath, my body relishing in his touch, his oh-so-perfect touch.

His mouth and fingers continuing to work their magic on me.

"Ah, fuck! Oh my god! I'm so close!"

I can no longer keep quiet as Trent proves his oral skills are *a-fuckin'-mazing*. I fist my fingers in his hair, guiding his face, thrusting my hips into his mouth, begging for my release.

He gazes up at me, his eyes dilated, his mouth wet from my arousal, my nipples even harder from the sight of him. Goose bumps of desire sprout across my body like wildfire as I watch his face between my legs, his mouth, fingers, and tongue pleasuring me, bringing me to heightened rapture.

"Don't come yet. I want to feel you come when I'm inside of you," Trent whispers huskily as he quickly unzips his jeans and pulls his still-hard cock out. In an instant, he sits down on the couch and has me straddling him. I ease myself down, reaching between my thighs and guiding his thick, rigid shaft home.

And then I saddle the fuck up and ride. I ride his hard cock with one goal in mind.

"Yes. Ride me," Trent says as he guides my hips up and down.

I'm meeting him thrust for thrust, plunge for plunge, and each hard, deep penetration has my pussy tightening around him.

"God you're so beautiful," he says breathlessly.

That one statement is my undoing and I feel my orgasm take control. Waves and waves of pleasure roll through my body and I can no longer maintain my movements. I melt into him as he continues to thrust hard and fast inside of me until I can feel his orgasm take over. He yells out my name, and I can feel the warm gush of fluid release. We are both sweaty and breathing heavily as he holds me tightly to his chest, my thighs still straddling his.

"Can we stay like this? You feel so fucking perfect around my cock that I don't want to leave."

I laugh lightly into his neck and lean back to look into his eyes. "I think the strip club would frown upon this."

"I don't fucking care." His bright blue eyes are shining with delight.

After I clean up a little in the bus bathroom, we head back into the club hand in hand, our faces probably making our most recent escapade known. Trent looks sated and thoroughly fucked, and I'm sure my expression is mirroring his. Amy and the rest of our crew are seated near the stage and enjoying the entertainment the strippers are providing. I take a seat next to my crazy best friend as Trent heads to the bar to order us more drinks.

"So did you get your fuck on in the party bus?" Amy asks as she places several singles in a stripper's G-string.

I let out a small laugh and give her a demure smile.

"You dirty little slut! I can't believe you and Dr. Thrust Me banged on the party bus! Did you give Ed the driver a good show? I couldn't be more proud of you right now by the way."

"Aw, don't get all emotional on me now, drunky. And no, Trent paid Ed the driver an obscene amount of cash to step off the bus while we 'got our fuck on.'" I emphasize her direct quote with the universal air-quote gesture.

"I'm surprised you two didn't screw right here while Candy was showing us her pole skills."

"Sorry to disappoint. I know you have a voyeurism fetish, but we decided to avoid being arrested for public indecency."

"Not to sound like a sappy idiot, but Elle, I'm so happy to see you so happy," Amy says before jumping out of her chair and practically suffocating me with a tight hug. During her public display of affection for me, she also happened to spill her entire glass of vodka and cranberry all over my white tank top.

"Shit! Sorry, Ellie Belly!" Amy is giggling uncontrollably, and I just look back at her with an annoyed stare.

"Where's the bathroom, idiot?"

"It's in the back near the strippers' dressing room," she says as she points towards the back of the club.

I head to the bathroom only to find out it's not *near* the strippers' dressing room; it's actually *in* the strippers' dressing room. I make my way toward one of the wall-length mirrors and see that my white tank top is covered in pink cranberry stains. Fuck, there is no way to remedy this situation.

"Uh oh. Looks like someone needs a new shirt." I glance up to see Candy, the stripper from earlier in the night, standing behind me.

"Yeah. My friend Amy got a little hug crazy and ended up spilling her entire drink on my shirt."

"Here, let me give you a shirt." Candy turns around and pulls something out of her locker, her bare ass staring back at me. *Yes, her fucking locker.* This club is as classy as they come.

"This is all I have for you to borrow. It's a promotional tee for the club, but at least it's dry," she says as she hands me a black shirt.

"Wow. Thank you so much. You have no idea how much I appreciate this."

"Sweetie, I've gotta get back out there, but I hope you enjoy the rest of your night," Candy says before striding out of the dressing room on her ridiculously high stripper heels.

I replace my ruined tank with the black promotional tee that Candy, the hot and seemingly friendly stripper, gave me. I see my reflection in the mirror and can't help but to laugh. I'm now sporting my black mini skirt and a tight black tee that is short enough to reveal my belly button. The shirt just has the word *Trixie's* written over the chest, accentuating my boobs with sparkles.

Oh my, Trent is going to have a field day with this one.

I head out of the dressing room and make my way back over to my friends. Trent is sitting down next to Amy, and a huge grin spreads across his face when he takes a gander at my new shirt.

"Damn, I leave you alone for five minutes and you're now promoting this club. Did you get a job here? When I said I wanted you to dance for me, I meant for my own personal entertainment, baby." The asshole is grinning so hard, I can't help but to smile back at him.

"Shit, I thought you wanted me to dance for you. I've agreed to go on stage next, and there's no backing out now I already signed a stripper contract."

He roughly grabs my hips and pulls me to his lap. "No fucking way anyone is going to watch my girl dance or see any part of her naked. These tits, this hot ass, and your sweet, tight pussy are mine and mine alone."

I giggle at his demands and find myself swooning over the idea of only being his. This was definitely a night to remember. I look down at the man staring back at me with his sexy, dimpled grin and mentally take a picture of him for my Trent album.

Click.

Chapter Twenty-Eight

"If the chicken shit shoe fits, go ahead and wear it, you pussy."

"Honey, I'm home!" I holler to Trent as I walk into his apartment. I see him sitting at his kitchen counter, laptop in front of him, and he's motioning for me to come over towards him.

"Wow! That's awesome, Mia. Do you like your kindergarten teacher?" Trent is talking into his laptop.

I just got done taking a yoga class with Amy and Lizzy. We just started this new hot yoga class that, no joke, kicked my ass. I've never sweated so much in my life. My hair is haphazardly thrown into a messy bun and I'm still sporting my yoga pants and tank top. I'm a hot mess right now and planned on taking a quick shower once I got to Trent's place. I set my gym bag down near the kitchen island and stand behind him, my hands resting on his chair.

"Miss Ann is so pretty and so nice and she brought us cupcakes today!" A sweet little girl's face is on Trent's laptop screen. He's Skyping with his niece Mia, and this is the first time I've actually gotten to see her cute dimpled face in person—in a virtual perspective at least. She looks so much like Trent, with dark black hair thrown up into adorable pigtails and the brightest blue eyes I've ever seen on a child.

ADORABLE. So freakin' adorable.

"Cupcakes! How many cupcakes did my Mia eat today?"

Mia holds up two fingers and smiles. "Two! I wanted three, but Miss Ann said no." Her bottom lip puckers out into a heartbreakingly loveable pout. That one little look has Trent wrapped around her little finger.

"Aw, baby. Next time I'm in Seattle, I'll buy you five cupcakes and you can eat every single one of them. Just don't tell your mom."

Mia claps her hands excitedly. "Yay! I love you, Uncle Trent! You comin' home soon?"

"Yeah, sweet girl. I'll be coming home for a little bit really soon. We'll have an entire day to spend together."

"Who's that?" Mia is now looking at me through the screen. "Is that Ellie? I've heard Mommy talking about your girlfriend Ellie." She giggles excitedly.

Trent laughs and leans to the left, allowing me to get closer to the screen. "Mia, this is my girlfriend, Ellie. Isn't she pretty?"

Mia nods her head several times. "Very pretty! Hi, Ellie! My name is Mia and I'm four" She holds up four fingers, grinning widely.

"Hi, Mia." I'm smiling back at her cute dimpled grin through the screen. "Four years old? Oh my gosh, you're so grown up!"

"I know. I'm going to drive my daddy's car soon and I have a boyfriend at school and my mommy painted my fingernails pink because she says I'm a big girl!" She holds up her hands to the screen, showing the already chipped pink fingernail polish on her cute little fingers.

"You're such a big girl! I love your pink finger nails—"

Trent cuts me off before I can say anything else. "Boyfriend? No way. My Mia is not allowed to have a boyfriend until she's thirty. What's this little asshole's name?"

"Trent! Language please!" Trent's sister Leah is now standing behind her daughter's chair, scowling at him, while Mia bursts into a fit of giggles.

"Mia is four, Lee! No way should she have a god damn boyfriend!" Trent's response makes me chuckle out loud, and Leah just grins back at me.

"Mia baby, tell Uncle Trent and Ellie good night then go upstairs and get ready for bed. I'll be up in a few minutes to read you a book." Leah glances down at Mia with a warm smile.

"Good night, Uncle Trent! Good night, Ellie!" Mia kisses her sweet little hand and blows us a kiss before hopping off of her chair, her pigtails swinging lightly as she quickly walks away from the laptop.

Leah sits down in front of the screen, her pretty face in full view. I can now see why Mia looks so much like Trent—Leah and Trent also share an uncanny resemblance. Leah is gorgeous with jet-black hair cut into a short, layered bob, contrasting her sky blue eyes in a very striking way. "Trent, you're right, Mia is only four years old, so I'll stop letting her go for drives in Matty's car and staying out past her one a.m. curfew. I probably shouldn't have been so lax on her punishment when I found beer in her bedroom…" Leah is grinning like the Cheshire Cat, and I honestly think I just fell in love with this woman. She is a total ball-buster, and I love that she gives her protective brother such a hard time.

"Not funny, Lee." Trent runs his hand through his tousled hair, causing it to become a hot mess of inky-black deliciousness.

"Actually…" I can't help the laugh the escapes my throat. "I think it's very funny." Trent peers back at me and gives me an annoyed look. Leah starts to chuckle hard on the other side of the screen.

"I'm glad to see my sister and my girlfriend are finding humor in screwing with me."

"It's only because we love you so much, little brother."

"Yeah, yeah. Now you're just patronizing me." His lips quirk up into a smirk.

"So this is Ellie? I'm so glad I get to finally put a face to the name and all of the wonderful things you've been telling me about her." Leah's eyes lock with mine. "Seriously…he can't stop talking about you. Every phone conversation I've had with him since he got to Charlotte has revolved around talking about how awesome you are." Her face is beaming with amusement.

"Please don't hold anything back on my account." Trent flushes with embarrassment as he gives Leah an exasperated look before glancing back at me with a tight smile.

"Awww, you talk about me? You know he started stalking me the moment he stepped foot in Charlotte—" I quickly say before Trent cuts me off again.

"Jesus…" He is shaking his head in exasperation. "I should've known you two would get along so perfectly." Leah and I snicker at Trent's expense. He's just so damn easy to get riled up, and it seems that we both have a way of giving him a hard time.

I hear my phone ringing loudly from my purse. "Leah, it was so nice to meet you! I hope we can do this again really soon!"

"You too, Ellie! Get my number from Trent so you can call me, and I'll give away *all* of my little brother's secrets and most embarrassing stories." Leah gives a smile and light wave before I leave the kitchen to go grab my phone from my purse.

I take a quick phone call from Amy. She just wants to know if I am going to come back to the apartment tonight or stay at Trent's. I guess she and Lizzy have an entire night planned of Chinese take-out and sappy romantic comedies. I'm happy they have become really good friends.

I've felt extremely guilty at times since Lizzy moved in. I've been so wrapped in Trent over the past several weeks, spending the majority of my time with him, and I kind of feel like I haven't really been there for Lizzy.

She's going through so much with everything between her and her husband, Matt. She's in a foreign city and most of her friends and family are still back in Louisville. The guilt was building up, and finally last night,

I had dinner with her in hopes that I could make up for all of the times I've felt like I've let her down. She reassured me that everything is okay, that she's actually happy here in Charlotte, and she's been using this time away from Louisville to find herself again.

Lizzy has started taking online classes through a local college; she has dreams of finishing her teaching degree. She's also shown a big interest in working out at a nearby gym. Ryder, her personal trainer, is beyond delicious. Someone that good-looking should not be allowed to walk around in a gym all day flexing his muscly biceps, making women cream their panties. Because seriously…he's that fucking good-looking. I'm not sure how Lizzy is managing to get through her training sessions without dry humping his leg. Amy and I got to meet him tonight at the gym after our hot yoga class. Let's just say I had a hard time convincing Amy to leave.

After I end my conversation with Amy, I start heading back into the kitchen, but I stop when I overhear Trent and Leah still Skyping.

"So things with you and Elle seem pretty serious?"

"Yeah, I guess you could say that… I love her, Leah. I really do."

"Wow… I never thought I would hear those words come out of my little brother's mouth."

Trent lets out a small laugh. "I know. I never thought those words would come out of my mouth either. My career has always been my focus, and I couldn't have given two shits about getting into a relationship, but she's just so perfect… I can't wait for you to meet her in person."

"What about Seattle? Dad told me University Hospital has made you a big offer. Head of Trauma Surgery. That's a huge deal, Trent."

Head of University Seattle's Trauma Surgery? Oh my god.

Just hearing Leah say that has my stomach turned up in knots, and I have the urge to run to his bathroom and vomit. I start to hear Trent's voice giving Leah a response, but I just can't do it. I just can't eavesdrop into their conversation. I quickly walk into his bedroom, away from hearing distance, because I definitely can't hear what he's going to say to Leah. I just…*can't.*

I'm a fucking chicken shit and more than aware of this. I'm just too scared to hear him say he's taking University Seattle's offer.

I mean, who wouldn't accept their offer?

Why in the hell would he refuse an offer like that to stay in Charlotte to play house with his girlfriend?

A girlfriend he's known all of two months…

Push it down. Way…way down.

Fuck my life and my shitty, shitty way of handling things. If I had some god damn balls, I'd just ask him straight up what his plan is. But, no.

I'm a flaky, fickle, *chicken shit.*
Someone just go ahead and smack me.

Chapter Twenty-Nine

"It's okay to break down. Pent-up emotion will find its way out no matter how hard you fight it. So don't fight it. Cry. Scream. Be angry. Let the grief come out. Don't put up walls. Don't hold back, because holding back will only get you...nowhere."

I pull into my designated parking spot near my apartment and put my Mustang in park without cutting the engine. My mood is somber. Devastation and defeat are creeping through my thoughts. I glance at the clock and see that it's already midnight. *Something I Can Never Have* by Nine Inch Nails is blaring through my speakers as I watch raindrops slowly drip down the window shield. My mood is falling deeper into the black abyss. The combination of music and rain is only taking me further.

My sixteen-hour shift in the ER ended with several victims of a highway auto accident coming in by squad. Four compact cars and one semi-truck were involved. One of the victims was a three-year-old boy who had been in the backseat of his mother's car. A beautiful blue-eyed, brown-haired baby named Tommy who happened to be sitting on the side of the car that took most of the impact. Tommy's injuries were critical, and when I left the hospital, Trent was still in the OR with him.

Flashbacks of the boy's mother are front and center in my mind. Her bloodcurdling screams and bone-chilling sobs seem to be on constant repeat. I can still visualize her outside of trauma bed one on her knees with her head in her hands, visibly breaking down while we were performing CPR and intubating her lifeless child.

I don't know if he's going to pull through.

I shut my eyes to keep the tears inside and lean my head back on my seat while silently praying to God that he wraps his arms around Tommy and gives him strength to survive.

I cut the engine and slowly walk toward my apartment, attempting to push back the mental flashbacks of Tommy's lifeless body underneath my hands while I performed chest compressions. My mind is numb. I am in shock and running on autopilot. I am hanging on by a mental thread as I shakily put my keys into the lock and open my apartment door.

I throw my keys on the kitchen table and sit down. I'm thankful that Amy and Lizzy aren't home tonight. Amy is working the late shift in the ER and Lizzy went home to Louisville to see Matt. I am just blankly staring off into space, trying not to think. Trying to shut my brain off and not replay every detail of my night. But I can't do it. I'm running through every aspect, every sound, and every visual. I can even smell the remnants of the chocolate ice cream that was on Tommy's shirt before I had to cut it off of his little body. I am usually better about shutting my emotions off and just doing my fucking job, but I can't do it this time.

This was a baby.

A sweet, helpless child whose life might have been taken away. All of this because one asshole decided that drinking and driving was a good idea. A man that chose to drive home from the bar when his alcohol level was way beyond the legal limit and was lucky enough to walk away with only minor injuries.

I feel the bile start to rise in my throat. I quickly get out of my chair and run toward the bathroom. I make it just in time before emptying all of my stomach contents into the toilet. The combination of adrenaline, nerves, and mental exhaustion is eating away at me. I sit on the bathroom floor and put my head in my hands in a pathetic attempt to regain control.

Time seems to stand still as I remain seated on the cool, hard bathroom tile.

Eventually, I find the strength to stand up and turn on the hot water. I'm hoping a shower will help relax all of this emotional energy that is coursing through my body. I avoid the bathroom mirror. I'm afraid that once I see my red-rimmed eyes and tired face I will break down. I'm not ready to lose it. I feel guilty for even thinking about crying. I don't have a baby that is lying on an OR table, fighting for his every breath. I don't have to attempt to perform a miracle to save a small child's life. I am one of the fortunate ones. I am home. I am alive. I don't have a loved one whose life is hanging on by a mere heartbeat.

I strip off my soiled scrubs. As I throw them in the trash, I see the bloodstains all over my pant legs. *Tommy's blood.* I feel the bile rising again and quickly put my head over the toilet, dry heaving several times until I have nothing left. I rinse my mouth out at the sink and step into the hot, steamy shower. The water makes me realize I am bone-chillingly cold. Placing my face directly under the soothing water, I feel a small sob escape my throat. I attempt to force it back, but it's too late. The tears are freely flowing down my cheeks. I can taste the saltiness on my lips as my sorrow slides down my face with the water.

My body is shaking uncontrollably, and I hear the gasping sobs coming more quickly from deep within my chest. I rest my back against the shower wall. My body slowly slides down on its own accord until I am seated directly underneath the showerhead. As the water pelts down, I let my mind release all of the pent-up emotions I have unsuccessfully avoided since I left the ER.

I sit on the floor of the shower until the water runs cold, my fingers pruning. I put on my plush white robe and wrap my long auburn locks in a towel. I use the hand towel by the sink to wipe the steamy residue off of the mirror. I slowly lift my eyes until I am looking at myself.

Red-rimmed and dark-circled, I am visibly worn down.

I decide to forgo eating and brush my teeth in hopes that I can sleep this night off. I don't even worry about turning off the lights in the living room. I walk slowly down the hall, step into my bedroom, and fall face first onto my bed and into my pillows.

"What a fucking night," I mumble to myself before falling into a restless sleep.

***

Waking up to several large knocks at the door, I groggily get out of bed and pad down the hall. The clock above the TV says 3 a.m.

It must be Trent.

I open the door and I am immediately startled by the man standing on the threshold of my apartment. My body is overwhelmed by fear. Deep within my gut, I know that something is very, very wrong with this scenario. My breath quickens and pulse speeds up as adrenaline pumps into my veins.

I am face to face with Frank.

ER patient Frank.

Paranoid Schizophrenic Frank.

He is staring at me with cold, soulless eyes.

Fuck.

Chapter Thirty

"Fear is a difficult emotion. It can either make you unable to do anything or force you to dig deep within yourself and fight. Fight with everything you have. Fight for your every breath, your every heartbeat...fight for your life."

Frank roughly pushes his steel-toe boot into the door, blocking any attempt at keeping him out of my apartment.

"It's bad manners not to invite someone in when they come to see you."

I take a deep, shaky breath and try to calm my nerves before attempting to answer him. Maybe I can talk him down off this proverbial ledge he's on and avoid the dark, tragic scenarios that are passing through my mind.

"Frank, it's three in the morning. I apologize for my rude behavior, but I was a little startled to have someone knocking at my door at this hour. I think it would be best if you went home."

"Desperate times call for desperate measures, Nurse Ellen."

"Well, I think it would be best if you went home," I say before quickly attempting to close the door to my apartment.

Frank roughly pushes the door back open, wraps his hand around my neck, and pulls a gun from his jacket pocket.

Oh fuck.

"You keep doing that, Nurse Ellen. Bad manners are not becoming of you,"

The barrel of the gun is now pressed into my right temple.

Double fuck.

He pushes me backwards into my apartment and slams the door shut with his boot. His revolting mouth is breathing harshly into my face as his hand increases pressure on my throat.

My mind is in panic mode.

I am frantically thinking of ways to defend myself or call for help. I can see my cell phone on the kitchen counter, but it's not within my reach. I am praying that Trent or Amy don't come home right now. I'm not really sure what Frank would do if they were to walk through that door.

Frank shoves me into the kitchen and sternly instructs me to sit down in the chair. He is mumbling to himself and pacing back and forth. In the light of my kitchen, I can see just how disheveled this man looks. He has most likely been living on the streets for several days; he reeks of alcohol and his entire appearance is unkempt.

"Frank, why are you doing this? If you need help, I will help you. You don't have to do this."

"SHUT THE FUCK UP!" He is boring holes into my skull with his dark, disturbing eyes. They are black, lifeless pits that make you feel like you're falling into the depths of hell. "You don't want to help me. You never did, you stupid bitch. I don't fucking need help. I came here for a reason and I'm going to get what I want." Frank is looking me up and down, undressing me, violating me. His eyes stop near my chest, and he slowly steps toward me before sharply pulling my robe open and crudely grabbing my breast. My body jerks violently away from his slimy hands.

"Get off of me!" I scream into his face as I try to put distance between us by standing up and moving away from the chair.

Then he places the barrel of the gun into my temple again, and dread fills my gut.

"You need to sit back down. You try that again and I will fucking blow your brains out."

I sit back down into the chair. My mind is shouting for me to make some quick decisions or I am not going to walk away from this alive.

This man will kill me in my own apartment.

Frank is leaning back against the kitchen counter with his gun pointing directly at me. His hands are trembling slightly, and his left eye keeps twitching at a rapid pace. He is muttering to himself as he stares at my open robe. I attempt to close my robe shut so my naked chest isn't exposed to him, but he quickly stalks towards me, ripping my hand away with brutal force.

"Put your hands behind your back," he demands as he pulls a roll of duct tape from his jacket pocket.

No...No...NO!

I have reached that critical moment where I need to fight.

Fight with everything I have.

I know I cannot let this man tie me down or else I will be left for dead. I quickly stand up and grab for his gun. I manage to get one hand on the barrel and push him back toward the kitchen counter, but I am no match for his strength. Using his elbow, he quickly swipes across my face. The impact causes me to stumble back and Frank takes advantage. A quick, forceful punch to the stomach makes me immediately loosen my grip on his gun, the feel of bile rising in my throat as all of the breath is pushed out of my lungs. My eyes water and my jaw clenches. I weakly lift my eyes up and face the vicious impact of a hard blow to the face…knocking me out cold.

Pain… So. Much. Pain.

I feel disoriented as I slowly blink my eyes. The throbbing ache in my head is intensified. My vision is blurred, and it takes a few minutes before I'm able to focus on my surroundings. I can make out that I'm still in the kitchen. I glance down and see that I'm actually lying on the floor, my robe open, and I'm left exposed in nothing but my cotton panties. My hands and ankles are bound together.

FUCK. FUCK. FUCK.

My heart is practically pounding through my chest as I take in my surroundings and come to understand the dire situation I'm currently faced with. I am lying vulnerably bound and exposed while a fucking psychopath is loose in my apartment. I glance up at the clock on the stove and see that it's only 3:30 am. I was out long enough for him to tie me up. Overwhelming fear washes over me, and I'm left vulnerable, contemplating the fact that I'm not going to walk out of this alive.

He's going to kill me. This man is going to fucking kill me.

Frank is standing over me. He is a fairly large man—at least six feet tall and probably pushing two hundred pounds. His eyes are rabid and his breathing is rough. He straddles my stomach and places all of his weight on my midsection. His jacket is off, and he's wearing a white t-shirt that is severely filthy and has several holes throughout. He pushes his long, greasy black hair out of his eyes, and that's when I notice he no longer has a gun. He is holding one of my kitchen knives.

Frank slowly runs the tip of the knife down my sternum along my midsection, the cold, sharp tip causing my nerve-endings to stand on end, making my body shudder in anticipation…in fear. I don't realize I'm holding my breath until he lifts the knife off of my stomach, spurring a deep, shuddering breath to escape my lungs.

Frank laughs coldly as he stares down at me; his face is evil, demonic. This man has far passed the point of return. He has fallen over that proverbial ledge, and Frank is not the same Frank I have taken care of in the ER. I'm not even sure if he is human anymore.

He scoots down my body so he is now sitting on my thighs. Taking the knife, he deliberately starts to cut my panties off. My breath is coming in quick, shallow spurts, my breasts heaving up and down as I'm desperately trying to pull in oxygen, fighting the urge to pass out again as my body threatens to hyperventilate.

"P-P-Please stop this, Frank. Please, please, please stop this!" I'm begging, pleading for him to stop the inevitable.

His knuckles make impact with my right cheek bone, which makes my eyes tear up and sting intensely. "You *need* to shut. The. Fuck. Up." His putrid breath hits my face, stirring nausea in my gut.

Frank stands up and gives several hard kicks to my ribs with his steel-toe boots. The last rigid thrust of his boot is so forceful that I can audibly hear a sickening crack. The pain is so penetrating that tears slide down my cheeks, and a low wheeze boils out of my chest. My breathing is shallow, and I suspect that Frank has not only fractured several ribs but also punctured my right lung. He glares down at me as a deep, menacing laughter consumes him.

"Nurse Ellen, I can't stop now. I finally have you exactly where I want you."

He roughly pulls my threadbare panties off of me and gawks down at my exposed body.

Tears continue to stream down my cheeks as his eyes move upwards and lock onto my face.

"Why are you crying, Nurse Ellen? Don't worry, I'm gonna make you feel *real good*. We're both gonna feel *so good*."

Bile rises from my stomach and hastily fills my throat; the urge to vomit is overwhelming. I attempt to sit up but he just pushes me back down to the icy, hardwood floor. I turn my head to the side in just enough time before I retch violently, bitterness pouring out of my mouth.

Frank seems to be ignoring the fact that I am spewing all over the place and lays his body down on top of mine. I can feel his arousal pressing into my pelvic bone. He is grunting loudly as he begins to grind himself into my defenseless, naked body. He does this for several minutes before sitting back on my thighs and pulling his erection out of his repulsive sweatpants.

"Now you're going to take care of me." He begins to stroke himself while watching me struggle to breathe.

I hear footsteps coming near my apartment door.

Oh god… Please don't let that be Amy. Or Trent. Oh god, no…

Panic washes over me, and I know I have to do something to warn whoever is planning on walking into my apartment. I take a feeble gasp and attempt to yell loud enough so whoever is near my door can hear my struggle.

"AHHHHHHHH! Get off of me!" I shriek at the top of my lungs.

My ribs protest in agony, and I instantly feel like I'm suffocating.

Frank smacks me across the face with his free hand and tells me to shut the fuck up again through clenched teeth. He continues to fondle himself and doesn't seem to notice the door knob to my apartment turn, little by little, indicating that the visitor is hesitant, aware that something very bad is occurring inside my apartment. Frank's back is to the door, and although, I'm lying on the floor, bound and exposed, I still have the door in view.

The door opens slowly and then my vision is blocked by Frank lying down on top of my body. He attempts to thrust himself inside of me, but the way my ankles are bound together prevents him from being able to penetrate. He's grunting loudly and aggressively, trying to push his length inside of me. I close my eyes tightly, lock my thighs together, and try to move my hips away from him in pure desperation.

I'm petrified and consumed with fear. Each inhalation of my lungs is getting shallower as my body screams for oxygen. I'm starting to feel lightheaded as I open my eyes again. I see Trent with the gun, standing behind Frank. A thousand different emotions are all over his face. My vision begins to tunnel as my ears are filled with ringing.

"GET THE FUCK OFF OF HER!" Frank stills and turns to see Trent pointing the gun at his face. He speedily stands up off of my weak, helpless body and tries to lunge at Trent.

BANG!

My body jerks from the startling, ear-splitting sound of a gunshot.

The intense, all-encompassing sound echoes deafeningly throughout my apartment.

The sensation of blood spurting across my face and chest instantly causes my stomach to recoil. Frank's body falls to the ground in a crashing tumble.

His lifeless body bleeds onto the hardwood floor of my kitchen.

Trent drops the gun to the floor and immediately collapses to his knees, draping himself over me. "Ellie, I got you baby. I got you baby. Hold on for me…"

That's the last thing I remember before my world goes completely black.

Chapter Thirty-One

"When life gives you dilemma, you should fight. Fight for every breath, every beat of your heart, and every chance to live another day."

Ellen...Ellie... Open your eyes, baby. Please open your eyes.

Someone is grasping my hand tightly, lifting it up, and I can feel soft, warm lips touch it tenderly.

You're going to be okay, Ellie. I can promise you that.

Muffled voices are around me, and a faint *beep beep beep* is insistent in the background. I try like hell to open my eyes, but the pounding in my skull is refusing to stop. Constant aching and pounding and aching and pounding... *Where am I?* My body doesn't feel like my body. I feel as if I'm having an actual out-of-body experience. My mind searches for some sort of memory, something to pull me out of this nightmare.

Search...

Find something...

Come on, Ellen. Remember what happened...

Then a vision of Frank straddling my thighs fills my brain and I remember. I remember everything—every crushing blow I received underneath his cold hands, every fear that overwhelmed me, the fear of never walking away from him alive. Adrenaline starts to rush through my veins, my breathing is fast, and my heart is nearly pounding out of my chest. *Beep beep beep beep...* That insistent beeping in the background has gotten louder, quicker.

Ellie, calm down baby. Someone get her physician and nurse in here.

Warm hands touch my cheeks, softly caressing them, attempting to calm me down, but it's too late. I'm stuck in the nightmare that is Frank. The memories are flooding in like a hurricane and I'm scared. Terrified. Cold fluid is pushed into my vein and my brain is getting foggy... Frank is drifting away into a dark abyss. Far from me, far enough that he can't touch me, hurt me...*rape me...kill me*. That's what he was going to do. He was going to violate me in the worst possible way and then leave me for dead. I squeeze my eyes tighter, fearful that if I open them he will be there. Standing. Waiting. Watching. Ready to hurt me.

Beep...beep...beep.

The beeping is slowing, and I feel my body relaxing into nothingness. It's a safe place where my mind and body will be protected and I don't have to think about anything... especially *him*.

***

I flex my hand and relish in the ability to actually move parts of my body again. I don't feel like I'm disconnected from myself anymore. I just feel tired and *pain*—I definitely feel pain. My chest hurts and my head is still throbbing.

Throbbing incessantly.

I flutter my eyelids open and my vision in blurred. I strive to focus, attempting to figure out where in the hell I am. The blurriness is replaced by the gray stark walls of a hospital room—an ICU room actually.

I'm in the ICU? Oh my god.

I'm lying in a hospital bed, in the ICU. I make out a Regency Hospital logo on a frame hanging from the wall and turn my head slightly to the side to see Trent next to me. He is sitting in a chair, his head leaned back, his eyes closed. He looks tired, disheveled. Stress lines his face. I reach my hand towards his—its currently resting on the stiff white sheets of my hospital bed. God, just moving my hand alone feels like I'm using enough energy to move a Mack Truck.

How long have I been lying here?

How long have I been unconscious?

"Trent," my voice croaks out in a whisper. My throat is sore and drier than cotton balls. I lightly touch his fingers with my hand. His eyes blink a few times and then there they are, gazing back at me, those beautiful blue eyes. They wrap me up and I feel safe for the first time since *he* stepped into my apartment.

"Ellie! Oh, baby..."

Trent kneels next to my bed, grasping my weak hand in both of his palms, his warm, comforting hands. He leans his forehead down, touching my fingers to his face.

"God, I was so scared." His eyes reach me and lock my gaze.

"You saved me. You saved my life."

"I could hear your muffled screams when I was walking towards your apartment and I *knew*. I just knew that something wasn't right. And then, when I saw him on top of you..." Trent shuts his eyes tightly, his jaw grits, and he takes a deep, trembling breath. "When I saw him on top of you, my heart fell out of my chest and I was ready to do anything to save you. *Anything*."

"Is he... Is he..." I can't even let his name cross my lips. Thoughts of his putrid breath and vile hands touching me, hurting me, violating me... They are causing my chest to feel heavy. Pressure... So much pressure is pressing down on me, making me unable to breath.

"You're safe, baby. He's dead. He will never hurt you again. No one will ever hurt you again, I can promise you that." Trent leans towards my face, tenderly kissing my forehead, and I take a heavy breath. I think this is the first time since Frank walked into my apartment that I feel like I can actually breathe.

"I'm going to go get your family and Amy. They've been worried sick about you."

"My parents are here?"

Trent lets out a low laugh. "Of course your parents are here, Elle. We've all been worried about you. Rest your eyes. I'll go get them." He stands up, kissing my forehead one more time, his lips lingering.

"Thank you, Trent."

"For what?" His look is incredulous.

"For everything. For being here. For being you. For saving me." A tear falls from my eye and slowly slides down my cheek.

Trent catches the liquid emotion with his fingertip. "I thought we've already established that I love you. Now let's establish that I would do anything for you, always, Ellie. You're important to me. *So fucking important to me*." His smile is soft, gentle, and it caresses my soul. He leans down and softly presses his lips to mine. His kiss is tender and affectionate, and it grabs at my heartstrings. And thoughts of Trent moving to Seattle aren't even crossing my mind, because right now, in this moment, I'm just thankful that I'm actually here, *alive*.

Chapter Thirty-Two

"Sadness and grief can be all-consuming. They can eat you alive and leave a shell of your former self. The only resolution is to search deep within yourself and find the will to battle for your well-being. For your chance to be whole again."

Eight long days at Regency.

Admitted to the ICU for four of the days, I spent the other four days finishing my recovery on a Medical-Surgical floor. I suffered a concussion, several cracked ribs, and a small puncture to my right lung. My face and midsection were covered in bruising from the violent blows I repeatedly received from Frank. I'm lucky, so damn lucky. If Trent wouldn't have happened to come home when he did, I would have been gone. Dead. There is no doubt in my mind that Frank was going to kill me. He was going to violate me in the absolute worst way and then take my life; but Frank was the one who died that critical night. Frank is dead, and I'm alive.

Everyone has been watching over me, trying to help me get through this awful, horrible situation. Physically, I'm doing better, on the mend. Everything is healing, and the only visible remnants of my injuries are the faint bruises on my face and midsection. Emotionally, though? I'm not really dealing with things all that well. Amy, Lizzy, and Trent have been the best support system anyone could ask for. They've spent countless nights at my bedside while I was in the hospital, and they proceeded to help me with everything I needed once I was discharged home. I'm so thankful for them, their support, and their endless love.

It's been four weeks since my attack.

Four long weeks.

These weeks feel more like years. I haven't spoken with Trent all day. His surgery schedule was grueling and the gunshot victim that rolled in at 7 p.m. made it impossible for me to see him before leaving work tonight. My muscles ache and my entire body is carrying the weight of the past couple of weeks. My emotional state is... I'm not even sure what to call it.

Withdrawn?

Emotionless?

I know I'm introverted, closed off, and I'm not myself right now. I'm wallowing in a bottomless pit of grief and anxiety. My nights are sleepless, restless, and bringing me closer to my breaking point. Every day, flashbacks of my attack consume my mind and nearly choke me to death. Visions of Frank in my apartment wake me up at night. His cold, soulless eyes staring down at me while his vile hands are all over my body.

These thoughts, these recollections, are overwhelming. They are slowly taking pieces of my sanity, day by day, minute by minute. Every day a small piece of my heart, *my soul*, is stolen from me. Trent and I haven't been getting along all that well lately. I'm short and terse and would rather wallow in my own self-pity than spend time with him. I think last night was nearly the last straw for Trent. He came over to my apartment to spend some time with me and my detached, pathetic state just put a giant roadblock between us.

"Baby, let's get out of the apartment. I want to take you to dinner," he said as he sat on the edge of my bed, looking down at me with tenderness in his eyes.

"I'm not going out tonight, Trent," I said before rolling over in my bed, my back towards him. I could hear him sigh heavily in frustration. Or was it irritation? I wasn't really sure. I knew he was tired of this. Tired of the ginormous change in me. Tired of trying to pull me out of myself and help me get back to some semblance of normality.

I felt his warm hand rest gently on my back. "Tell me what I need to do, Ellie. Just tell me what I need to do to take this pain away for you and I'll do it." His voice was a whisper, nearly pleading.

"Nothing, Trent. There's nothing you can do. There's nothing you can say. You might as well just go home." I held back the tears as my voice cracked in a hushed tone. His hand gripped my shoulder, and I could practically feel him wince behind me when I told him to leave. Why was I still doing this? Pushing him away. Refusing to let him back in. I knew this wasn't fair to him, but for some reason, the wrong words just kept flowing out of my mouth. Trent went home last night after giving me a soft kiss to my forehead, and I was left wondering if that was the final push he needed. Did I just seal myself a fate without Trent by continually testing his patience? Continually avoiding, pushing away, closing off, and putting up giant walls.

My physician strongly encouraged me to begin therapy and take a medical leave of absence from Regency. He could see the grief and depression engulfing me whole. Empathy and concern filled his eyes at my appointment today. I know I need help. I know what I need to do. I know this, and yet, here I am, taking no action. Making no effort to help myself, *heal myself*. I dial the number to the one person who understands me, who will listen, who will lend a willing ear, who will be my shoulder to cry on.

"Hey, sweetie. It's so good to hear your voice."

"Hi, Mom." Tears start to fill my eyes.

"How are you?"

"I'm all right…" My lips tremble with sadness and a sob bubbles up from my throat.

"Oh, baby girl, what's wrong? Your father and I have been so worried about you." My mom's voice is etched with concern. My parents came immediately when they got news of my attack. My mom stayed with me in the hospital for several days and even helped me get settled back into my apartment. It was hard to see her head back home to Louisville, but responsibilities of the family diner were causing a strain. I could tell she was torn and didn't want to leave my side, but Amy, Trent, and Lizzy made sure she knew I would be well taken care of.

"Everything. Absolutely everything." The waterworks have started, and I feel no end in sight. My chest burns with each gasping breath.

"I'm here for you, Ellen. I'm always here for you. Take a deep breath, try to calm down, and tell me what's going on, sweetie."

And with that, I tell her everything. Everything that is bothering me. Trent. The attack. The grief and depression that's consuming me. I'm desperately screaming for help, for guidance, for someone to just fucking tell me what I need to do. For someone to tell me that everything is going to be okay. And that's what she does. She throws me a lifeline, an inflatable life vest to save me from drowning. She helps me see what I know I'm avoiding, what I'm running away from, what I'm sadly attempting to squash down and ignore.

She's right about everything, and deep down, I know this. I already know this. I know what I need to do, what I have to do, what I *will* do. I'm not weak. I've never been the type of girl to let something take over my life, ruin me every minute of every day. I've never been that girl, and I refuse to start being that girl now. For the first time since the attack, I feel renewed, invigorated with hope that things can get better, that I can get through this. I can get past the horrible things Frank did to me. I'm thankful to be alive, and for that, I should be on my hands and knees thanking God. I should be relishing every second of every day, grateful for how things actually turned out.

I'm not sure what will happen with Trent and me. I obviously love him. I love him so much that I can literally feel my heart trying to escape from my chest, aching for him, screaming for him. He saved my life in more ways than one. He saved me from the girl I was turning into after John. He saved me from myself. He saved me from my mentally disturbed attacker who had my life in his cold, careless hands. I may not get to stay with Trent, but at least I got to *be* with him. I got to experience his love and endless kindness, even if I feel like it was too short.

I'm lying in the bathtub, warm water soothing my tired, achy muscles.

Relaxing me.

Calming me.

I close my eyes and slide farther down into the bathtub, only leaving my head peeking above the water line. I place my foot on the faucet, feeling the cool metal graze my skin. My head is clear for the first time in what feels like forever. I take a huge, profound breath, and it feels like it's been ages since I've been able to breathe without my chest protesting. This feeling is wonderful. I hear the bathroom door open and shut quietly. My eyes flutter open to find Trent, still dressed in his navy blue scrubs, gazing down at me; his smile is breathtaking.

"Getting naked without me, I see?"

My lips turn up into a grin. I think this is the first time I've smiled in days. "Sorry, Casanova. I couldn't wait. My muscles needed some soothing."

Trent squats down near the tub and rests his elbows on the porcelain edge, dipping his hands in and splashing a few bubbles towards my face. "I could help with the soothing…"

"I don't doubt that." I flick water towards him with my index finger.

"I missed you. How's my Ellie girl?" I see concern cross his eyes for the briefest moment. I can only imagine the hell I've been putting him through over the past several weeks. I've been so closed off, so distant; I'm sure he feels like I've completely checked out from our relationship. Deep down I'm scared that my emotional state has given him reason enough to leave Charlotte and go back to his life in Seattle. I fear that I've ruined us. Ruined this amazing thing we've shared. I just want to enjoy the time I have with Trent from here on out, even if the time is short, nearing an end. I want to savor him, relish in the way he makes me feel.

"I'm better actually. I had a nice conversation with my mom. She made me finally open my eyes. I've got some work ahead of me, but I'm not letting what Frank did take over my life."

Trent lets out a breath, almost like a massive weight has been lifted off of his shoulders. "You're so strong, baby. So god damn strong. I'm always here for you no matter what, okay?"

I don't let the fact that I know Trent is going to go back to Seattle soon crush this moment. I take his words for what they are right now, right this very second. "Thank you." My eyes are kind, appreciative for what he's done for me. "You have no idea how thankful I am that you came in that night and saved me. You saved my life, Trent."

His eyes close and he shakes his head back and forth subtly, running his hands through his tousled, jet-black hair. "I will never let anything or anyone hurt you. *Never*." His eyes open and the intensity nearly rips my heart out of my chest.

I reach my hand out of the water and place it upon his cheek. "I love you." Water droplets slowly drip onto his skin.

"I love you too." Trent places his palm over my hand, his warm caress causing the tips of my fingers to tingle. "I'm not sure if you remember, but I leave for Seattle tomorrow. I'll only be there until Friday, just a few things to get settled with University Hospital and my old apartment. There are some things I want to talk to you about…"

I immediately place my fingers over his lips, quickly shutting him up before I have to hear that he's leaving me for good. I adjust a little in the tub, lifting my chest above the water, my breasts in full view above the bubbles. His glances down and a lustful smirk crosses his face, my lips returning the favor. I want to savor this time with him, bring back the fun, witty banter we're so good at. We haven't been intimate since before my attack, and my body craves him.

"Let's talk about those things later. Where's my kiss, Dr. Thrust Me?" I giggle a little before pushing my bottom lip out, giving him my best pouty face.

He leans in to give my lips a small peck, and I immediately pull him off balance when I wrap my arms around his neck and drag him into the tub with me, water and bubbles splashing everywhere. "Shit! Ellie!" He yells before he starts laughing.

I'm still giggling with a very shocked and still fully clothed Trent lying on top of me, soaking wet. "Whoops!" I say, feigning innocence.

Grinning at my attempt at being coy, he starts to tickle my ribs, making me laugh even harder. Now I'm begging him to stop. "I see how it is, little spitfire!"

I'm cracking up and gasping for air. "Stop! Please stop! Trennnnnnt!"

He is beaming down me with his beautiful blue gaze. He kisses my lips, gently entwining his tongue with mine. My nipples are instantly hard at the feel of his mouth on mine, his warm skin piercing my body through his wet scrub top. I kiss him back intensely, ardently, as I wrap my legs around his waist.

His arms embrace me before sliding around my ass, pulling my body closer to his. Trent takes me off guard by quickly standing up with me still in his arms. Water is sloshing out of the tub, onto the bathroom floor.

"Trent! What are you doing?!" I squeal when the cold air hits my nude body.

He steps out of the tub and heads for my bedroom, a lascivious grin etched on his face. "I'm getting ready to give that sexy body of yours some serious attention."

"Oh my god! You're getting everything wet!" I whine as he stalks through the hall, sounds of squeaky shoes echoing off of the hardwood floor. Once he steps into my bedroom, he throws me down on the bed, and I laugh as my butt hits the mattress.

Oh god, how I've missed him.

Being with him. Letting him take charge of my body and do wicked, delicious things to me.

"I most certainly am going to get *everything* wet." He gives me a mischievous grin before starting his assault on my now very wet and stark-naked body. All thoughts of Frank and Trent moving back to Seattle are long gone. Right now, I'm only thinking about how good he feels, how much my body is yearning for him to be inside of me.

And my body gets exactly what she desires for hours and hours and hours...

Chapter Thirty-Three

"In order to get what you really want, you have to take your balls in your hand and put yourself out there, vulnerable and exposed."

Trent's flight was delayed for a few hours, and Amy decides that it's high time I enjoy a Friday night out with her. *Friday night Karaoke at Murphy's Pub.* This used to always be our little October ritual. Johnny started this tradition a few years back, and every Friday night in October, we'd get sloshed and watch people make fools of themselves singing *Like A Virgin*, as if they were actually Madonna. I agree fairly enthusiastically to the much needed night out, and I'm extremely happy to see my sister Lizzy tag along.

Things have been really rough on her over the past few months, but I've seen a change in her. She's different, in a good way, a better way. She's really taking time for herself, finding out who she is and what she wants. I support her in anything she decides, and right now, Lizzy has decided to divorce Matt.

She just recently got back to Charlotte from another week-long trip to Louisville. She spent time with Matt, with my parents. Things were said, feelings were expressed, and it sounds like divorce is her final decision.

She broke this news to me yesterday. I held my breath, prepared for her to be a sobbing mess, but I was surprised to see that she was calm, collected, and completely rational. I just want her to be happy. I just want Lizzy to have the life she wants, not the life someone else wants for her, and that's what I think really happened with her and Matt. He had an idea of who he wanted Lizzy to be in his head, and well, that wasn't the person she wanted to be.

I've only had a few, far too short phone conversations with Trent over the past couple of days while he's been in Seattle. I'm avoiding the whole conversation of Trent moving back home. Dr. Grey is due to come back from his medical leave of absence in less than a week, and the thought of Trent leaving me is pretty much eating me alive.

I hate it, and I'm too scared to hear him say the words, so what do I do? I continue to be a chicken shit and avoid. I'm avoiding the conversation, I change the subject whenever he brings it up, and I can feel it in his voice that this is driving him crazy. The last time I talked to him, he sternly told me, "Damnit, Ellie. You can't keep avoiding this conversation. When I get home tonight, we are going to have a nice long chat and you are going to listen to every single word I have to say, even if I have to scream it through a god damn megaphone."

What could I say to that?

Trent is a patient man, but when the time comes for him to make his message known, his patience goes out the window. I'd say we're at that point. I just hope I can hold it together when he breaks my heart. I know what you're thinking…

Why don't you just move to Seattle with him?

And I would do that in a heartbeat if he wanted me to, but I'm not sure he does. The past few weeks have been rough, and my subconscious keeps telling me that Trent Hamilton needs a break from Ellen James's craziness. I know the attack and my closed-off, emotionless state I was walking around in for weeks have been a huge strain on him. I could see it in his eyes as each day passed.

So what am I going to do about it?

I'm not sure of my exact plan of action, but giving him some time and then stalking him in Seattle is on the list of possibilities. I just don't think I can let him go.

He's *it* for me.

Amy, Lizzy, and I take a seat at one of the high top bar tables toward the front of the makeshift stage. Johnny brought us over a few beers and now we're just sitting here, enjoying the ambiance that is drunken karaoke. The song list has ranged from *Don't Stop Believin'* to *Baby Got Back*. A whole lot of classiness all up in this pub.

I'm enjoying this time with my best friend and my sister. We're laughing and cutting up about each boozed-up singer that graces the stage. There is nothing like a good night of watching people who think they are the next Adele, sing their little hearts out. There has yet to be any true talent, but enthusiasm and interesting dance moves help to make up for a lot.

Amy's mouth gapes open as James slides into an empty barstool at our table. Yes, the very same James she refuses to speak to, acknowledge, or even talk about. Dr. Limp Dick, as she so fondly calls him. She's still pissed that he refused to sleep with her drunken vagina after the Regency golf charity function. Amy is the type of girl who is proud of her pussy.

And I mean this in the most extreme form possible. *Vaginal hubris.* She owns her shit, and the fact that James didn't take her up on the offer for a little boom-boom after the charity function, well... That didn't go over to well with Amy.

"What the fuck are you doing here?" Amy nearly gives James whiplash with her curt tone.

Shit, even I felt that sting of that one...

James smiles, which makes my jaw drop. If I were him, I think my balls would have crawled up inside of my stomach. "Everyone keeps talking about these famous karaoke nights at Murphy's and I figured I'd come out and see what all the fuss is about. Plus, I heard you were going to be here... So here am I."

"What makes you think I'd want to see you?" Pissed off isn't even the word for her look right now. I think she might start shooting laser beams from her eyes.

"I didn't think you wanted to see me, but *I* wanted to see *you.*"

Damn, he's good.

I glance at Lizzy, and we both exchange a knowing grin. I know that James has just dropped the gauntlet on her ass. She's been left a little speechless, and I'm just dying to see what she does with his response.

"W-W-Whatever," Amy stutters. She is scowling while James is still smiling as silence consumes our table. The bastard is just sitting there, completely relaxed and without a care in the world. A laugh escapes me, and I think Amy is about to shoot daggers into my chest.

God, she's stubborn.

I've attempted to have several chats with her about James, trying to get her to open her obstinate eyes and see that he showed that he is truly a nice, respectable guy when he didn't have sex with her that night. Let's just say theses attempts at conversations about James did not end well. His nickname of Dr. Limp Dick is still going strong, and she's still continuing to be a total and complete cunt whenever he tries to talk to her. I was honestly feeling bad for the guy, but now seeing the way he handles himself around her, I can see that Amy has for sure met her match with him.

"I'm going to head up to the bar. Anyone need anything?" James asks before standing up from his barstool.

Lizzy and I both thank him for the offer but politely decline. Amy, well...

"Nope, and no one fucking cares where you're going."

Remind me to never piss Amy off. Ever.

James just smirks at her cuntiness and walks towards her barstool, standing close to her. Amy takes a deep breath and closes her eyes. He softly brushes her hair behind her ear, leaning down slowly and whispering loud enough for Lizzy and me to hear. "You look beautiful tonight."

And with that, he turns around and walks away, leaving a *very* shocked and speechless Amy.

"What an asshole," Amy spits out once she regains her equilibrium.

Lizzy and I both look at her with questioning expressions.

"Right? He's such an asshole!" Amy glances back and forth between us, trying to get us to agree with her absurd comment about James. Because seriously, she's completely off her rocker. She can be so stubborn sometimes, especially when it comes to her ego. And let's face it, James gave her vagina's ego a hard blow, and unfortunately for him, Amy's vagina apparently holds grudges. Big. Time.

"I'm not touching that with a ten-foot pole. That shit is between you and him. I'm staying out of it." I raise my hands in the air, showing my refusal to give her my opinion on the entire situation.

"Elle! Seriously? You're not going to agree with me that he's a total asshole?"

I vehemently shake my head no.

"Lizzy? What about you? I know you have to agree with me!"

"I'm also staying out of this one, Amy."

"All three of you are assholes!" Amy screams in frustration.

I give Amy a minute to reel in her anger before testing the waters a little. I know my best friend, and I decide to throw a little comment out there just to see if James has managed to loosen her guard at all.

"Did he really tell you that you looked beautiful tonight?" I take a sip of my beer and watch Amy like a hawk, waiting for her reaction.

She's looking down at her beer, slowly peeling off the label from her bottle. For a split second, her eyes light up a little and the corners of her lips threaten to turn up into a smile. I start to grin in response, and then she looks up, locks eyes with me, and replaces that happy look with a death glare. "Fuck him and his limp dick."

Damn, he really is good. Somehow, James has actually managed to get Amy to let a little bit of her guard down. My money says that James has his work cut out for him when it comes to winning over Amy's affections, but the man has for sure managed to put a few small cracks in her iron-clad wall of grudge-holding and never-ending stubbornness.

After a few more displays of drunken hilarity on the karaoke stage, I notice Amy look down at her phone. She glances up at me and a huge grin spreads across her face. Her fingers are quickly typing out a text message, and once she hits send, she rests back in her seat, takes a swig of her beer, and seems to have a smug look about her.

"What's going on over there, dickhead?" My eyebrow is quirked at her.

"Nothing you need to be concerned about, sweet cheeks." Her eyes are amused, and I get the feeling that she's hiding something from me. I know Amy almost better than I know myself, and believe me, I know when this chick is trying to keep something from me.

"You didn't start another online Twitter relationship with a fictional character, did you?" My fingers are peeling the label off of my beer bottle as I slyly glance up at Amy.

She slams her beer bottle on the table, foam dripping from the top. "Shut up, asshole! First of all, I thought we agreed to *never* talk about that little mishap again, and secondly, NO, I have not. I learned my fucking lesson the first time."

Lizzy is looking at Amy with curiosity on her face. "Online Twitter relationship with a fictional character? I need details. I really, really need details."

"Well—" I start to say before Amy curtly cuts me off by slapping her hand over my mouth.

"We agreed. End of discussion. You talk about it, and I swear I will shove this beer bottle straight up your ass," she says with far too much attitude while giving me a pointed stare.

Lizzy and I start laughing at Amy's very serious demeanor. She's now glowering at us, completely pissed off that I even brought it up, but I couldn't help myself. That has got to be one of the funniest situations I've ever seen my best friend a part of. Yes, Amy fell in love with a fictional book character on Twitter and proceeded to have a two-month love affair through tweets, direct messages, and emails. The book character was a guy named Grant Evans. The book is *Love & Forgiveness* by E.M. Marks. Fantastic book, by the way. I wish I could let you in on this little story, but Amy would quite literally cut off my right labia if I spilled the beans.

Well, I guess a few more details wouldn't hurt anyone…

Amy and her online fictional book boyfriend were going strong and quite possible in some sort of fictional relationship on Twitter. *They were an item.* She was incessantly messaging, emailing, and sending him tweets throughout her day, until her fictional book boyfriend's mother sent her a nasty email…

Come to find out, Amy's love interest was actually a sixteen-year-old boy who started a Twitter account for a book character he knew about from reading one of his mother's smutty romance novels. Yes, the entire ordeal was quite traumatic for my dear friend, Amy, but unquestionably one of the funniest things I've ever heard. In her defense, the kid knew his book character, and I'm pretty sure he had that romance novel memorized.

I can't avoid the fact that Amy is *still* glowering at me. I choose to raise my hands in the air, indicating that I'm throwing the white flag and I'll keep my mouth shut on this topic. Amy turns back towards the bar to let Johnny know we could use a few more beers at our table. I make eye contact with Lizzy and mouth, "I'll tell you later." She quickly smiles and winks at me before Amy is facing us again. Amy glances back and forth between my sister and me, making sure we've really stopped talking about her ex-fictional book boyfriend. She didn't seem to notice our little exchange, and for that I'm extremely thankful. I think she would have honestly attempted the whole beer-bottle-up-the-ass maneuver.

Johnny drops a few beers off at the table, and his dimples are standing out from the giant smile on his face. "You guys are going to love this next...*singer*." He looks directly at me. I'm a little creeped out right now. Johnny isn't one to dish the smiles around, and when he's flashing his dimples, something is going on. The last time he flashed those cute little dimples at me, I had to stand on top of the bar while he serenaded me with *She's a Jolly Good Fellow*. It wasn't my birthday. I'm obviously not a fellow, and Johnny loved every second of embarrassing me in front of the entire bar.

"Stop being so weird, Johnny. You're creeping Ellie out," Amy quickly says before flicking her wrist, indicating for him to leave our table. She's such a bitch sometimes, but right now, I'm more than appreciative.

"What's going on? He's not going to make me stand on top of the bar while he sings again, is he?"

"I don't have a clue, but I got your back, girlfriend. No way in hell will I let him pull a stunt like that again."

I start to say something to Amy but stop when I hear the first beats of one of my favorite Ray LaMontagne songs start to play over the bar speakers. I'm a little pissed off at the asshole that is going to attempt this song; I mean, who in the hell thinks they can even come close to Ray LaMontagne? I've decided that if they really screw this up, I have no qualms with heckling them on stage. I'm not afraid to be the cunt in the crowd. Ray LaMontagne is my man. He's the best, and when you try to mess up the best, well, you have some hell to pay. I look over at Amy and Lizzy and they are both grinning like Cheshire Cats, staring at me. I give them a "what the fuck" look before hearing a very familiar voice start to sing the first lyrics.

My eyes quickly dart up toward the stage, but no one is standing up there.

The husky voice continues the song, and I know exactly who is singing. I'm in shock and I think my heart may have stopped beating for a moment before quickly speeding back up and nearly pounding out of my chest.

I look back at Amy and Lizzy; they are both knowingly watching me, letting me know that they were in on this.

And then I see him. Trent.

His bright blue eyes are beaming as he belts out the lyrics to my favorite song. He is now standing on the makeshift karaoke stage, front and center.

His eyes are on me. He's watching for my reaction, and all I can do right now is gawk at him. My jaw is basically sitting on the table. I can't believe he's doing this. He's singing this song, of all songs, to me. The song he knows is my favorite, the song he's heard me gush about. The song I've told him is the most perfect, most romantic song. Tears are filling my eyes as realization hits me. This isn't goodbye. Trent is forcing me to hear what he has to say, what I've been avoiding for fear that he would reject me. He's not rejecting me; this is his way of screaming through a megaphone and making me hear how he really feels.

He's a terrible singer by the way, completely ruining the song. He's missing verses and his voice cracks as he attempts to hit notes that only Ray LaMontagne could make sound good, but I don't care. This is the biggest, most romantic gesture anyone has ever done for me. This is *Jerry Maguire* on steroids. This is un-fucking-believable. This man deserves a thousand blow jobs for this.

I feel Amy wipe a few of the tears off of my cheeks, but I can't even take my eyes away from Trent's to look at her. He's got me riveted. His horrible, terrible, off-key singing has me so hooked that I can't even notice anyone else in the bar.

Baby
We've come a long way
And baby
You know I hope and I pray
That you believe me
When I say this love will never fade

Trent finishes the song and I'm still sitting on my barstool, gaping at him. Shocked. Surprised. Elated. I'm more in love with him in this moment than I have ever been with anyone in my entire life. *I love Trent Hamilton.*

My thoughts are interrupted by the hoots and hollers from the bar, then Trent clearing his throat loudly. Oh god, first he serenades me and now he's got a speech?

He raises his hand, smiles at the crowd. "Thank you. My album will drop next month." He nervously laughs with the bar before locking his eyes on me. "Ellie, is this loud enough for you?" He smirks at me and continues talking into the microphone. "I know I said megaphone, but Johnny wouldn't let me, said it would clear out the bar."

Johnny yells from behind the bar, "Even with just the mic you almost accomplished that, dude!"

Trent laughs and gives Johnny the middle finger. "Anyway, where was I before that rude bartender interrupted me?" He grins at Johnny and then sets his sights on me again.

I'm still in astonishment and even feel Amy give me a quick nudge to make sure I'm still with her. I just nod my head yes and intently watch Trent, waiting for what he's going to say.

"Ellie, I don't want to be your knight in shining armor, your prince on the white horse. You don't need saving, baby. You're the strongest woman I know. The last few weeks have been rough—*really rough*—but together we're going to get through it. You're everything I could have ever hoped for, and just knowing you has made me a better man. I'm in awe of you, Ellie. Your beauty, your grace, your feistiness, your adorable charm, and your kind heart. Your outspoken personality and spitfire attitude that constantly keep me on my toes, mostly for fear of what you'd do to my balls if I pissed you off." His eyes beam with amusement and I'm internally giggling. "I know you have your doubts, I know you're scared, baby, but I'm still going to ask you, *beg* you. Be with me. Love me. Let me stand by your side and experience this crazy life together. I want you, Ellie girl. I want all of you. I want every piece of the incredible jigsaw puzzle that makes you the amazing woman that sits before me. I can tell by the look on your face right now that you're a little shocked, a whole lot surprised, but I just needed you to hear me out. I needed you to hear that you are it for me. No hesitations, no doubts, no second thoughts. I'm staying in Charlotte because I love you. I love you so much that I can hardly breathe—"

"Stop! Stop!" I abruptly jump up off of my barstool, knocking my beer bottle over, liquid spilling down the edges of the table. Keeping my gaze locked on Trent's, I walk towards the stage. He's so beautifully nervous right now and probably scared to hear what I'm going to say, yet he still gives me a small smile as he watches me move through the bar. This man has me. Owns me. I'm his and there's no doubt in my mind that this little thing between us has turned into so much more than I could have ever imagined. I know in my soul that this is forever. I hate sounding like a total douchebag sap, but I can't help it. I'm blaming it on the Hamiltonian Effect.

I take a step up onto the stage and stand in front of Trent, looking up at him, drinking in this instant in time. This moment I will most likely remember for the rest of my life. I sense the bar has gone quiet, intently waiting for me to say something, but I honestly have forgotten about them. They don't exist right now. Right now, it's just Trent and Elle. I'm wrapped up in his blue, piercing eyes.

"Please say something. Say anything. Wait, no, not anything. Don't say goodbye. Anything but—"

I place my fingers on his lips and his mouth immediately stops moving.

"You're a terrible singer."

I feel Trent's lips quirk up into a smile against my fingertips as he nods his head in agreement.

"But you have fantastic taste in music." I smirk at him and his eyes shine with amusement. "And you have fantastic taste in women." My fingers slide down his chin and lie gently over his heart. "No goodbyes, Trent. *Never* goodbye. You and me, we're forever, and as much as that used to scare the shit out of me to think about, I'm not scared now. You own me, all of me, even the part of me that sports twelve-inch strap-ons at Halloween parties." His chest vibrates against my palm with quiet laughter. "You are all I could have ever hoped for and a million things I never knew I even wanted. You are mine, Casanova. This right here…" My fingers gently tap his chest. "This is mine and I will never let it go."

Trent drops the microphone to the ground, a loud bang echoing through the speakers. He places his hands on my cheeks and pulls my face closer to his; we're nose to nose, staring into each other's eyes. "Fuck, you made me nervous." Wrapping his arms around my back, he takes a shuddering breath and pulls me closer, pressing his lips to mine.

I giggle against his mouth. "I'm sorry…" I kiss him deeper, showing him how much he means to me. "I love you."

"I know you do, but you still have a lot of making up to do tonight." I lean back and he waggles his eyebrows at me suggestively.

"You're incorrigible."

"You love it."

"That I do, pervy. That I do." I tenderly kiss his cheek and snuggle into his chest.

And then our little romantic moment is ended with a certain obnoxious dickhead yelling out from the crowd.

"Are you two going to fuck on that stage or let the rest of these asshole give us their best Tina Turner impressions?!" Amy yells from the table her and Lizzy are still sitting at.

I flip Amy off and proceed to kiss Trent with everything I am, everything I have, everything I can give to him, because he is *everything* to me and…*we are forever*.

Epilogue

"Every happy ending starts with a bumpy ride, a rough journey. That beginning will most likely throw some unexpected surprises your way, but in the end, it'll all be worth it."

Cutting the engine, I slowly get out of my truck, tired and ready to crash for hours.

I've been in surgery for the past eight hours, and it's now past two in the morning. I'm starving and exhausted, and I see some much needed sleep in my future.

Making my way into my apartment in Uptown Charlotte, I throw my keys on the foyer table and head for the bedroom. The lights are off, and the apartment is silent, *peaceful*. I haven't seen Ellie in the past forty-eight hours. The combination of her work schedule and the numerous surgeries I've scrubbed into has only made it possible for a few text messages and short phone conversations here and there. I miss my girl. *My girl*. My soon-to-be wife. I beam inwardly like a pining idiot. I know I sound like a lovesick fool right now, but I don't give a shit. Ellie is my world, the most important person in my life. And now she's going to be Mrs. Hamilton. Mrs. Ellie Hamilton. She's got me by the balls and I love every minute of it.

Grinning like the pussy-whipped asshole I proudly I am, I stride into the bedroom and see Ellie sound asleep on our bed. She's serene and devastatingly beautiful. Her auburn hair is spread all over her pillow while the blankets are strewn all around her body, most likely from the constant tossing and turning that is Ellie's sleep cycle. She's a kicker. An occasional snoring, tossing, turning, kicking, cover-hog whom I'm desperately in love with. Countless nights I can recall of her waking me up with hard blows to the shins. I instantly grab my nuts, remembering the last time she woke me up with her insistent movements at night. I may not be able to have children anytime soon, but I still love her all the same.

Ellie lets out a soft snore and abruptly turns over in the bed, her arm hastily thrown to the side and now currently hanging off the bed. I hear a quiet whine from the ball of fur that is curled up near her legs, obviously upset with the interruption in her sleep. Georgia's big brown eyes open and she glances my way, her tail instantly starting to wag.

"Shhhhhhh, Georgie. Don't wake Ellie." I head over to the bed and attempt to calm our six-month-old Boxer puppy's excitement with soft pats to her silky coat. I rub her soft, brown puppy ears and she closes her eyes in contentment, instantly laying her sweet little face back on Ellie's leg. Ellie mumbles something in her sleep and I snicker a little at another one of her many nocturnal habits.

Heading into the walk-in closet that's conveniently attached to the bathroom, I start to strip off my scrubs, more than ready to call it a night. I see the black fuck-me heel that Georgia chewed on the first day I brought her home sitting in a box, a box with evidential proof that our dog has a predilection for Ellie's shoes. Thoughts of the first day Ellie met Georgia flood my mind…

"I can't believe you're going to propose to Ellie by bringing home that mutt and wrapping the engagement ring around its fucking collar," my brother Josh said through the screen.

I was Skyping with him with Georgia impatiently sitting in my lap. On a whim, I'd come up with a plan—a proposal plan. Ellie had fallen in love with this Boxer puppy at a local pet store and I couldn't help myself. I'd never thought of myself as a sappy, romantic kind of man, but she just brought it out of me. Doing a terrible rendition of You Are The Best Thing *by Ray LaMontagne is proof of this—incriminating proof at that. If anyone had caught that on video, I would have offered my left nut to get it deleted. It was worth it though. The stunned look on Ellie's face when she saw me belting out the lyrics in front of an entire bar was one hundred percent worth it. She'd attempted to get me to re-enact that night, that moment. The instant in time when I'd poured my heart out to her.*

When I'd laid eyes on her for the first time in Charlotte, I'd been interested. Well, my cock had been interested. She was beautiful and sexy, and her quick wit had me begging to be with her in every way physically possible. I'd been besotted to say the least. I'd wanted her and I'd had my sights on being with her, even it was just for one night. Then I actually got to know her. I guess I'd always felt like there was someone out there for everyone. You know, that one perfect person to make your life complete and all that other happy horseshit.

I'd honestly never put much thought into it. It just hadn't been a priority. Being a surgeon had been at the forefront of my mind for a very long time. I'd worked my dick off in med school and then nearly killed myself slaving away during my surgical residency. I'd had my sights set on my final goal of becoming a trauma surgeon, and thank god Ellen James did not come into my life until after this goal had been accomplished because she would have made it difficult to stay focused. Extremely difficult.

This woman, this beautiful, hilarious, highly intelligent woman, owned me. Within a few days of spending time with her, she'd had all kinds of strange, foreign thoughts crossing my normally testosterone-filled brain. A brain that generally focused on work and then sex. No-strings, one-night stand sex for the most part. I hadn't had time for intimacy, for a relationship. My job was my life. Then lucky for me, Ellen James walked into my life in all of her fuck-me heels and twelve-inch strap-on-wearing glory. She changed me almost instantly. Her mere presence had my brain processing terrifying thoughts of forever. Thoughts of her being a permanent fixture. This had scared the shit out of me at first, but the more time I got to spend with her, to be with her, these thoughts became comforting. I found myself savoring the idea of being with her—forever. She was scared, downright terrified, and she didn't do the best job of hiding this. My girl wore her heart on her sleeve, and whatever emotion was running through her mind was plastered on her face like a giant neon billboard. I was patient. Very patient.

Just like I'd set my sights on accomplishing my ultimate goal of becoming a surgeon, I'd set my sights on Ellen. I was convinced that I would do anything to make her mine, even if that included an endless amount of patience, an impromptu karaoke session, and a giant romantic gesture that belonged in a John Hughes film. Yes, I realized I'd looked like a complete and total pussy. My brother would most likely never let me live this down, but this just proved how much Ellie had changed me. She'd come into my life in a whirlwind of auburn hair and adorable awkwardness, altering my life forever. I thanked my pussy-whipped stars every day for this woman.

So here I was, conversing with my brother on how shit was going to go down in relation to the subject of "The Proposal." He called me a dickless idiot more times than I could count and seemed to find this entire production hilarious. I was glad I could be his comedic relief today. Asshole.

I placed Georgia on the bed and attempted to tie the engagement ring I'd bought for Ellie on her collar. With Amy and Lizzy's help, she'd unknowingly picked this one out. This was a two-carat princess-cut diamond ring solitaire set in a gold band and adorned with tiny diamonds throughout. It was beautiful and had cost a shitload of money. Good thing I loved her so much. Georgia was an eight-week-old brindle Boxer puppy, cutest fucking puppy you'd ever meet. She'd already been named by a lady at the pet store, and honestly, I thought it was perfect for her. Her insistent curiosity and overall loving demeanor made the name fit.

I'd brought her home last night while Ellie was at work. Amy and Lizzy had been kind enough to keep the puppy at their apartment so the surprise wouldn't be ruined. I was pretty sure the girls had had a rough night with Georgia. I'd received several angry text messages from Amy indicating that she wasn't really a dog person.

Amy: *You're fucking dog is an asshole. She just shit on my carpet.*

Amy: *This god damn dog just pissed on my bed!*

Amy: *I thought surgeons were supposed to be smart. This plan of proposing marriage to my best friend with a pissing, shitting, shoe-eating mutt seems like the worst idea you've ever had.*

Yeah. Note to self: never let Amy watch my dog in the future.

I heard Ellie walk in the door, and her footsteps headed into the kitchen, lightly padding on the hardwood floor. "Trent! I'm starving! Feed me now!" She yelled as she walked past the hallway.

"Babe, I'm in the bedroom. Come in here for a minute," I shouted back as I was furiously attempting to hold the squirming puppy in my lap, keeping her from running out of the bedroom and into an unsuspecting Ellie.

"No! You come out here and cook dinner for your exhausted girlfriend!" The fridge door opened and then slammed shut. Maybe this wasn't the best time for this proposal? I ran my hands through my hair in frustration, freeing Georgia to jump off the bed and run down the hallway, her little paws pounding loudly on the floor. Son of a bitch!

I attempted to grab the puppy before she ran down the hallway, but she wiggled out of my reach, and I was left looking like an idiot. "Shit! Georgia! Come here, girl!" I whisper-yelled behind the puppy. This dog was eight weeks old, so there was no way she should have been able to outrun a grown man. A small bark escaped from her snout and echoed off of the walls of the apartment. I was rethinking this brilliant idea at this point.

"Bark! Bark!" Georgia raced towards Ellie, whose back was turned toward the pantry, furiously looking for something to eat. Ellie turned around at the unfamiliar sound and her eyes widened in surprise when she spotted Georgia.

"Oh my god! Is this the dog?! Is this the puppy from the other

day?! Ahhhhhhhhhhh!" She squealed in excitement as she wrapped Georgia in her arms and pulled her close to her face. The puppy licked her nose and cheeks as her tail wagged excitedly. Ellie was grinning and laughing, and a few small tears filled her eyes.

Did she spot the ring?

"Trent! I can't believe you bought me the puppy!" She stepped toward me and wrapped her free arm around my back, pulling me in for an awkward hug with a squirming puppy squished between our chests. "You're going to get so many blow jobs for this!" I couldn't help but smile at this statement. I mean, I might have been a fucking sap, but my cock still loved blow jobs.

Ellie continued to kiss and croon to the puppy, and I was left to stand there...waiting. Waiting for her to spot the ring so I could start my proposal speech. And I waited and waited and waited...

Still waiting.

Still waiting.

What the hell? How could my soon-to-be fiancée not notice the giant rock of a ring hanging from Georgia's neck? This dog was so cute that she was ruining my proposal plan. Ellie was so wrapped up in rubbing her soft ears and hugging her tightly to her chest that she wasn't even looking at the ring hanging from her collar.

"What do you think of her collar?" I was grasping at straws here, shamelessly hinting for her to look for the ring.

"It's great. I love pink! Great choice, baby! Awww I love you so much, Trent!"

She places a soft kiss on my cheek and doesn't even glance down at Georgia's collar.

"Who's my girl? Who's my pretty girl? Let's go to Mommy's bedroom so she can get changed and then we'll go for a walk!" Ellie kissed Georgia's head and began padding down the hallway to our bedroom. I swear, that fucking dog just looked at me, her eyes laughing at my expense. Ellie headed into the hallway, completely clueless. I was generally a patient man, but I only had about a thread of patience left.

Sighing heavily and doing the only thing that was left, I walked into the bedroom and found Ellie sitting on the floor, playing with the puppy. Georgia's nub of a tail was wagging ninety miles per hour as she and Ellie played tug-of-war with a sock. I was standing in front of them, arms crossed in front of my chest. I thought I needed to get Ellie's vision checked. That was the only thing I was certain of at that moment. That and the fact that I was still feeling like an idiot.

"Would you look at the fucking collar, Ellie?" I was exasperated, my dreams of the perfect proposal was squashed because I'd brought home *a dog whose cuteness well surpassed the appeal of the shiny engagement ring.*

Ellie looked up at me with annoyance. "What crawled up your ass?" she huffed out.

This was not how this was supposed to go. What crawled up my ass? This was not supposed to be a thought that was crossing her mind right now. She should have been crying and smiling and begging for me to fuck her all over our bed after she threw herself in my arms screaming, "Yes! Yes! I will marry you!"

Screw this. I was throwing in the towel; this obviously wasn't the perfect moment to propose to my girlfriend. I stalked into the bathroom and used the sink to splash cold water on my face. I placed my elbows on the sink, my head in my hands. My heart was racing, the nerves of the entire proposal fiasco had worn me down. And I'm not going to lie, I was disappointed. Oh well, I'd come up with something.

Maybe I should have just hung the ring from my dick...

I lifted my head to the sound of Ellie clearing her throat behind me. I locked eyes with her in the bathroom mirror. She had the ring in her hand, and tears were streaming down her cheeks, the most beautiful, breathtaking smile on her face. She'd never looked more perfect than in that moment. I turned around so I was facing her, continuing to drink her in with my gaze.

"Now what do you think about Georgia's collar?" My lips smiled down at her as I stepped closer to Ellie, our chests mere inches away from each other.

"Are you... Is this... Wha... Oh my god!" She was stuttering and had apparently lost the ability to form coherent sentences. YES! Finally the reaction I'd been looking for!

"Ellie, I have something I want to ask you." I got down on one knee and pulled Ellie's hand into mine, grasping the ring between both of our palms. "I love you. I love you so much, and I want to be with you for the rest of my life. I want your laugh, your smile, all of you. Everything, with me...forever. Will you marry me?" I lifted my hand and removed the ring from her grasp, holding it out, waiting for her response. More tears streamed down her face, and she blinked her eyes shut for a moment, inhaling a shaking breath.

Ellie opened her eyes slowly and pierced me with the most intense, passionate look. She nodded her head yes as a smile hinted at her lips.

Before I was able to slide the ring on Ellie's finger, she tackled me to the bathroom floor, laughing and smiling and raining kisses all over my face. I wrapped my arms around her, holding her tightly to my chest, nuzzling my face into her strawberry-scented hair.

"I love you so much, Trent," she whispered into my ear.

"I love you too, baby, but I think we need to get your vision checked."

She smacked my chest and started giggling. "You asshole! How was I supposed to know you tied an engagement ring to that ridiculously adorable puppy!"

I crushed my lips to hers and my heart was ablaze. This girl had just made my life with a simple nod of her head. We continued to kiss and caress each other, enjoying the moment, savoring this memory. My mind was already letting my cock know it was high time we headed to the bed. Ellie had already promised me a lifetime of blow jobs, and I was ready to bury myself in her all night long.

I heard heavy panting and something drop to the bathroom tile beside my head. Ellie glanced up and anger crossed her face. I tilted my head to the side to try to figure out what had caused this sudden change in mood.

"That dog just destroyed my favorite pair of heels!" Ellie hopped off of me and proceeded to chase the puppy into the bedroom. Georgia was barking loudly, jumping up and down, thinking that Ellie was going to play with her again. I sat up and saw the battered shoe that was sitting beside me. It was one of the infamous fuck-me heels Ellie had worn in Nashville and on our first date.

Damn dog. I'd really loved those shoes...

The sound of Georgia getting up and trotting into the hallway pulls me from my reminiscent thoughts. She frequently wakes up in the middle of the night, too hot from Ellie's body heat, and finds a cool place to sleep in the kitchen. I throw on a pair of flannel pants and walk into the bathroom to finish getting ready for bed. I grab my toothbrush from the holder, and as I go to pick up the toothpaste, I'm stunned.

Shocked.

Speechless.

The word *pregnant* is staring back at me.

The word *pregnant* is front and center in the window of a pregnancy test. A pregnancy test that's sitting on my bathroom sink, our bathroom sink, my and Ellie's. *Ellie's pregnant?* I lift my eyes when I hear a throat clearing behind me. My eyes meet Ellie's in the mirror, and I'm smiling but still too stunned to form sentences, much less words.

I turn around, toothbrush still grasped in my hand, surprise etched all over my face.

"Wha... You're... What?"

Ellie's smile nearly knocks me on my ass.

"Trent, I'm pregnant." She says the words slowly, giving my brain time to process this monumental bombshell. *Ellie's pregnant. My Ellie's pregnant? Holy shit! Ellie's pregnant!*

Dropping my toothbrush to the bathroom tile, I immediately grab her around the waist and clutch her against my bare chest, her soft breasts pressing into me. My lips tremble slightly as tears fill my eyes. I lift my hands, placing my palms on her cheeks, pulling her lips to mine, attempting to tell her how happy I am right now through physical affection. My mind is still unable to function, still unable to process coherent words.

"Dr. Hammer has superhero sperm." Ellie giggles against my mouth, her breath warming my face. "Your superhero cock's superhero spunk somehow managed to surpass my birth control."

A husky laugh vibrates my chest as a single tear slides down my cheek.

"I'm so happy, baby. So. Fucking. Happy." In an instant, this girl has changed my life again.

She's turned my world upside down and given me the most precious gift I could ever ask for...

I'm going to be a father.

-THE END-

***

Coming Soon from NA Alcorn

Are you ready to hear Amy's story?

The Infamous Amy Jackson (The Infamous Series #2)

February 2014

Acknowledgements

THANK YOU

This book could not have been completed without the never ending support from my wonderful family and friends. You guys rock. You've picked me up more times than you probably even realized and for that, I will forever be thankful.

Thank you to my husband Rob for always being my biggest fan. The endless nights of listening to me talk about book characters and dialogue and plot lines. I love you, forever and always.

Thank you to my mom and sister. I love you both to the moon and back. Your ability to make me smile and give me confidence is something I will forever be grateful for. Angela, our endless phone conversations and your speedy reading abilities got me through some serious self-deprecating moments. You're the best sister a girl could ask for. Belinda, you're the best mother in the entire universe. You've been my biggest supporter and I don't know what I would do without you. I told you you'd get mentioned in this book!

Thank you to my wonderful blogging friends whom I've spent countless hours chatting books with.

My best friend Mo at Fifty5Cents Book Blog, otherwise known as author M. Mabie. You're my writing partner in crime. You make me laugh and I seriously love you. Like love you love you. You're my domestic partner and I'll never forget our night in Columbus. I don't know what I would do without you. Have we really only known each other for a year? No way. I feel like we've been friends forever. You get me like no one else. You're the jelly to my peanut butter. The nacho to my cheese. The wind beneath my wings. I might start singing for you in a minute… But seriously, I love you. Your support and encouragement and uncanny ability to motivate me are a huge reason I was able to jump into this crazy writing world.

My favorite girl Nataleeeee! From Read This Hear That. Who would've thought all it would take is for us to have the same name to become lifelong friends! I love you, lady. You're the best!

My favorite drinking partner and soul sister, Malory from Loverly's Book Blog. I love you. Your quick wit and uncanny ability to find the very best pictures makes my day. EVERY DAY.

My Kitty Kat. Kat from Momma's Romance. You, my dear friend, there are just no words to even describe the support you've given me. I love you so much and your friendship means the world to me. You're willingness to help me and encourage me well…you're awesome. It's as simple as that. You rock my world lady!

Sandie and Dee from Book Boyfriend Reviews. These ladies showed me what the blogging world was about. These awesome chicks whose feisty personalities have made me laugh more times than I could even count. Your friendship and support mean the world to me.

Heidi and Steph. Two ladies who've expanded my creative horizons just by letting me be a part of something truly amazing. I love you both. My day isn't complete without our Kik conversations. You realize that we're basically friends for life now, right?

Amber & Tara. I love you both. I don't know what I would do without you two. Your support, encouraging words…well, it pretty much rocks. Thank you. Thank you. Thank you.

My Mercy Girls. The ladies who've inspired me to write some interesting stories. The ladies who keep me up at all hours of the night. The awesome ladies who deliver babies like it's no one's business. You rock!

Reader Thank You

I just want to take a moment to thank you, the wonderful readers! You're amazing and I am forever grateful to you for giving me a chance. Thank you for your support of indie authors! You rock and I hope you enjoyed Ellen's story just as much as I enjoyed writing it. I can't wait to give you Amy's story and I truly hope you come back! –N.A.

About the Author

N.A. Alcorn is a wife, mother, labor and delivery nurse, writer, and blogger. She lives in Cincinnati with her husband and three-year-old son, Sid. In her spare time she enjoys reading, writing, running, and having inappropriate conversations with her blog besties. She also has a serious addiction to music and her all-time favorite band is Incubus. Her ability to eat an ungodly amount of Reese's Cups in a fifteen minute time frame would quite literally blow your mind.

Feel free to message or contact this author through her social media sites. She would love to hear from you!

http://www.facebook.com/naalcorn
http://www.naalcorn.wordpress.com/
https://twitter.com/NAAlcorn

Sneak Peek for M. Mabie's book Fade In

Coming Soon in 2014

Please enjoy this sneak peak of *Fade In*, a contemporary-comedy romance from debuting author M. Mabie.

Tatum Elliot is a successful writer on a hit television show. She lives in an Upper East Side apartment and loves her life. She wouldn't change a thing. Unfortunately, she doesn't have a choice.

As Tatum trips over her tongue and her four-inch heels, she all too quickly realizes that the things that appeared so important are slowly slipping out of sight. With the support of her best friends, family and colleagues, she begins to see that there's much more to life… and herself.

When Ben Harris enters her life as her new personal assistant, she can't tell if it's his good looks and charm that are working on her libido, or his kind and helpful nature working on her heart? Whatever it is, neither one of them can resist it.

As her vision fades out, a world of love and happiness just might…Fade In.

Fade In is a contemporary-comedy romance about laughing through tears and telling life to, quite frankly, "Suck it." This novel is vulgar and contains wickedly, sexual situations that the author may or may not have tried at home… for your safety, of course. Research is research.

M. Mabie lives in Illinois, NOT Chicago, with her husband. She loves writing for Fifty5Cent Book Blog, which she owns and operates, usually poorly. She cares about politics, but won't discuss them in public. She uses the same fork at every meal, watches Wayne's World while cleaning, and lets her dog sleep on her head. M. Mabie has never been accused of being tight lipped or shy. She's THAT girl.

And now… **Fade In**- Chapter 1: Masturbating Makes You Go Blind

1

Masturbating Makes You Go Blind

"Date of birth?"

"Are you fucking kidding me, Charlotte? You know my date of birth. You just told me happy birthday when I walked in! I know you have to ask, but do you really have to ask? I've been coming here since I was fourteen. It's a little redundant. Don't you think?"

Charlotte is Dr. Meade's receptionist. She's about a hundred years old and wears "slacks," and a lovely parka that could be fashioned from the cat hair hanging from her blouse. She's my favorite brand of old lady. Don't tell anyone I said that.

"I'm sorry. I'm just anxious. I didn't mean to cuss you out for doing your job." That's me. I blow up and then apologize. I have no filter when I'm nervous. "Four, twenty, nineteen eighty-five."

"Thank you, Tatum. Doctor is on schedule. It should only be a minute. Are you doing anything fun for your birthday? Is Kurt taking you anywhere?" She waves her hand in a big way to let me know I can sit.

"I think we are going to dinner with Winnie and Coop. They are picking me up here in a while. Any recommendations? I'm supposed to be deciding where to go. I hate that. Deciding where to eat. It's like…" And mid-sentence, on my way to the seat, that, mind you, I've sat in almost every time I've been here for years, I slam my shin into something. "Son of a bitch!"

I look down and see that I hit it hard enough to shove the coffee table back a foot or so.

"Charlotte, when did this piece of shit get moved here? Ouch." Oh, yeah. I'm losing my sight. Seems cruel to move furniture on an almost blind klutz, doesn't it?

I sit, and she comes around her desk to check on me. Moving the offending table back to its rightful position, she picks up the magazines that fell off.

"I'm sorry, dear. I put that there the other day. It was by the window. Then the fichus was dying and—oh dear. I'm so sorry. I should have said to mind the coffee table." Looking as guilty as the cat that ate the canary, she stands before me, all apologies. Like it's her fault I can't navigate around a four-foot-long inanimate object.

"It isn't your fault," I say, rubbing my battered leg. It isn't like that is the only bruise I have earned myself. Today.

As if on cue, Dr. Meade walks through the door that leads back to the patient rooms. "Tatum. Happy Birthday. Did Charlotte finally get sick of your potty mouth and kick you?"

Ha. Ha. They look between each other and have a nice chuckle at my expense. No pity from him.

"No, Dr. Evil. I whacked my leg on that wretched table," I replied in an innocent singsong voice. "Real classy to shift around the furnishings before your favorite handicapable patient arrives. Bravo."

He comes to me and offers me a hand up. I accept and limp my lame ass toward the door with him. His hand is warm and big. He lets go so I can follow him down the hall to the examination room toward which he is steering us.

He stops just short of exam room four and waves me past him. He smells like rubbing alcohol and cologne. Strangely it smells good to me. It's familiar.

I have tried to figure out how old Dr. Meade is many times. When I first met him, he seemed way too young to be my doctor. If I had to guess, I would say late thirties or early forties.

I've always thought he was handsome. His dark hair is beginning to lighten around the edges, and his kind and easy smile has left charming laugh lines around his eyes and mouth.

Of course, I get to look at him closely during my visits, and I have been his patient for a long time. I can see pretty well up close if I'm looking directly at something. That is the strange thing about my condition.

I have RP, or Retinitis Pigmentosa if you're fancy. Let me break it down for you. It started when I was a teenager. I had poor peripheral vision—not awful but poor. I was diagnosed then with RP. It didn't seem like that big of a deal. Who needs peripheral vision?

It sort of stayed the same for a long time, and other than that, my vision was pretty good. I made it fine through college, sight in tow. I landed a great job. Bought a fabulous apartment on the Upper East Side, and everything was smooth sailing.

Then around the time I turned twenty-six, it started getting worse. I always came to see Dr. Meade on a regular basis to monitor the condition.

He could tell, too. I suppose he'd be a pretty crappy eye doctor if he hadn't noticed.

Our plan was to just monitor it, and then he would let me know if treatment became available. So far, it's just a good dose of vitamin A. Seriously. That is all the remedy they have.

I can still see pretty well. Although, it is not as good as it was six months ago. Simply, it's like tunnel vision. For a long time it has just been a fuzzy gray edge around my field of sight.

Then it got darker and the rim got wider. Now it is about thirty percent gone. So it's still better than it could be, but it's a lot like looking through a port hole on a ship, and my night vision is really starting to suck a big one.

"I like your haircut, Tatum. It looks nice for summer. I don't think I have ever seen you wear it this short."

"Thank you. You can't help but flirt, can you?" I wink, and he lets my flirting slide. He always does. "It is just easier to fix in the morning. We've been busy at the show, and it was just a pile on my head by the end of the day anyway. I had no use for it."

"Well, I'm glad you are cutting out the unnecessary. Simplifying." Dr. Meade smiles as if it were his idea to have Luis, our staff stylist, cut nearly a foot off my blond hair. He motions for me to sit in the chair and I do.

"You look pleased. Should I have my stylist send you the bill?" We laugh—him in earnest and me sarcastically.

"No. I'm just glad that you're making things easier for yourself." I know he's just being honest, but I don't like it. It makes me uncomfortable being real about what's going on.

Sitting in his chair, he wheels toward me with his clipboard. "How have you been feeling? Any headaches?"

"Only when I smack it off something. Same goes for my toe aches and leg aches." That earns me a look. "No. I still haven't had many headaches."

"Good. Have you noticed your peripheral vision getting worse? Is your tunnel vision narrowing more? Are you more tired than normal?" He's writing and lifts his head up. "Just answer, Tatum. I can't say anything to anyone. You can tell me."

"It is getting narrower, but not by a lot. I've been measuring it sort of. Like at work. I use to be able to see both of the cameras from offstage. Now it's like I'm looking right in between them. My night vision is almost nonexistent. If I wake up in the middle of the night, and there isn't a light on, I can barely see to get to the bathroom without waking up Kurt by bumping around. It isn't like he wants to sleep with the light on. Who would?" I sigh, knowing that I didn't really need to tell him all of that, but again, I'm nervous and can't help it.

"Well, we were expecting that. If the light is on, can you see better when you wake up?" He asks like he is talking to a child.

"Yes, but it takes a minute for everything to focus. It comes back in a few seconds and everything is back to shitty-ass normal. Tell me the truth. Is this because of my adolescent masturbating? I was told that leads to blindness."

"This again!? Would you quit with the masturbating!" He almost shouts.

"I wish I could. It's just that I'm so good at it." I know its bad timing, and timing is supposed to be everything. It's just that sometimes my dirty mouth rescues me with a perverted life jacket and it's always just my size.

Why should I be the only one uncomfortable? If you can't beat me, I'll make you join me.

"You know what I mean. You need to talk to someone. Have you considered seeing a therapist that specializes in people who are visually impaired? Would you use a referral? You always do that, you know? This is serious."

"Do what?" I know I'm baiting him again to say something I can twist around into dirty word play and embarrass him into changing the subject, but it isn't as effective as it used to be. Have I desensitized my optometrist?

"You know what. I think you could benefit from seeing someone who can help guide you through this transition. You should also consider going to a facility that can teach you practical ways to deal with how your life is going to be."

"Like a fat farm? No way. I'm not going to blind camp. Not going to happen." This isn't the first time he has approached me with the idea of therapists and blind school. I'm not ready for that, and I don't mean to sound like a better-than-somebody snot either. I can hardly see me keeping my mouth shut around other people who would probably benefit from me not being there.

"Don't totally dismiss the idea of getting help with this. I will try to think of some alternatives for you. You wouldn't last a day there anyway. They wouldn't be able to handle you." And there is my Dr. Meade. Swinging it right back at me.

"Great idea. Alternatives. You think on that. I will hire another assistant for my personal life and start interviewing housekeepers. See? This is compromise. You said make life simpler. You do your thing and I'll do mine."

We finish up the standard exam with him agreeing that he could see more degeneration and suggesting we not wait as long in between visits.

After I make the appointment with sweet, old-ass Charlotte, I sit in the waiting room, eager to get the text from Winnie that says they are outside. Winnie is my best friend, colleague, and soon-to-be sister-in-law.

Some say that if you let people go and you're meant to be with them, then they will come back. I say that if you have a smoking hot college roommate you love, then hook her up with your adorable brother and you'll never have to worry about that leaving shit.

My brother Coop—Cooper if you are our Grandma—fell in love with Winnie the first time he saw her. But then again, in a way, I did too.

She is dramatic and wild. Her body totally embodies her personality. And she has crazy curly brown hair, an ass that won't quit, and big brown eyes that make her irresistible. That's why she made a great actress with no training at all.

We are both writers. That's how we met in college. We had the same major, and admissions paired us up as roommates.

Following graduation, we landed a couple of jobs as pages at one of the biggest television stations in the country, ABN. Don't ask me how that seriously lucky turn of events unfolded, because I will never tell. Neither will the two-pump chump, Derek, the lead page at the time, who I ironically met on my birthday my senior year.

Then after slumming it for a year or so, we both were promoted to different floors in the building and on different shows. I was hired on as a junior writer for a late-night talk show, and Winnie was hired to a sketch comedy show to write and perform. We made friends with people, both of our shows came and went, and born was Just Kidding.

That is our show. Winnie and I would like to take credit for the entire show, but it actually is a three-way—me, Winnie, and Wes Ruben. Winnie and Wes worked on the same show before Just Kidding and had great on-camera chemistry.

If they were in a scene together, then it was gold. Their characters were always fan favorites and that made them a hot-ticket commodity in the entertainment business. When they approached me as a writer for the spin-off of their canceled show, I was more than happy to say yes.

First of all, I was unemployed. So that was a no-brainer.

Second of all, I knew working with Winnie and Wes would be fun, profitable, and an opportunity that wouldn't ever come around again.

If I were a betting person, I'd bet they will both be on the big screen in leading roles within the next five years. They are that good.

My phone buzzed with a text from Winnie.

She asked, "Birthday Slut, are you ready yet? We are 3 blocks away."

I reply, "I'm not Birthday Slut anymore. You can call me Birthday Bitch from here on out. I'm walking out the door."

"Oh, I bet Birthday Slut is in there somewhere," she coyly replied.

So, there was a time before Kurt and I got together that I may or may not have had some casual sex. I wasn't a whore or anything. I dated and had casual boyfriends. Nothing too serious. Dating within the business is like that. Here one minute and kiss my let's-be-friends ass the next. Every year on my birthday, if I was dating someone, I would break up with whomever and not look back.

Then, Winnie and I would go out and Birthday Slut it up. Well, I would. She faked it by just going home with Coop and telling me she called him by a different name. She has the best logic.

Look for Fade In on Goodreads and M. Mabie at mmabie.com, Facebook.com/AuthorMMabie and on Twitter @AuthorMMabie.

46874364R00138

Made in the USA
Lexington, KY
18 November 2015